When he pulled away, she moaned, suddenly bereft. She opened her eyes, a trembling hand reaching up to touch her swollen lips. Her breath was coming fast, as if she'd just finished a four-minute free skate. "Why…why did you stop?"

Michael nuzzled her jawbone. She trembled. He smiled against her cheek. "Because you're definitely not a backseat woman. We should go inside to finish what we started."

She was having difficulty concentrating. "Finish?"

"Finish." He ran a finger down her bare arm. "I want to kiss every centimeter of your beautiful, sexy body. I want to make you scr…"

"No." It was a strangled, frightened sound.

"What?"

Yvonne quickly slid away from him, taking a deep breath to clear her head. "It wouldn't be a good idea," she managed to say.

NO COMMITMENT REQUIRED

SERESSIA GLASS

Genesis Press, Inc.

Indigo Love Stories

An imprint of Genesis Press, Inc.
Publishing Company

Genesis Press, Inc.
P.O. Box 101
Columbus, MS 39703

ISBN-13: 978-1-58571-222-9
ISBN-10: 1-58571-222-1
Manufactured in the United States of America

First Edition 2000
Second Edition 2007

Visit us at www.genesis-press.com or call at 1-888-Indigo-1

ACKNOWLEDGEMENTS

So many wonderful people have helped in the development and publishing of this novel. My "sisters" in George Romance Writers deserve a big thank you, especially Emily Sewell, Elisa White, Carmen Green and Stephanie Hauck. Your encouragement and help has gotten me here, and I'm grateful.

To my family, for being as excited as I was when I got the news.

And to Jon, for being you.

— *Seressia*

CHAPTER ONE

Michael Benjamin didn't see the slap coming, but he sure saw the stars afterwards. He touched his cheek gingerly, golden eyes glinting with genuine regret. "I'm sorry, Diedre…"

"Sorry?" the seething redhead repeated, her voice rising several octaves. "First you tell me that the only way I'm going to get an engagement ring is to buy it myself, and then you have the nerve to tell me you're sorry?"

A heavy sigh escaped him. This wasn't the way he wanted to end his relationship with the model. He hadn't meant to snap at her, but pressuring him for something he wasn't capable of giving had brought out the cutting remark.

"I'm not the marrying type," he said quietly. "I told you that when we started seeing each other. I wish you had believed me."

His furious ex-lover laughed hollowly. "What woman in her right mind believes a line like that? That was a challenge, not a confession. What you should have told me is what a cold-hearted son of a bitch you are."

True, but that wasn't something that could be brought up in casual conversation. Or bed. "Look, I know I've handled this badly. Maybe if we went to dinner?"

The statuesque woman who commanded thousands of dollars per photo shoot leaned over his desk, her teal dress revealing the creamy swell of her cleavage. "The only way we're having dinner together is if they're serving your magnificent specimen roasted on a stick!"

She stalked to the door, then turned. "Did you love me at all?" she asked, her voice becoming plaintive. "Even just a little?"

He wanted to tell her yes. She was a beautiful, vibrant woman. It should have been easy to love her, but he couldn't. He couldn't love anyone. "Diedre ..."

"Who is she?"

"Who?"

"The woman who ruined you for the rest of us."

Just like that, memories ambushed him, kicking him viciously in the gut. "I ..." he trailed off, unable to speak past the guilt and anger that clogged his throat.

Diedre nodded, as if his lack of answer was answer enough. "I never stood a chance, did I?"

He thought about explaining, but that damned tightness kept his throat securely closed. Wordless, he shook his head.

Diedre sighed. "I know it's wrong to speak ill of someone I don't know, but I hate her." She left without a backwards glance.

Regret mixed with relief as he rose then turned to gaze out the window behind his desk, not seeing the afternoon sunlight. "Sometimes I do too," he whispered.

"Trouble in paradise?"

Turning back to the door, he saw his partner, Thom Sebastian, in the doorway. "She wanted something I couldn't give her."

"So how many does that make for you so far this year, Casanova?" Thom chuckled. "You should try a temp agency. Maybe they can find the right woman for you."

"I'm not looking for Mrs. Right. I'm convinced she doesn't exist."

Thom crossed the room to stand beside him. "It's been nearly ten years," he said soberly. "Don't you think it's time to put the past behind you?"

"Do you have anything good to say, or did you just come to gloat?" Thom had been happily married for four years. Michael didn't begrudge him his happiness, but he himself had no desire to go down that road again.

"Actually, I have bad news. I just got off the phone with Gredinger. He's taking his account to another firm."

"Damn!" Michael slammed his fist onto his desk. Gredinger's small information systems company was a lucrative account for their consulting firm, Better Business Concepts. "Did he say why?"

Thom shook his head, pushing his glasses firmly onto his nose. "He was vague, but when I pressed him, he said he wanted an established firm to handle his account."

"Established?" Michael gave a snort of disbelief. "BBC has been in business for eight years!"

"As I said, I didn't really buy the story. Conrad was handling Gredinger. He's sitting in my office right now. Do you want to chew him out? You look like you could stand to blow off a little steam."

"No, you should handle it. It scares them when you fly off the handle, especially since it so rarely happens." The phone buzzed. "Yes, Connie?"

"Mr. Maxwell, line two."

"Thanks." Michael turned to Thom. "I'll call Gredinger myself tomorrow, see if we can salvage anything out of this.

Meanwhile, I'll see if Jeff has any leads he can throw our way."

Jeff Maxwell had been his best friend since high school, and the financial advisor networked with a wide variety of people. If anyone knew of a company needing marketing and management consults, it was Jeff.

"You do that. We need to replace that account in a hurry." Thom's benign expression hardened. "Meanwhile, I'll go have a little talk with Conrad."

Michael sat at his desk with a sigh. What else could possibly go wrong today? He picked up the receiver. "Jeff, tell me you have some good news."

"Mike. I need a favor. A big one."

"Where the hell are you? You sound like you're stuck in traffic."

"I am stuck in traffic. Some idiot in a Pathfinder just rear-ended me!"

Michael winced. Jeff treated his car like a child. "Need me to come get you?"

"No, I'm going to make sure the tow truck gets my car to the dealership in one piece. I need you to go to the airport for me."

"The airport?" He could feel a headache coming on.

"I have a friend coming in, and I promised to pick her up. Will you get her for me?"

"Did you say 'her'?"

"Yeah! Hey man, watch my fender!" Jeff yelled at the tow truck operator. "Look, Mike, I need to go before they hurt my car worse. Her name is Yvonne Mitchelson, and she'll be on Delta flight 1504 from New York in about an hour." He disconnected.

Disbelief scoured Michael as he stared at the phone. "Jeff? Come on, man, don't do this to me. Dammit!"

He slammed the receiver down. The last thing he wanted to do was to fetch a woman from the airport. That usually entailed four or five massive cases—designer, of course—filled with enough clothing to stock a small department store.

God, he did not want to do this! But he owed Jeff more than a few favors. Going to the airport during rush hour to pick up a woman would definitely even the score.

Resolute, he stood, slipping into his jacket. Things were definitely going to hell in a handbasket. Losing a lover and an account within five minutes of each other. How could the day possibly get any worse?

Yvonne Mitchelson looked out the tiny window of the jet, relieved to see Hartsfield International Airport come into view. She hated flying almost as much as she hated cars. New York was now running a close third. She'd been in negotiations with textile suppliers until an hour before her flight left, and if she had to listen to another supercilious male in a tailored suit tell her what she couldn't do, she'd scream.

Being a five-foot-four minority female was supposed to make her easily intimidated, but Yvonne didn't place faith in that theory. If everyone that told her no intimidated her, she wouldn't be walking, much less the owner of three successful boutiques.

Reaching this point hadn't been easy. Fifteen years ago, she and her twin sister had dominated pre-Olympic figure skating trials until the night a truck struck their parents' car. Yvonne's sister and parents had been killed instantly, and she was left temporarily paralyzed. Her mind, body, and spirit broken, it had taken three grueling years to heal.

Learning to walk again had been easier than learning to live with the loss. There were days when it became overwhelming, days like anniversaries and birthdays. Those days she gave in to the need to grieve, remembering, honoring, then moving on.

The darkness and pain never completely left her, but she persevered. She was a survivor. Her love of figure skating led to designing costumes and exercise gear which evolved into designing lingerie and opening her own stores. As always, the thought of her boutiques, Your Heart's Desire, brought a smile to her lips. They were posting record numbers again. The sales rush from Mother's Day to the end of June promised to be bigger than ever.

But something wasn't quite right, and the artist in Yvonne knew it. Her designs weren't leaping out of her head the way they used to. They didn't sizzle on her sketchpad either. She was entering a creative funk. Her partners, Gwen and Angela, had a simple solution.

Yvonne needed a man.

She didn't trust their opinion onthat; after all, the last man Angela introduced Yvonne to, her personal assistant Lawrence, turned out to be homosexual. But it did give new life to an old idea: a men's line. Perhaps finding a local Adonis to turn into an overnight sensation and serve as creative inspiration was just what she needed.

The plane taxied to a stop, and she retrieved her briefcase from the overhead compartment. Hopefully, inspiration was all Your Heart's Desire needed. But just in case, she had a meeting next week with Better Business Concepts, a hot consulting firm in Midtown. She didn't know much about them, but her best friend, Jeff Maxwell, said the firm was great with young companies. Her plan was to thoroughly question Jeff about it over dinner.

Yvonne smiled to herself, resolutely joining the mass of humanity teeming for the exit. Perhaps Desire was too small for the players in New York, but there was always more than one way to skin a cat. She would get what she wanted and she wasn't going to let anyone stand in her way, especially some jerk who wouldn't know a demi-cup if it hit him in the behind.

"Excuse me, I'm in a hurry." An older man, his jacket barely fastened over his protruding belly, pushed past her as she disembarked. She glared at his receding back.

"Probably needs to get rid of some of that hot air he's full of," a tall brunette standing next to her remarked.

Yvonne grimaced in agreement. "I know what you mean," she answered, her eyes scanning the crowd. Jeff was supposed to pick her up. Where was he? She wanted to stop by the Buckhead store before dinner.

"I wonder whom he's waiting for?" She couldn't miss the predatory tone of the woman beside her and followed the direction of her stare.

He was the epitome of tall, dark, and handsome. In his early thirties perhaps, with dark hair slicked back and broad shoulders draped in a navy Armani jacket, the man leaned against the column with all the arrogant sullenness of a *GQ* model. He had every woman on the concourse salivating, and he knew it.

She regarded him with a purely professional eye. He was fine, for a white man. Definitely inspiring. She tried to imagine what he would look like in boxers and briefs and began to blush. Not that she had any experience by which to judge, but she was sure he was more than adequate in that area.

Intrigued despite herself, she thought about approaching him, but quickly abandoned the idea. What would she say? "Hi, I want to design your underwear"? He would probably think it was just a line at best, or think her crazy at worst. Besides, she had more important things on her mind, like finding her ride home.

Just then, her name coursed through the address system. Clutching her briefcase, she moved to the attendant's desk.

Michael leaned against a column, impatient. Where the hell was this Mitchelson woman? Her name sounded familiar, but he couldn't place it. He had her paged; the attendant had been most helpful until he told her he was looking for a woman. And Jeff had been too busy yelling at the tow truck driver to give a good description.

His attention was snagged by a bright red pantsuit. A black woman carrying a briefcase and black coat sported the body-conscious suit. She moved toward the attendant's booth with a feline grace.

Curious, he watched as more than a few men slowed their hurried pace upon catching sight of her. He couldn't blame them—he'd almost forgotten why he was in the airport. She wasn't Naomi or Tyra, being just below average height, but that suit and that walk demanded and received attention. He wondered who the woman was and if she was having someone paged. Maybe she was new to Atlanta. Maybe she needed to know where to pick up her luggage. Better yet, maybe she needed someone to take her to dinner.

To his surprise, the Delta clerk pointed in his direction. The woman turned, and Michael could feel her eyes, hidden behind sunglasses, assessing him. Then she turned back to the attendant, shaking her head. But the clerk nodded and again pointed to him.

The woman in scarlet walked toward him. Instinctively, he checked his tie. When she was close to him, she removed her sunglasses.

Their gazes met and he was brought up short. He forgot about Jeff, Jeff's girlfriend, and losing his patience. He forgot all that because he was losing himself in that gaze.

Her large, almond-shaped eyes were expressive and syrupy- soft, the color of fine brandy. They caught him and held him, mesmerized.

She broke the silence. "You've been waiting for me?" she asked, the Yankee of her accent softened with a slight drawl.

It was the perfect line and he couldn't resist. "You have no idea how long." He gave her his best smile.

Completely unfazed, that's what she was. Michael could feel his day taking another downturn. A wry smile twisted her lips. "I'm sure you've waited all your life, and from the look on your face a few minutes ago, you don't like it much."

Her expression was wary. "Why don't you tell me who you are and why you paged me."

It took a moment for that to sink in. "You're Yvonne Mitchelson?"

She took a step backward, wariness deepening to suspicion. "Who are you? How do you know my name, but not what I look like?"

"I'm Mike Benjamin. Jeff Maxwell asked me to come get you. Your name's familiar, but Jeff didn't tell me you were African-American."

"That's probably because I'm not from Africa, and neither were my parents."

Michael could feel his ears turning red. "I'm sorry, I'm still confused by the political correctness of it all. But if Jeff had told me you were black…"

"You'll have to forgive Jeff," she cut in, her voice heavy with sarcasm. "He has this annoying little habit of not categorizing people by their color. I told him not to be so blind to other people's hang-ups, but he…"

"Wait just a minute," he interrupted. "I don't have a hang-up about color."

She held up a hand. "Let me guess. Some of your best friends are black, right?"

He looked down at her, feeling his face flush in a mixture of anger and embarrassment. Yvonne Mitchelson didn't top his shoulder, but she was primed to take his head off. Damn, today definitely wasn't one of his better days. What the hell did Jeff see in this woman anyway?

"Actually, that was not what I was about to say, Ms. Mitchelson," he said coldly. "But if you must know, Jeff happens to be my best friend. My business partner is black, and I was best man in his wedding to a beautiful woman who is from Africa. What I was trying to say is that it would have saved a hell of a lot of trouble if Jeff had told me what you looked like."

He dug into his jacket pocket, then dropped his cell phone in her hands. "Why don't you give Jeff a call and verify my credentials? And while you're at it, call a taxi."

Ready to leave her where she stood, he folded his arms and counted back from fifty. Instead of answering him, she massaged her temples with her free hand.

"Look, I'm sorry," she said thinly, obviously not used to apologizing. "I've had a day from hell."

"You're not the only one capable of having a bad day," he informed her. "In fact, I think it's pretty contagious."

To his surprise she smiled, a dazzling display of teeth and dimples that nearly blinded him. "You're right. That was kind of bitchy of me, pissing off my ride home. I really do know better, so why don't we start over?"

She stuck out her free hand. "I'm Yvonne Mitchelson, but you can call me embarrassed!"

Michael took the proffered hand, and felt a surge that was almost electric. One look at her face, he realized she felt it too. The pulse at the base of her throat actually jumped. With a subtle tug, she attempted to extricate her hand until his fingers hit the big diamond she wore.

Without seeming to, he examined the gem. A lot of money had gone into the ring. A whole lot.

"You can call me your ride home." Trying to keep disappointment out of his voice, he caught himself. Why the hell was he disappointed? He decided he didn't want to think about it.

They headed for the baggage claim, Michael explaining Jeff's bad luck. As they walked, he assessed the woman beside him. She was petite, barely five-five, yet the elegant confidence she exuded as she walked made her seem taller. Her skin was a rich warm caramel and her shoulder length hair a mass of dark brown curls. And somewhere under the pantsuit, he was sure, was a body that could stop traffic on the Downtown Connector.

He frowned slightly. Why did her name seem so familiar? Jeff, also a confirmed bachelor, would have told him if he was engaged. They even had a running bet on who would get married first. But someone had put a rock the size of Stone Mountain on her finger. He suddenly wanted to know who.

"So what brings you to Atlanta, Yvonne?" he asked, retrieving the luggage she pointed out, surprised to see only a large rolling suitcase in addition to the briefcase she held. "Visiting your fiancé?"

They left the airport for the parking lot. "Jeff really hasn't told you about me, has he?" she asked. "I mean, it's not a big deal, but you should at least be aware that you're not playing taxi for a mass murderer."

He stopped before his pride and joy, a pristine black '65 Mustang convertible that he'd restored himself. "You're definitely not a mass murderer," he stated matter-of-factly, putting her cases and coat into the trunk. "Ballet maybe?"

He came around to hand her into the car. She hesitated, then got in. The graceful way she swung her legs inside made him warm. Some women practiced that forever without mastering it.

She turned to face him when he entered the car. "I've been living in Atlanta for about eight years. I'm not a spy or a dancer or even engaged."

The gem on her hand sparkled as she held it between them. "This is my 'keep away' ring. It helps deter unwanted attention. I'm too busy with work to maintain a relationship."

The day was looking up after all! "So what kind of work keeps you so busy?"

When he started the car, she fastened her seat belt and pushed her seat as far back as it would go. "Have you ever heard of Your Heart's Desire?"

"Those local shops giving Victoria's Secret and Frederick's a run for their money? Yes, I know them—the one in Buckhead turns Peachtree Street to permanent gridlock around Valentine's Day."

He paid the parking fee and pulled into the traffic heading for the highway. "Wait a minute! Are you that Yvonne Mitchelson? Of Gemini Enterprises?" She nodded. "Well, I'll be damned! No wonder Jeff said I'd recognize you when I saw you. You were the cover story in *Georgia Business* magazine last month."

"If you read that, you're more than a pin-up guy," she said, smiling.

He grinned back. There was a compliment in there somewhere, he supposed. "I hope so. Thom wouldn't like it if I didn't pull my share at BBC."

"BBC?"

"Better Business Concepts. It's a…"

"Well if this isn't the mother of all coincidences!" she exclaimed, turning in her seat to face him again. "I have a meeting scheduled with your firm next week."

"You're kidding."

She shook her head, her gaze on the Atlanta skyline as it came into view. The last of the sun gleamed on the dome of the Capitol, turning its gold cap into a burnished copper. The rest of the city proper spread along the skyline like an electric rainbow. "I've heard a little about your firm, so I called and set an appointment with Kyle or Conrad or someone like that. Jeff said he knew someone at the firm, and he was going to pick me up so that I could pick his brain over dinner."

Forcing down the surge of excitement at her words, Michael kept his eyes on the highway. "It must be fate, because I'm a senior partner of Better Business Concepts. If you believe Gemini Enterprises is at a level where a management firm would be a benefit, then BBC would certainly like to be considered."

"Spoken like a true businessman," she observed with laughter. "Where's the sales pitch?"

"I've definitely got one. Care to hear it over dinner?" That slipped out on its own, but now that he thought about it, dinner was a good idea. He certainly wasn't ready to say goodbye yet.

He stole a glance at her. Her profile was determined, and her hand had the armrest on the passenger door in a death-grip. "I really should call Jeff," she said, her voice hesitant. "We were supposed to go out to dinner, but if that precious Lexus of his got hit, he'll probably want to baby-sit it."

"We can call him from the restaurant. That way, he can join us and explain how we both know him and not each other."

She had to laugh at that. "Sounds like a segment on *Unsolved Mysteries*. But surely I'm keeping you from more important pursuits this evening? I'll be more than happy speaking with Kevin or Carter next week."

A little frisson of worry had him tightening his grip on the steering wheel, his only outward display of emotion. "What could be more important than discussing a terrific business over a wonderful meal? And given our mysterious mutual friend, I must ensure that you receive the best consultation BBC has to offer." Besides, the only consulting Conrad's going to be doing is with the classifieds.

"All right." She settled firmly into her seat, rechecking the seatbelt. "On to dinner. I can see Jeff tomorrow."

Michael watched her watching the skyline and hid a smile. The day was definitely ending better than it had started.

CHAPTER TWO

Yvonne surreptitiously eased her grip on the door handle and exhaled as the car rolled to a stop. Michael Benjamin wasn't a bad driver, but it was hard to feel safe in the heavy convertible that didn't even have airbags. Of course, it was becoming hard to feel safe around the man himself.

Sitting beside him in the cramped confines of his car, Yvonne felt as if she had just taken a load of sweaters out of the dryer. Every nerve ending was tensed, waiting for the static charge of his personality to zap her.

Try as he might, the man just couldn't be inconspicuous. As they walked out of the airport, she had scrutinized him closely. Her practiced eye recognized Armani when she saw it, and he wore it well. Muscles, defined but not ostentatious, flexed smoothly beneath the tailored jacket, the navy and gold striped tie did dangerous things to his eyes, and the long legs encased in navy trousers were lean like a runner's.

He was, to say the least, a big man. How he was able to move so gracefully amazed her. And she was sure that he could intimidate anyone he wanted to, with his size or his lightning-bolt looks. Still, it was difficult to look at him and not think of taking his measurements. All of them.

Suppressing a sigh of relief, she let him help her out of the car. "Do you take your clients out in that?"

He accepted a ticket from the valet and ushered her up the walk. "Only if they love classic cars. My working car is a Mercedes."

Of course it is, she thought to herself. If he and Jeff were anything alike, a Benz was more his style. The women he dated probably wouldn't set foot in less. If he dated. She bit back laughter. If?

"Yvonne?"

She glanced up, startled, and saw that they were at Marco's, a trendy Greek-Italian bistro a few blocks from the Arts Center. "I'm sorry. You were saying?"

"I was asking if you drive at all." He held the door to let her through.

"Not if I can help it. Traffic makes me nervous. I have an assistant who drives me around when I need it, but I do most of my work at home."

Michael looked at her strangely, and she supposed she couldn't blame him. How many twenty-eight-year-old women were afraid of driving?

The blonde hostess took their coats and gestured them to a low divan, giving Michael a wide, inviting smile. "Is there anything I can get you?" she queried, leaning over him.

He must have some sort of radar, Yvonne mused. Or maybe he was releasing pheromones, or pure magnetic energy. Whatever it was, he certainly had the attention of every woman in the alcove. It didn't seem to matter that she had come in with him.

Well, she had, so they'd just have to deal with it.

"Is Nicolas here tonight?" she asked in a brisk tone.

The hostess glanced at her, assessing, then back to Michael. "Yeah, he's here."

"We need a table in his section." It was not a request.

The hostess straightened, a frown bending her dark brows. "There aren't any tables free in his section," she said flatly.

Undaunted, Yvonne gave her a sunny smile. She ran her left hand through her hair, giving the hostess a good look at the diamonds on her finger. "We'll wait for one, thank you."

The hostess froze, her eyes widening. She shot Michael a resentful glare, threw their coats over her arm, and stomped off.

He dipped his head towards her. "What was that about?"

Yvonne shrugged, but inside she was grinning like the Cheshire Cat. It was her first territorial skirmish, and she was feeling a little giddy. "Don't know. Do you come to Marco's often?"

Michael stared at her a moment before answering. "I'm addicted to Mediterranean food. I come in probably twice a month, sometimes bringing clients. My favorite restaurant right now is Creole." He looked at her again. "If you have a favorite waiter, I suppose you come in pretty often."

"I'll admit it, I'm an addict too," she confessed morosely. "I eat here more than I eat at home."

"That hostess should have recognized you, then."

"That hostess is—"

"Ms. Mitchelson?"

A waiter came from the main room, a smile on his face. "Hi, Nicolas," she said, standing up with a grin.

Nicolas shook her hand. "What are you doing sitting out here? Your table's empty!"

She nodded toward the hostess stand. "Your hostess thought you were full."

"Did she?" Nicolas turned to the stand, shooting the guilty hostess a frown. "She's new," he explained. "I'll talk to her."

He led them to an intimate corner table lit by a muted overhead lamp. "When did you get back?" he asked as he seated her.

"A little while ago. Jeff's car broke down, so he had his friend here picked me up." She introduced Michael. "Is Marco here?"

Another waiter delivered a basket of breadsticks and dipping sauces, two glasses of water—with a lime twist for Yvonne—and menus. "When isn't he?" Nicolas answered, fussing over the table. "Do you want a minute, or have you decided on the usual pasta dish?"

"No, I think I'll munch on these breadsticks for a bit, then try something different. Thanks."

When Nicolas left, she occupied herself by dunking the tip of a breadstick into the marinara sauce, aware of Michael's gaze on her. She glanced up. Those eyes! Did eyes really come in the color of liquid gold? And why had God decided to give such long, thick lashes to a man? It just wasn't fair.

He propped his chin in his hand, as if trying to keep his mouth from dropping open. "Okay, Yvonne, 'fess up."

She paused, the breadstick poised at her lips. She decided she liked the way he said her name, sort of shy and breathy sounding. "About what?"

The innocent routine obviously wasn't going to work, not if the way he folded his arms and leaned towards her was any indication. Her tongue darted out of her mouth, licking sauce from her lips.

His gaze immediately zeroed in on the movement, following her tongue back and forth. Something deep inside her began to quiver. She hastily put the breadstick down and covered her lips with her napkin. "What?" she asked again.

"That waiter couldn't help you fast enough. And he seemed to want to do bodily harm to that hostess for ignoring you."

Managing a nonchalant shrug wasn't easy, but she did it. "You heard Nicolas. She's new. She doesn't know I'm a frequent diner."

"That's not it. At least that's not all of it. You're more than a frequent diner, aren't you?"

Nervous, she wiped her fingers with the cloth napkin. "Well, it's not widely known, but if we're going to do business together, you'll see it in my portfolio."

His hand jerked, as if he had the urge to grab her by the shoulders. "See what?"

"There really is a Marco—Marco Piccione. We knew each other before there was a restaurant."

"Really." His tone was completely noncommittal, but Yvonne saw the tiny muscle tick beside his eye. She'd put him off some way, but how?

She was about to ask him when Marco himself appeared. "Yvonne, cara mia!" he exclaimed, pulling her to her feet to kiss both her cheeks. "Nicolas said you were back!"

Laughter broke from her as she was swallowed in an exuberant hug. "Marco, I've missed you! How is Sofia?"

"Bene. I can't keep her out of the kitchen. She cooks, she eats, then she and Liza go exercise my food away, just like you." He held her away critically. "And look at you! Did you not eat in New York?"

Yvonne spread her hands. "I tried, but the food there doesn't taste like yours. In fact, I came straight from the airport, and I'm starved!"

"Marco will feed you, you know that," the chef said affectionately, one arm draped about her shoulders. "And who is the Signore with you?"

"Oh my goodness—I'm sorry!" She turned as Michael got to his feet, his expression closed. "This is Michael Benjamin. He's president of a consulting firm in Midtown. He also happens to be a very good friend of Jeff's."

A beep sounded. All three reached for their pagers. "It's me," Yvonne said, glancing at the readout. "Speak of the devil. I'll give Jeff a call and let him know we're not abducted or stranded. Excuse me."

Both men were silent, watching Yvonne weave her way across the full dining area. "Welcome to Marco's," the restaurateur said, giving Michael a strong handshake. "I remember now, seeing you before with Signore Maxwell— and very nice ladies."

He paused. "Mr. Maxwell is a good friend to Yvonne."

Michael took a sip of water, wishing like hell it were something stronger. Marco was in his forties, the dark curls of his hair turning silver at the temples. He was dressed in chefs' whites that only enhanced his cultured mien. He was the epitome of the Italian male, and Michael didn't like him one bit.

"Yvonne said she knew you before there was a Marco's." He barely kept the accusation out of his voice. Here was another man falling over himself for Yvonne. How many others were there?

"My daughter Liza works for her," the older man answered easily. "We became friends, and she made all this possible."

Michael thought he was going to choke on a chunk of bread. Did Marco know the Heimlich Maneuver? Would he use it if he did?

Somehow he got the bread down. "What?"

Marco grinned. "Yvonne is a silent partner of Marco's," he explained. "When my daughter told her of our struggles to open a restaurant, Yvonne arranged the investment."

He drew in a deep breath and released it. "I owe the success of Marco's to her. She's a remarkable woman. Excuse me, Mr. Benjamin, but I must get back to my kitchen. I have a dish I would like Yvonne to try. It was a pleasure to meet you."

He moved off, leaving Michael more than a little dumbfounded. Who in the world was this woman, and how in the world was she able to bankroll a restaurant? The income from three boutiques couldn't do that, no matter how successful they were.

Nicolas returned with a choice red wine, and he accepted it gratefully. He was still pondering the mystery that was Yvonne Mitchelson when she returned. "Jeff's relieved that I'm okay. He says he owes you one."

"I'd agree with that." He seated her, returning to his own chair as she reached into her briefcase for a notepad. "Where were we?"

"I think you were going to tell me how you bankrolled this restaurant for Mr. Piccione."

Her hands froze in the act of uncapping her prestige pen, and she gave him a measured, wary look. "So Marco beat me to the punch." He nodded. "And he told you I came on as a silent partner?" Again Michael nodded.

"Liza Piccione, Marco's daughter, has been working for me for about three years," Yvonne explained. "Her father was a chef at a little known and even less appreciated bistro in Roswell. Liza told me about how her father always wanted to have his own place, so I asked to meet him. His wife, Sofia, practically adopted me on the spot. We talked about it for hours, days, months. The more I heard, the more I tasted, the more I knew it wouldn't be just another Italian restaurant. Everything told me to go for it, and when Jeff gave me the final okay, I gave Marco the start-up funds. But he and his wife put the blood and sweat into it."

Michael realized he had to reappraise her. First impressions didn't mean a thing with this woman. What he knew about her didn't begin to compare to what he was learning. Talk about the tip of the iceberg!

"That was damned risky," he pointed out, but there was nothing but admiration in his voice.

"I'll be the first one to admit it was dangerous—no, the second," she acknowledged. "Jeff thought I was financially hanging myself, especially since Desire II had just opened. But, as I'm sure you're aware, white males dominate the business world. I wanted to climb the ladder without a coffeepot in my hand. To make my mark, I've had to be unorthodox. But it paid off. Marco's is in the Top Ten best restaurants for the second straight year. And Jeff didn't even blink when I suggested investing in Creole."

The Cajun-inspired restaurant, Michael knew, was also voted one of the ten best in Atlanta. And she had a hand in that too? He gave a low whistle of appreciation. "Do you habitually risk everything on dreams?"

Her eyes sparkled as she gazed at him. "Oh yeah, it was a risky dream. But dreams are worth the risks, don't you think, Michael?"

At that moment, every woman he had ever known, ever thought about, packed her bags and left his mind. They were evicted by some dreams he definitely wanted to risk, dreams involving a certain stunning beauty who wanted to do business with him. Business!

Soft candlelight bathed the curves of her face, lighting the sensuous sincerity of her eyes and accentuating the dimples in her cheeks. Was her skin as satiny soft as it looked?

"You're right," he finally answered, his voice soft. "A dream isn't worth dreaming if you aren't willing to risk anything—everything—to see it become a reality."

Her smile grew, and she impulsively reached out and squeezed his hand. "You understand! You see it the same way I do. I knew you would."

Absurdly pleased, he smiled back at her, turning his hand to clasp hers more firmly. "I'm glad."

Yvonne suddenly found herself engrossed in the study of his eyes. First liquid gold, now flashes of topaz and even citrine, glinted in the candlelight. Those eyes beckoned to her, promising her all manner of delights.

She saw his mouth moving but couldn't hear his words over the pounding drum solo her heart had begun. She sat back, extracting her hand. "Pardon me?"

He gave her a knowing smile. "I was wondering why you feel you need a marketing firm. With the successes of your boutiques and the restaurants, I don't think you need me."

Still dazzled by his eyes, Yvonne blurted the first thing that came to mind. "I need a man."

He coughed into his wineglass, dribbling a good bit down his chin. "Who— what did you just say?"

"Oh, my God, I can't believe I just said that!" She covered her eyes with her hands as mortification engulfed her. Waiting a heartbeat, she darted a peek between her fingers. Yep, he looked as if she'd sprouted an extra head.

She forced her hands to her lap and smiled through her blush. "Really, Michael, it's not like it sounds. I design a lot of the lingerie in my boutiques, and the private line has been holding its own with the other lines. But I'm thinking of branching out into menswear. Nothing major, just a few basic pieces women would want to pick up for their partners while shopping."

"And you need a man because ... ?"

She could feel a tingling in her cheeks that had nothing to do with the sip of wine she just had. "I prefer to use fit models when I'm ready to produce the finished product, and I hope to find someone to, well, to inspire me to create vibrant designs."

Didn't any of her male friends fit the bill? Michael wondered. It didn't matter. He knew he could be positively inspiring when he wanted to. "So you want a marketing firm to compile a feasibility study for you?"

"Among other things. I want to expand my horizons. I think it's about time."

So did he, but they probably weren't thinking about the same thing. "I think I, that is, BBC, can give you what you're looking for."

"Great." She opened her leather notebook. "I think we can work well together, Michael, but I want to ask you a few questions first, if you don't mind."

But he did mind. Business was the last thing he wanted to be questioned about. "Don't you ever mix pleasure with business?"

"My business is my pleasure," she retorted, then softened her words with a smile. "I'll be brief though. Business is definitely off limits once Marco brings the food out."

He leaned back, graciously waving a breadstick. "Shoot."

And with that, she proceeded to interrogate him about Better Business Concepts. She questioned his background, degree, experience, and his company's track record. She speculated on the percentage of minority-owned businesses in his clientele, the rate of new contracts acquired, the number of satisfied clients. As he talked she made notes in her notebook, nodding agreement or acknowledgment at times, pursing her lips with concern at others. He knew it wasn't just an act; if he asked, he was sure she could tell him anything he'd said verbatim.

It was with obvious relief that he welcomed Marco and Nicolas back, bearing trays loaded with steaming tidbits.

"Marco, I have to hand it to you. You can't help but be a success with this woman on your side."

"I agree with you," the chef answered, pouring their wine. "Yvonne is wonderful in the office, but the kitchen?" He shook his head ruefully. "Dio mio!"

"Marco," Yvonne protested. She shifted in her chair uncomfortably.

"It's true," the restaurateur insisted. "Our first night, she invites so many people, the place is overflowing. So, she decided to help."

Marco spread his hands. "Burned all the breadsticks— and right after the fire marshal left! We made her an honorary hostess instead!"

Michael turned to her. Even with her skin tone, he knew a blush when he saw one.

"All right, I'll be the first one to admit that I'd starve to death if God hadn't invented takeout," she said defiantly. "But I'm getting better. The last time I used my stove, I made tea. And I did it without setting off the smoke alarm!"

"That's how you tell if it's a good day?"

"Hey— you gonna eat that food, or do you wanna wear it?"

The car rolled to a gentle stop, and a saxophone was cut off in mid-wail as the ignition was turned off. The console was full of other jazz discs, and even some blues. That he liked jazz was a surprise to her; she expected an eclectic heavy metal-Top 40 mix. But then, she was learning not to expect what she expected when it came to Michael. He proved her wrong every time, which was refreshing to someone who could make a career out of picking a fake person out in five minutes or less.

"So it's a done deal?" he asked, helping her out of the car before retrieving her bag and coat. Hefting the case, he followed her up the walk.

Yvonne lived in a smart townhouse community that was not far from him. Of course, here in Atlanta, five miles put you into an entirely different community and culture. Knowing she lived less than fifteen minutes away was a pleasant thought.

"Don't sign the papers yet. I'd still like to meet your partner, and you haven't been behind the scenes at the stores or met my partners yet. One look at my humble enterprise may send you screaming to the hills." She opened the door, stepping inside to disarm the alarm.

"Somehow I doubt that." She didn't say he couldn't, so he followed her in, admiring the polished hardwood of the foyer and a tiny mahogany table boasting a sculpture of an African tribal dance.

"If you like, we can hammer out details over dinner tomorrow night. After all, I'm not afraid of my stove."

"Insulting me is not going to get you my business," she reprimanded primly.

Michael took a mental step backward, wondering if he had gone too far. Calm down, moron, he told himself fiercely. You just met her and you're already inviting her to your place. What's gotten into you? "A thousand pardons, O deity of take-out."

To his relief, she laughed. "I'd like nothing better than to get everything settled, but I'd like you to at least pretend that I'm shopping around. And with this aggravating trip to New York and the advent of the bridal season, my weekend's going to be stretched between the boutiques and my girls."

He dropped the Pullman with a thud. Girls? She had children? That meant there was—or had been—a husband or something in her life. If there were a boyfriend, he would have picked her up at the airport. Michael knew he wouldn't let another man pick up his girlfriend, not if that girlfriend was this exotic, intelligent, financially independent woman.

All this took a split second to run through his head. "Your girls?" he repeated, knowing he sounded redundant but not caring.

Her smile was radiant as she hung her coat in the closet. "I work with mentor Atlanta," she explained. "It's almost like the Big Brother and Sisters organization. I mentor a core group of three, but one weekend a month I have as many as fifteen girls over. We go to exhibits, they talk to Jeff about their financial future, and I give them projects to do based on my workweek. And this is the weekend."

She turned to face him. "Mondays are usually a recovery day for me, and I'll probably be meeting with my partners for most of it, rehashing this trip. How about a meeting on Tuesday? Tuesdays are typically slow, and I can adjust my schedule. And that's what I agreed to with your associate."

He didn't know what he had scheduled for Tuesday, and he discovered he didn't care. The president of Microsoft would be rescheduled to accommodate her.

"Tuesday would be great. Eleven o'clock okay?"

They agreed on the time and Yvonne extended her hand. "I've kept you long enough. Thank you for playing chauffeur," she added, her voice low. "And for dinner. I really needed that."

Michael took her hand. It was small and warm in his, but there was strength in the grip. "My pleasure, especially if it means your business!"

They shared a laugh again, like old friends. She remained in the doorway as he walked to his car. "See you Tuesday," she called, then was gone.

Michael drove home slowly, replaying the night in his mind. Yvonne Mitchelson had a way of pervading his senses that confounded him. Even though he'd only known her a few hours, he was sure he could find her in a crowded room blindfolded. Her fragrance was a combination of jasmine and spices, sweet and exciting. Her smile lit up a room. Her voice flowed sexy and warm. And those eyes …

Yvonne wasn't afraid to look at a person straight on. And the looks she gave him! If she looked at him that way while talking business, how would she look at him when he kissed her?

With a jerk, Michael pulled his car over to the curb. He ran his hands over his face, eradicating the grin he'd worn since leaving her house.

"What the hell do you think you're doing? Ms. Mitchelson—" he had to force himself to call her that— "is a client. She isn't even that yet! Get a grip!"

He exhaled harshly, forcing himself to face reality. Reality was, he needed Yvonne's business more than he needed her body. Reality was, he wasn't looking for a relationship. Reality was, Yvonne's social life was probably so full she needed a personal secretary to keep her dates straight. Reality was, she was black, he was white, and she was only interested in business.

Reality was, he had a hard-on the size of Montana.

CHAPTER THREE

Jeff spun around Michael and executed a perfect lay-up. "Hey man, I wasn't trying to cut you out. Yvonne asked me about marketing firms a few weeks ago. Naturally I mentioned yours, but I didn't know she was seriously searching. I can't tell you what I don't know."

Jeff Maxwell was tall, athletic, and a dead ringer for Denzel Washington. He had gone to the University of North Carolina on a basketball scholarship but had always hit the books. When a knee injury sidelined hopes of a pro career, he was able to convert to an academic scholarship and graduated in the top ten of the class. Now he was enjoying life as an obscenely successful financial advisor with the possible dream of retiring at forty. Women elbowed each other aside whenever he entered a room.

"So tell me what you do know," Michael suggested, tossing the ball back to him. They were playing one-on-one in front of Michael's garage, sweating in spite of the cool temperature. He was trying to be as casual as possible, but was glad that Jeff was paying more attention to the game than him. "How long have you known her?"

"Yvonne and I have been friends for about ten years. Met her at a wedding—her cousin, my brother Jeremy. She was quiet, intense, and seemed kind of lonely. When I found out that she had been a junior figure skating champion, one of three black skaters at the time, I had to meet her. I don't know how, but we hit it off. We exchanged letters for years, and after her uncle died, I convinced her to move here."

Michael knew there was more to the story, but decided not to push it. He stole the ball from Jeff and slammed it home. "Why didn't you tell me she's a co-owner of Marco's and Creole? Everyone's raving about both of them."

Jeff dribbled by him on a fake and hit a jumper off the backboard. "Yvonne's extremely low-key about her finances. But yeah, since I handle her portfolio, she came to me with the idea of backing Mr. Piccione. Creole actually is run by one of her mother's distant relatives from Louisiana. At first I was against her getting into restaurants, even for family, but it's hard to tell Yvonne no when she sets her mind on something. I was glad she didn't listen to me. Both places are still raking it in."

Impressed, Michael caught Jeff's one-handed lob. "She seems to know her business."

"Sure she does. That master's degree from Spelman didn't come cheap. She devotes her life to those stores and being a mentor to about fifty girls. I was out with them yesterday, and I tell you, I don't see how she does it. I don't see her as much as I want to, since one of us is almost always out of town. She barely has time to meet me for lunch."

Is she seeing anyone?

Jeff stopped short, stealing the ball and tucking it under one arm. "Why do you want to know?"

Why did he want to know? Michael didn't have a clue. "Just natural curiosity."

Jeff eyed him for a moment. "Don't try and play me, Mike. I've been your friend for too long."

He didn't need to hear the explicit warning in Jeff's voice; his friend's expression said it all. If he showed the slightest interest in Yvonne, Jeff would shoot him down in a heartbeat. He threw up his hands. "Hey, ease up. Like I said, I'm curious. I like to know as much as possible about the people behind the companies I deal with. You know that."

Jeff's frown shifted to a slight smile. "All right. Don't mean to come off like that, but Vonne's like my little sister, and I guess I'm a little overprotective. But she's not seeing anyone." He passed Michael the ball with a hard, double-handed thrust. "All she makes time for are her girls and her business."

With a surge of elation, Michael hit a twenty-footer, nothing but net, and won the game. "So how is she able to bankroll two restaurants, take care of fifty girls, her stores, that condo, and pay you to make her money grow?"

Jeff stopped bouncing the ball and wiped an arm across his dripping forehead. "That's privileged info, buddy. I'd like to say it was all my expertise, but she had plenty of cash before I got my hands on it. Let's just say that if the restaurants and all three stores went belly up, she'd still have enough assets after paying off her employees and other losses to not ever have to work again."

He turned his back, absently flicked the ball over his head, and was rewarded with a gentle swoosh. "You'll probably find all of this out on Tuesday. Yvonne sounded excited about doing business with you. Guess it was good luck my car broke down. In fact, I'd say you owe me big."

Michael clapped him across the shoulders. "Beer and a couple of Cajun steaks at Creole?"

"Good. Better bring your credit card though. I'm hungry and thirsty."

By 10:45 Tuesday morning, Michael's calendar was cleared and he allowed himself fifteen minutes to ponder his next appointment. He moved to the huge window of his Midtown office. Atlanta's skyline twinkled at him, but he didn't see it, replaying memories of the past few days.

Yvonne Mitchelson. He had thought of little else all weekend; her image assaulted his senses. Thick dark brows danced above molasses-soft eyes framed by mile-long lashes, a round nose and full, soft lips begging to be kissed. In fact, Yvonne's whole body—or what he had imagined of it—was screaming for hours of wild passion.

"Down boy," he muttered, rocking on his heels. He exhaled slowly, deeply. He couldn't deny that he was extremely attracted to Yvonne, like lightning to trees. Granted, there had been other attractions and other women, but never one who had grabbed him like this.

Priding himself on being a straightforward, blunt man, he asked himself if he was attracted to Yvonne solely because of her color. He immediately dismissed the idea. He had been around enough black women, especially when he and Jeff prowled the Buckhead bar scene together. But none of them had caught his interest like Yvonne did. No woman had.

Correction. Maybe one had. Only one, and she had died in a seven-car accident. It had been more than ten years ago, but there were moments when it seemed like yesterday. For his entire adult life Michael had been in an emotional exile that habit made home.

Still, Jeff's warning notwithstanding, he hoped that Yvonne was just as willing as he was to explore other sides of their relationship. She didn't seem to be one of those women who needed to keep a man constantly at her beck and call. In fact, she didn't seem to need a man at all, save for creative inspiration. Her obvious independence made her all the more appealing to him. She wouldn't want emotional entanglements cluttering her life, any more than he did. But if she wanted sex—mind-blowing, wake the neighbors passion—he would, and could, provide it.

The phone buzzed, halting his reverie. "Sir, Ms. Mitchelson has arrived," his secretary informed him.

Michael slipped on his jacket and straightened his tie. "Thank you, Connie. Please show her in."

If possible, Yvonne was even more stunning than he remembered. She wore a slim lavender skirt that stopped a few inches above the knee and matching jacket with ivory cuffs. A single strand pearl choker was about her neck, with an amethyst drop dangling from it. The dark waves were pulled up and held by pearl combs, making her expressive eyes more noticeable. A faint, spicy fragrance teased and beckoned him.

The overall view had a powerful effect on Michael. He sighed deeply and wondered how long he would last.

He shook her hand, then led her to a sitting area by the large window. "My partner, Thom, will be with us shortly. How was your weekend with the girls?"

She beamed as she settled in a burgundy armchair. "Wonderful and exhausting. I had about fourteen girls over. I try to combine something educational with all the fun, so Saturday Jeff and I took them to the history museum and to the bank to check on their savings accounts. Between that and skating and trying on clothes, they wanted to know all about boys—questions I didn't have answers to!"

She shook her head in disbelief. "But I love being a Mentor. It's an honor to have those girls look up to me, to be living proof of what they can achieve if they try."

Her gaze was mildly abashed as she balanced her briefcase on her knees. "I'm sorry, Michael, I get a little preachy when I talk about the Mentor Atlanta organization. But if your company can help mine, I'll be able to devote more time to them."

"I'm here to make you happy," he answered. "We'll do what we can to make it easier for you. Would you like something to drink?"

"A bottled water would be great." As he went to his desk to buzz his secretary, Yvonne reflected on the little that Jeff had told her about him.

She knew that he and Jeff had been friends since high school and kept in touch even when Jeff's scholarship took him to the University of North Carolina and Benjamin money had taken Michael to Yale for law. In his junior year he had abruptly switched to a business major. Jeff described him as a brilliant businessman, dependable, extroverted, and a good friend.

But Jeff had also warned her about Michael's tendency to go through women like bargain hunters through a clearance sale. Women, it seemed, had a habit of throwing themselves at him, and red-blooded male that he was, he hardly ever refused them. Not that he wasn't conscientious about it, Jeff said, but Michael never had a relationship last longer than a year.

Of course, Yvonne hastily told herself, she didn't care that much about his personal life. As long as he took care of her company, he could do what he wanted off the clock.

"Penny for your thoughts."

She accepted the proffered bottle and glass. "Just comparing notes."

"On?"

She gave him a level look. "On what Jeff told me about you versus what I know myself."

He took the chair next to hers. "Was his recommendation less than glowing?"

His posture was deceptively casual, but she wasn't fooled. His eyes betrayed his concern. Setting aside the briefcase, she crossed her legs and settled into her chair. "He praised your business acumen, if that's what you want to know."

"Anything else?"

She didn't bother hiding her smile. "Fishing for compliments, Mr. Benjamin?"

"Call it curiosity."

"I don't take stock in what people say. People will say anything to get what they want. It's what they do that impresses me."

He leaned toward her. "And have I impressed you?"

His voice was low, and to her, unbelievably seductive. "Well, you have to admit that chauffeuring a less-than-grateful passenger around would certainly earn you brownie points."

He laughed with her. "Hopefully you'll give me and my company the opportunity to earn a halo."

"Can I ask you a personal question?" she surprised herself by asking.

"Only if I can ask you one," he replied, his gaze steady on hers.

She fought the urge to squirm. There was something about the way Michael Benjamin looked at her, the direct-ness and intensity of his gaze, that made her feel as if he were having another conversation about her in his head. But it would be rude to ask him to stop. Besides, she wasn't sure if she wanted him to.

"Jeff told me that you were going to work in corporate law. What made you decide against it?"

His gaze did flicker away then. "I'm surprised Jeff didn't tell you," he finally said, his voice without inflection. "It was expected of me, but after my wife died, I decided I didn't want to do what was expected of me anymore."

He had been married? She looked down at her hands, clasped firmly in her lap. Though he had answered her question readily enough, she could almost feel the fence going up between them. "I'm sorry, Michael. That was tact-less of me."

"It's all right," he said. "It was a long time ago."

It was also a closed subject. She could tell by the way he sat back in his chair, as if distancing himself from the memory. She copied his gesture, preparing herself for what-ever question he had. "Guess it's my turn now. Shoot."

She could almost see the gears in his head turning. It was a wonder smoke wasn't coming out of his ears. Could he possibly have that many questions he wanted to ask her, or was he trying to decide how to ask it?

"Jeff told me that he handles your investment port-folio," he began, then paused.

"And here I thought you were going to delve into my personal life," she said, forcing a smile. "I guess you're wondering how could I possibly afford to fund two restau-rants, three gift stores, a print shop, and live in a pricey Buckhead condo? Not to mention being able to afford Jeff to make more money for me. You want to know where the money came from?"

She leaned forward, dropping her voice to a stage whisper. "It's drug money."

She watched his eyes widen in surprise, then narrow with suspicion. "I don't believe you. You're too intelligent for that crap."

"I was just seeing if you'd bite." She reached to tuck a curl behind her ear and gave him a mildly reproachful look. "My father's family was reasonably well off, and he was a successful businessman in his own right. He started invest-ment portfolios for me and my sister when we were born."

"So he helped you start your business?"

She reached for her water, then put her hand in her lap to hide the sudden tremor. "Jeff didn't tell you?"

"He told me he met you at a wedding, and that you were a junior figure skating champion. That's all."

Her hand crept to her throat, fingering the pearls there like a rosary. "Jeff is like the brother I never had. My twin sister and I skated competitively on the junior circuit until we placed first and third in the nationals. Our coach was prepping us for the Olympics until ... "

She paused, swallowed. "I lost my family in an accident when I was thirteen," she finally said, her voice without emotion. "A tractor trailer went through a red light and plowed into our car. I was temporarily paralyzed, but after two years of therapy I had regained some sense of normalcy. My inheritance, plus a settlement from the trucking company, ensured that I wouldn't want for anything. Financially speaking, anyway."

Financially speaking, she was set for life. But money couldn't fill the emptiness her family's deaths left her, and she knew it. Neither would spilling her history to a stranger.

A large hand closed over hers. "I had no right to pry. I'm sorry I resurrected bad memories for you."

Yvonne looked down at their clasped hands. She didn't like to talk about her past, for many reasons. She didn't like to talk about herself at all. But somehow, it was easy with Michael. It was probably part of his charm.

She released his hand and stood up, distancing herself from him. No one had gotten to her so quickly, and it unnerved her. "There were good memories too," she softly, to remind herself.

Giving herself a mental shake, she turned around briskly. "In fact, Your Heart's Desire is a testament to the love my parents had for each other. If I impart just a little of the magic of their relationship to someone else, then I honor their memory."

There was a knock on the door, and Michael's partner entered. Thom Sebastian was tall and coppery, with honest hazel eyes smiling behind gold glasses perched on a straight nose.

He gave her a pleased smile as he walked to her, and his handshake was firm.

"Welcome to Better Business Concepts, Ms. Mitchelson," he greeted her warmly. "I have you to thank for my idyllic marriage. My wife adores your stores. She's bought several books there, and I know better than to go to a drugstore for a greeting card."

"So people do shop my stores for more than lingerie," she remarked, completely at ease with him. "And please, call me Yvonne—especially since we'll be doing business together."

"Mike did the sales pitch already?"

"He didn't have to," she replied, reaching for her brief-case. "Jeff Maxwell is a very good friend of mine, and he gave your firm a high recommendation. That's enough for me."

"Then you know that in eight years we have created a tradition of service and excellence surpassed by no one," Thom said.

"Your record speaks for itself. I took the liberty of talking to a few of your clients. They're pleased with your firm and the business you've created for them."

She pulled several files from her briefcase, smiling at their expressions. "Don't be surprised, gentlemen; I told you I did my homework. I know your firm is best suited to my needs. And my needs are simple: increase the profitability of the boutiques and my other concerns, and make it all more efficient."

"Here's a bio of Gemini Enterprises," she said, passing each a file. "Feel free to look it over at your leisure, but I'll give you a verbal rundown now, if you don't mind."

She launched into her second favorite subject. Both men listened attentively as she waxed poetic about her company, but she was highly aware of Michael following every movement she made from hand gestures to her less-than-perfect stride. She quickly summed up then sought the refuge of her chair as Thom began to speak.

Attempting to focus on him proved difficult, since her thoughts kept straying to his partner. She'd never let business meetings unnerve her before. Why now? Michael had a way of mixing personal and professional that made her want to run for the hills. She couldn't believe that he was attracted to her, but something had sizzled in the air between them the first time they touched.

It didn't matter. She couldn't turn down his firm. They were the best. She needed their youth and their expertise, and she needed inspiration. Badly.

She caught Thom's last remark. "I agree with you about the hands-on approach. I'd be happy to give you a tour of my humble enterprise, if you'd like."

"Does than mean we're on board?" Thom asked.

"It does indeed. I was sold before I even entered the building, but I liked hearing the pitch anyway."

Thom laughed. "Well then, all we need is your handshake and I'll have our secretary draft a contract. I can have it completed and couriered to you by tomorrow morning."

"Perfect." She shook their hands. "Here's my card with my home office and fax numbers. And here's a gift certificate for each of you. We call them 'Desire Dollars'."

"My wife will love you," Thom thanked her. "In fact, we're having a small dinner party this Friday. Brianne will have my head if I don't invite you. We can celebrate the contract, and perhaps even toss a few proposals around."

Her eyes unconsciously strayed to Michael. "Sounds wonderful ... " she began.

He took the hint. "I can pick you up. People tell me I'm a great chauffeur."

Yvonne gathered her papers and sealed her briefcase. "Then I will see both of you on Friday, but please feel free to visit my stores before then. Just give my assistant a call to set it up."

She shook hands with Thom; then Michael escorted her to the elevator. "I'll definitely see you before Friday. Somebody has to help me spend my 'Desire Dollars'."

"Well, if one of your girlfriends can't make it, I'm at your service, Mr. Benjamin."

He gave her a very private grin. "At the moment, I am completely unattached."

"Not a common occurrence, I'm sure. Still, that's good news for the single women of Atlanta, isn't it?"

His voice was low. "Not all of them." The elevator opened and she stepped inside. "I'll call you."

"I'll answer," she quipped, fluttering a barely-there wink before the elevator closed.

Realizing she had the elevator to herself, Yvonne sagged against the back wall. What the hell was she doing? She had just become Michael Benjamin's client, not his date. She was acting like a giddy sixteen-year-old! The man was obviously a natural-born flirt and a womanizer of the first degree! Women prettier and paler than she probably stalked him wherever he went. She wanted his business skills, not his sexual acumen. She needed to get a grip.

Boy, she wanted to get a grip. On him.

CHAPTER FOUR

She was never good at social gatherings. As a child she had watched, mesmerized, the elegant dinner parties her parents orchestrated. The black elite of Detroit had convened in their huge three-story home like a post Academy Awards gala. She remembered feeling awed and inspired, knowing that they were people to look up to and learn from.

But aside from treating her managerial staff to dinner once a month, Yvonne detested going out. Her loathing was deeply seated in her own introverted inadequacies. She had never learned the art of small talk and superficial being. After all, she had spent her adolescence struggling to live, heal, and walk again. She didn't even attend high school; her uncle had hired a tutor to prep her for college. Even then, proms and pomp held little interest for her.

Now Yvonne stood in front of her walk-in closet, surveying the damage she had wrought. She was an obscenely successful entrepreneur. She could make decisions that affected the lives of a couple of hundred people in no time. So why was it that the only decision she'd made was what lingerie to wear?

Michael told her that the Sebastians' dinner parties were casually formal. What the hell was that supposed to mean? Jeans with a chiffon stole? Evening gown and Nikes? Jogging suit with elbow-length gloves?

Deciding what to wear had never been a problem for her. When she was sketching, leggings and a T-shirt were her uniform. Suits and skirts in bright colors served her well when she visited the stores and suppliers. She always dressed to please herself. This was the first time she was dressing to please someone else.

The thought had her stopping short. Was she really dressing to please Michael, agonizing over what to wear like a kid going on her first date? Realization washed over her in a wave. She wanted Michael to like her. She wanted to believe this was a real date.

Dropping the blouse she was holding, Yvonne stood in front of her cheval mirror. Her eyes immediately dropped to the network of scars that ran down her left side from abdomen to hip. They were faded now, but to her they were as fresh as if she had gotten them today. Combined with the mind-numbing pain she felt in her re-knitted bones whenever it rained or dropped below thirty, she was continually reminded that she would never be normal. She hated them for making her remember what she had lost and reminding her of what she could never have.

Michael's ideal woman was probably very tall, very beautiful, and very WASP. And even if Yvonne fit that mold, she packed enough emotional baggage to cruise around the world. No, Mike Benjamin only wanted her business, same as she. Besides, she had to admit, she would probably run screaming if he wanted more.

Unsettled by her thoughts, she grabbed another handful of outfits and held them one by one before her, critically assessing herself in the cheval mirror. She discarded every one of them in disgust. "This is what you get for not socializing in college," she scolded herself, flopping across the four-poster bed.

To de-stress, she thought back to her youth, watching with Yvette, her twin, as their mother went through her closets. Their mother possessed impeccable fashion sense, and even though her wardrobe always reflected the latest styles, Mrs. Mitchelson preferred simple classic looks.

"You want people to notice you, not your clothing," she would tell them. "You don't have to outdo everyone else. Not making a statement is a statement in itself."

"Okay Mom," she said aloud. "In this day and age, almost anything goes. So what should I wear?"

She got to her feet, surveying her bed and what was left in her closet. "Anything that looks like a suit is out; this isn't a business meeting. And you can bet a lot of people will be in good old basic black. So I should wear something bright, yet understated."

Eureka. A vintage tank dress of emerald green silk with a sweetheart neckline and a knee-skimming skirt. It fit like second skin, and she could wear her mother's emerald and diamond pendant and earrings with it. Even the wide silver and gold bangle she never removed looked good with it. Pull the hair up into a French twist, slip into black satin pumps and she was ready.

Just in time too. The doorbell chimed, causing her heart to lodge itself in her throat. How she managed to get down the stairs without falling, she had no idea. She was breathing and suffocating simultaneously, yet she was able to open the door.

Michael wore a black lightweight trenchcoat over mustard colored linen trousers with a matching shirt and geometric pattern vest. No tie. His hair wasn't slicked back, but fell over his forehead in soft dark waves.

She was going to faint. She realized that now. She was going to pass out on her own doorstep and hope like hell that he would catch her. She wasn't immune to him, despite his color. Why hadn't she realized before now how affected she was by him? And the way he was looking at her wasn't helping.

Speechless, she backed out of the doorway to let him in. He was still staring at her, and had yet to say a word. She rubbed her suddenly sweating palms together and picked a nonexistent piece of lint from her skirt. "You don't like it," she said in dismay. "It's too flashy, isn't it? I can go change."

He shook his head, as if waking from a dream. "No. God, no. You don't need to do that. The dress, it's beautiful. So are you." He stuck out his hand. "I, uh, brought these for you, to thank you for your business."

Ridiculously pleased, Yvonne reached for the bouquet—and not just any old grocery store arrangement either. Delicate orchids of indescribable colors poked out from assorted irises, baby's breath, and fern sprigs.

"They're lovely, Michael, thank you," she whispered, closing her eyes and breathing in their heady scent. "This is the first time anyone's ever given me any."

Unless you count all the ones she received during her stay in the hospital, and after skating in the nationals. This was the first time a man had brought her flowers, and she was going to cherish them—and not tell Michael how much the gesture meant to her. "Come in."

He followed her into the kitchen, where she removed a dried floral arrangement from a vase. He was still staring at her. Did she have scars showing that she didn't know about? Years of oils and creams had helped to fade most of the superficial scratches on her arms, and the bracelet covered the one that wouldn't fade. Had he noticed?

She grabbed her wrist, squeezing the cuff firmly to her arm. "W-would you like something to drink before we go?"

He blinked and shook his head. "No, thanks. This is a nice place. Do you live here alone?"

Was he asking for a tour? She hoped not. It was bad enough having him in her kitchen, a room she rarely used. She did not want the image of Michael standing in her bedroom imprinted on her thoughts.

"Yes, though it hardly feels like it. I usually work six days a week, so my assistant, Lawrence, is always here. The girls come every two weeks, and I have the Desire staff meetings here every fourth weekend. Technically, I only have the first Sunday of the month to myself."

She took the vase back into the living room, giving it a spot of honor on the ledge above the black marble fireplace, conscious of him looming behind her. "I like and I need the space. I do most of my designing and make most of the decisions of Gemini Enterprises here. Besides, I've been alone for a good fourteen years now. I'm used to it."

He frowned, and she knew she sounded as defensive as she felt. "I didn't mean to put you on the spot. I live alone myself, except for my dog, Cutter. Jeff and I tried living together once after college. It's a wonder we're still friends!"

Yvonne grabbed a black velvet wrap from her coat closet, and they were off. It was warm outside, one of those unseasonable yet typical beginning of spring days. Jazz set the tone for the twilight drive. The Sebastians lived in an exclusive swim and tennis community in Dunwoody. Their home was a beautiful two story beige stucco of Italian design. The cul-de-sac and the sweeping drive were overflowing with a rainbow of luxury sedans and sport cars: from Acuras to Volvos, every car manufacturer was represented.

Upon catching sight of the press of cars, the first crampings of fear arced across her abdomen. Belatedly she wondered if she could escape by pleading insanity. Or better yet, vomiting.

Michael must have sensed her discomfort. He gave the hand in the crook of his arm a gentle squeeze. "Relax. You'll fit in perfectly. And even though most of Brianne's friends are lawyers, they don't bite. In fact, they'll probably love you so much they won't let you leave and I'll end up going home alone."

He may have been kidding, but she felt her stomach churn into high gear. "Don't you even think about leaving without me!"

The front door opened with laughter and noise. "Mike! The party is not on the front stoop! How can you leave the guest of honor out in the dark? And trust you to be the last one to arrive!"

The voice belonged to a tall, striking woman dressed in African-inspired robes of gleaming white trimmed with gold. She wore her braids in twin twists framing her slender face.

Michael laughed. "Counselor, wouldn't it be bad taste for the guest of honor to be the first to arrive?" He kissed the woman on both cheeks.

"Guest of honor?" Yvonne squeaked. She felt herself growing faint.

"Tsk, it's not all that bad," the woman said. "I'm Brianne Okelu, Thom's wife. And you must be Yvonne Mitchelson of Your Heart's Desire. I love that boutique!"

"Brianne's from Sudan," Michael informed Yvonne as they stepped into the monstrous tiled foyer. "She and Thom met in England during an international student exchange in college."

"Thomas fell in love with me immediately," Brianne confided, guiding Yvonne by the elbow. "I thought he was too American for me. But we corresponded; then I was accepted to Emory's law school. The rest is history." She grinned mischievously. "I told Thom he should have been a lawyer. He was most persuasive."

Yvonne found herself smiling back, liking Thom's wife immediately, despite her pushiness.

"Why don't you go find my husband, Michael?" Brianne suggested none too subtly. "I'll take Yvonne around to our guests. Just because you chauffeured her doesn't mean you get to monopolize her."

Michael gave his hostess a frustrated look, then touched Yvonne's elbow. "I'll catch up with you later."

Her palms immediately began to sweat, and her hostess' throaty chuckle did nothing to soothe her nerves. From her quick glance around, the men at this gathering outnumbered the women. More than one man had done a double take when they entered, probably because of her escort. She made sure her mother's engagement ring was firmly in place, all the while wishing she was at home designing or reading a juicy romance novel.

She had a hard time keeping up with everyone Brianne introduced her to. If she remembered her parents' gatherings as elite, she would remember the Sebastians' dinner party as the epitome of haute elite. The who's who of Atlanta's twenty- and thirty-something population were present. Doctors, lawyers, several athletes, a few professors, a couple of media personalities, and a few politicians—all were present. They were men and women, some white, most of one color or another. And they all represented tax brackets Uncle Sam drooled over. The Sebastians' "small" dinner party was forty people as diverse as the animals in the ark. And if some didn't have money, they were well on their way to having it.

It wasn't until Brianne introduced her to an ethnic artist that Yvonne realized the true treasure trove she had been invited to join. Each guest could be of some benefit to another. This cocktail-laced networking was the equivalent to being told a smorgasbord was calorie-free.

"Vonne?"

She turned to see Jeff coming toward her, a statuesque model following in his wake.

"Jeff! I didn't know you were going to be here."

"I could say the same about you."

She laughed. "I know, this isn't exactly my usual Friday night thing, is it? I met Michael's partner Tuesday, and he invited me. Michael was kind enough to give me a ride."

Jeff didn't take that very well. "If I'd known you were coming, I would have picked you up. In fact, I can give you a ride home, in case Mike does his usual thing and decides to leave with someone else."

Yvonne tried valiantly to cover the dismay Jeff's words caused her. Would Michael leave with someone else? She didn't want to believe that of him—she couldn't imagine anyone being that callous.

"Don't worry about me," she said lightly. "If Michael decides to leave with someone else, he's more than welcome to. I can take a taxi home. After all, it wouldn't be fair to your lady friend to invite someone else along. Three's a crowd, remember?"

Before Jeff could answer, she moved past him to his date, who was clearly developing an attitude. "Hi, I'm Yvonne Mitchelson, Jeff's sister."

The towering woman immediately cheered up. "Oh hi," she gushed. "I'm Tironda. Jeff didn't tell me he had a sister."

"Actually, I'm his play-sister. We've been friends for years."

"Hey, are you the one who runs that store, uhm, what's it called? Everything Your Heart Desires?"

It was difficult to keep a straight face. "Something like that, yes."

Tironda was fairly spewing cheerfulness now. "I love that place. It's one of my favorites."

"Thank you." Yvonne reached into her evening bag and withdrew a business card and a pen. "Here, bring this card into the Buckhead store and we'll give you a discount. You can pick out something nice for my 'brother'. By the way, his favorite color is red." Just like the shade of his face right now, she thought to herself.

Jeff had the good grace to smile. "Okay, sis, you got me. I'm being way too overprotective again. Just keep your guard up."

No need to worry about that, Yvonne knew. Even though the men outnumbered the women, she didn't even compare to the glittering, sophisticated ladies around her. She felt like Cinderella an hour after midnight. Michael could probably choose any of them if he wanted to. She'd mingle a little bit more, then excuse herself, call a taxi, and wish she'd never come in the first place.

Michael took a gulp of his wine, staring silently at Yvonne's audience. With almost everyone else in the room in black, she stood out like a ray of sunlight on a cloudy day. He'd been right about her body. Her curves were generous, definitely able to stop traffic. Where the hell did she get a dress like that? She had flitted from group to group like an emerald butterfly, never pausing, not even once, to acknowledge his presence.

Hell, why would she when nearly every man in the place— present company included—kept his eyes firmly fixed on her generous cleavage, the impish eyes, or her kissable lips? Once they found out what she did for a living, they circled her like vultures over roadkill, hoping to become her next muse. And there was nothing that he could do about it. After all, he was just her friggin' taxi, not her date.

It didn't matter that she didn't encourage the attention. In fact, she either didn't notice the flirtation she was receiving, or didn't care. She didn't bat her eyes at anyone, didn't lay her hand on someone's arm, didn't even lean close to make a point. That didn't stop hordes of men from offering to refill her diet soda, get her a napkin, or see to any other need she might have. They were like courtiers fawning over their queen, and Yvonne was blithely unconcerned.

He watched with barely concealed irritation as Jeff and his date joined the group dominating the center of the room. The two friends engaged in a light-hearted verbal duel that soon had everyone exploding with laughter.

Yvonne had simply forgotten that he was alive; forgotten the five hours they had spent touring the boutiques; forgotten the leisurely but informative Thai lunch during which he had become a Desire apostle; forgotten how he had chauffeured her from one adoring crowd to another, be it her restaurants, her stores, or this dinner party from hell…

"With that scowl on your face, it's no wonder everyone's around Yvonne," Brianne remarked, standing beside him.

Michael frowned at her. The assistant DA wore a casual smile, but her eyes twinkled mischievously. "She's definitely the life of the party," he observed ruefully. "And to think, she tried to convince me that she was apprehensive about coming! I mean, does she look like she's nervous?"

He threw a hand toward the group. Indeed, Yvonne had turned her vibrant smile onto one of the football players, a huge brick wall of a man who towered over her enough to gaze raptly down the front of her dress.

Frustration mounted, and he could feel the tips of his ears becoming red. It didn't help when Brianne gave him a knowing grin as she answered, "No, she doesn't look a bit nervous to me."

"And she doesn't look like she needs a ride home either," Michael retorted, watching as Yvonne gave the athlete her business card.

He was furious, and the fact that it wasn't his place to be made him even more furious. It's not like he was dating her, he thought sourly. He couldn't tell her who not to talk to. Even as her lover he couldn't do that. And just because he had spent three days with her obviously didn't mean he had a claim on her time.

Resisting the urge to break it, he set his wineglass down. "Well, you were right, as usual, Counselor. Just because I chauffeured her doesn't mean I get to monopolize her. In fact, I don't even get to speak to her."

Unable to believe he was so upset yet equally unable to do anything about it, he said, "Please apologize to Yvonne for me. Tell her I got sick and left because I didn't want to spoil her evening."

"Lie to her yourself," Brianne shot back in her court-room voice. "She's coming over now."

Beautiful and smiling, Yvonne walked up to them. "Brianne, this was wonderful. Thank you for inviting me."

"No thanks necessary," their hostess replied. "You made the evening a hit. I hope you'll come back."

"You can count on it." Yvonne turned to Michael. "Would you mind leaving now?" she asked. "If you'd rather stay, I can call a taxi…"

"No problem," he cut in. "Let's go." He turned heel and stalked to the foyer, leaving Yvonne and Brianne trailing behind.

"Is something wrong?" Yvonne whispered.

"He's just a little out of sorts," Brianne whispered back. "He should be all right."

But Michael wasn't all right. He was silent for most of the journey to her house, leaving her to listen to music— rock, not jazz. Finally she couldn't stand the silence. "Thank you for taking me to the Sebastians'. I had a wonderful time. There were so many interesting people."

"You should see the crowd they have at cookouts," he began, then stopped. Even by the dim dashboard lights, Yvonne could see him frown.

"Michael?"

"I see you made a lot of friends," he said carefully, his eyes on the road.

His mood was unnerving. He was obviously angry, but she had no idea why. "I don't know if I'd call them friends," she said uncertainly.

"I guess not," he said curtly. "After all, you don't flirt with friends, do you?"

Surprised by the tone of his voice, she turned to look at him. His jaw was firmly clenched, proving her assumption true. But he was more than angry, he was downright pissed.

"Flirt?" she repeated in bewilderment. "I don't flirt. I wouldn't even know how to."

"Then what were you doing all night, especially with that football player?"

"Talking about becoming a mentor," she answered in surprise. "I was talking to everyone about it. He decided he wanted to mentor a couple of boys, so I told him to give me a call so that I could put in him touch with the right people."

Excited, she began to gesture. "And Brianne introduced me to an ethnic artist. I'm hoping to convince him to do an exclusive line of cards for Desire, especially for Kwaanza. Brianne showed me a couple of paintings she has by him and they're fantastic. If he can put that energy and emotion on the cover of a card … "

She sighed deeply. "That party was like a networking dream. I can't believe I made so many contacts!"

"Well, you could have stopped by and said hello," he said petulantly.

"Is that why you're upset?" she asked. "I'm sorry, Michael. I didn't think you wanted me hanging around you like some petrified kid. I thought there might be someone else you might have wanted to be with."

"Someone else?" Slowing to a stop, he bit back a laugh. "No, there's no one else. Why don't you have someone, Yvonne?"

The question came straight out of left field and left her momentarily stunned. She should have been expecting it. In fact that was the question she had expected him to ask that day in his office.

Best to get it over with. She took a deep, calming breath and whispered, "Is that the end-all and be-all for a woman? To have a man in her life?"

"No, that's not what I meant." His voice was equally quiet as he slid a knuckle down her arm. "What I meant is, just like this dress complements your figure, and your success complements your intelligence and drive, I wonder why you don't have anyone to complement you."

The touch of his hand on her arm unsettled her almost as much as the conversation. Taking another deep breath, she leaned her head against the seat, closing her eyes. Too many people were interested in her private life: Jeff, her partners, her assistant, and now Michael.

"My life is overflowing the way it is. I have my company and volunteer work. Those two things are the most important things in my life, and they take up twenty of the twenty-four hours in my day."

"That takes care of your need to succeed and your need to make a difference, but what about your need to care, to be cared for?"

"My girls give me all the care I want. I don't want or need anything else."

Maybe that was a lie, but he didn't need to know that.

It was definitely time to change the subject. "So what do your girlfriends think of the inordinate amount of time you spend with your new clients?"

"Touché," he said, throwing up his hands. "The last woman I was with bailed out the same day I picked you up at the airport."

What a convenient coincidence. She couldn't ignore the little surge she felt at his words. That didn't mean she was letting him off the hook, however. "And what made her do that?"

"She made some demands I could not, would not, fulfill. My situation is basically the same as yours."

"Oh." Yvonne's voice was small. "I'm sorry … " Yeah, right. Like hell I am.

Her insincerity must have been obvious, because Michael burst out laughing. "I'm not," he confessed. "It's a blessing in disguise. After all, it made me escape the office to play chauffeur."

"And you've gotten very good at it. Don't think I don't appreciate it, because I do." She laid a hand on his arm. "Thanks, Michael. I had a wonderful night."

He stared down at her hand, then slowly, so slowly that she could feel it, his gaze returned to her face. His eyes glittered in the dim light filtering into the car as he looked at her mouth. "So that's what it is," he murmured, half to himself.

If she was unsettled before, she was shaking now. She didn't like the way he was staring at all. Every nerve ending in her body stood on edge, waiting for his next move.

"That's what what is?" she asked, just to keep him talking. That way, he wouldn't do what she thought he wanted to do: kiss her.

"What makes every man you know fall at your feet," he said in a low voice.

His gaze was like a laser beam on her skin, searing her. "N-no one falls at my feet," she stammered.

"Oh yes, they do, and this is why." He dragged the pad of his thumb across her bottom lip. She gasped at the electric surge that shot through her center. "This mouth has haunted my dreams since the first time you smiled at me. I can't let you leave the car until I discover if your mouth is as sweet as it looks."

The way his gaze fixed upon her mouth elicited an involuntary shiver that had nothing to do with cold. Like a mouse bemused by a cobra, she was frozen, tingling with anticipation.

She didn't wait long. He moved in closer, molding her lips with his own, urging a response from her.

Heaven. Sheer heaven. His lips were wonderful. She didn't know that a man's mouth could be so soft. And warm. And honey-sweet. Tentatively, she opened her mouth to touch the tip of her tongue to his lower lip.

His response was immediate. Groaning with satisfaction, he pulled her closer, cupping the back of her head to deepen the kiss.

She was engulfed in flames. Did kisses affect everyone this way? She felt as if she was floating in a river of warmth, heading for a waterfall. It was a delicious, dangerous feeling.

When he pulled away, she moaned, suddenly bereft. She opened her eyes, a trembling hand reaching up to touch her swollen lips. Her breath was coming fast, as if she'd just finished a four-minute free skate. "Why ... why did you stop?"

Michael nuzzled her jawbone. She trembled. He smiled against her cheek. "Because you're definitely not a backseat woman. We should go inside to finish what we started."

She was having difficulty concentrating. "Finish?"

"Finish." He ran a finger down her bare arm. "I want to kiss every centimeter of your beautiful, sexy body. I want to make you scr..."

"No." It was a strangled, frightened sound.

"What?"

Yvonne quickly slid away from him, taking a deep breath to clear her head. "It wouldn't be a good idea," she managed to say.

"Why? Because of our business relationship? We're adults, Yvonne. We can have a personal life as well as a professional one."

She forced her tone to be cool. "Our business arrangement is less than a week old. I'd rather get to know you professionally."

Michael sat back and sighed harshly, pushing his hands through his hair. "So you're telling me you didn't feel anything in that kiss?"

She stared down at her hands, knotted around the straps of her purse. She couldn't tell him how starved she was for emotional comfort, how his kiss had rocked her to the core, how the taste of him had left her hungry for more. She couldn't tell him that the thought of being intimate with him scared her senseless.

Being intimate meant being naked.

No one would ever see her naked.

"It doesn't matter what I felt," she replied, failing to keep the futility from her tone. "I'm not going to act on it, and neither are you. It'll be best for both of us if we forget about it and concentrate on being friends. Better yet, we can concentrate on our business together. If you think about it, you'll see what I mean."

She opened her door. "I'll see you on Monday for the follow-up meeting. I hope you and Thom have some ideas by then. Goodnight."

"Yvonne, wait." Michael caught her arm. "I-I'm sorry."

Her expression in the overhead light was unreadable. "So am I."

She got out of the car and entered her house without a backwards glance.

CHAPTER FIVE

Michael jogged through Piedmont Park with Cutter, his German shepherd, at his side. He mentally kicked himself every step of the way.

He had way overstepped the bounds with Yvonne last night. The need to kiss her, to touch and taste her, had been overwhelming. Even now his fingers and lips tingled with memory.

Somehow, in a way he couldn't explain, she had gotten under his skin. Always, he had pursued his women with a charm that was relentlessly successful. And while he had enjoyed his partners fully, he had never been out of control with any of them. His senses had never been assaulted the way they were when Yvonne kissed him. If she had let him, he would have taken her in the car.

Angry with himself, he pounded down the path, pursued by his thoughts. The look in Yvonne's eyes when she exited his car swam in his memory. It had been a mixture of things: disappointment, anger, even some desire. Fear had been uppermost. She had wanted nothing more than to escape him.

Why? Why had she been afraid, terrified, of him? She didn't seem to be the shy type, considering the fun she had at Thom's party. So why did she leave his car as if she was being chased?

Slowing to a stop, he placed his hands on his knees and gasped for air. He probably wouldn't have the chance to get answers to his questions. Yvonne had made it perfectly clear that she wanted nothing personal from him. She was the first woman to tell him no in a very long time.

He couldn't believe she meant it. Their kiss had left her shaking. He knew it, and she knew it. She had to be playing some kind of game.

Determined, Michael straightened. If she wanted to play, so be it. He could play games with the best of them. And when he played, he never, ever, lost.

"Ouch!"

Yvonne sat back with a sigh. "Sorry, Jennifer," she apologized, watching her fit model rub the thigh she had just stabbed. "I can't seem to keep my mind on my work today."

Jennifer surveyed her leg in the three-way mirror. "What crawled up your butt and died? No, let me guess. Man trouble?"

"Is it that obvious?"

"Doctors out for blood don't stab as much as you have today," Jennifer answered. "Your man not behaving?"

She almost stabbed her again. "He's not my man," she retorted, giving the hem of the peach-colored lace chemise a convincing tug. "How does the bodice feel?"

"It's still a little loose," the model informed her, gathering her bust in her hands. "So he's off the market and still wants to go shopping?"

Yvonne got to her feet, stretching. "He's on the market and looking for a sale," she explained, tucking several pins between her lips. She pushed the bodice up. "I'm not interested."

"Are you sure about that? And stick that pin in place before you answer."

That was the problem—she wasn't sure about that. She was finding it difficult to think about anything else but Michael and his kiss for the rest of the weekend.

Completely and unabashedly male. That what he was. Not to mention sexy as hell. If she could bottle his charm, she could make a mint. Jeff had told her that Michael always succeeded when he set his sights on a woman.

That was the crux of the problem. While her intimate knowledge of the opposite sex was laughingly limited, even she knew that Michael Benjamin had Don Juan stamped all over him. He had just come out of a relationship because he wouldn't commit; he had told her so himself. So why was he coming after her?

It didn't matter. There was no way she was planning on being another notch on his bedpost. As soon as he realized that, they could get down to business.

"I need his mind," Yvonne said slowly, concentrating on the material before her. "I don't need his body."

Oh yeah? And that's why your showers were so cold all weekend? "Every body needs some body," Jennifer reminded her.

"I thought you were here to be seen and not heard?"

Jennifer shrugged, straining the fabric in Yvonne's fingers. "Hey, I'm a psych major. Butting in with our two cents is what we do." For some reason she went absolutely still. "Have you ever considered creating a men's line?"

Yvonne, glad that the model was standing still long enough for her to tackle the problematic bodice, stuck another pin through the scoop neckline. "Funny you should mention that. The idea's been running through my dreams lately." That wasn't the only thing racing through her dreams, but Jennifer didn't need to know that.

"If that's the guy after you, I bet that's not the only thing you've been dreaming about," she whispered with a grin, jerking her chin toward the door. "That man could make a nun quit her habit."

Yvonne froze. A shiver snaked from her hair to her toes as her body tightened in belated awareness of the subtle change in the air. She fastened her eyes to Jennifer's face. "He's here?" she mouthed.

When the model nodded, she almost gave in to the urge to flee. She wasn't up to facing him. With her hair knotted on top of her head, barefoot, and dressed in ragged leggings and a T-shirt that had seen better days, she knew she looked a mess. Well, if her words couldn't convince Michael to leave her alone, maybe her looks could scare him away.

"Drop your hands," Jennifer hissed sotto voce.

"What?"

Jennifer dropped her eyes to her bustline, which Yvonne still had a hold on. With a start, she let her go.

"Okay, Jen, that'll do it for this piece," she said in a false tone. Forcing her hands to her sides instead of her hair, she turned around.

"Hello, Mi-my goodness!"

She was amazed at how calm she sounded. She was amazed that she was still upright, because her knees were suddenly, deliciously weak.

Michael stood just inside her office. He was dressed for running in snug red shorts and a sleeveless tank. His legs were just as she imagined them, long, muscular, and beautifully defined with a light covering of hair.

Today may have been the first warm day of the year, but the temperature outside had nothing on the heat being generated in her office. Just like that, several designs popped into her head as her imagination took flight. A queen, resplendent on a low divan, being fanned by men who bore a remarkable resemblance to Michael, their bare torsos and muscular arms gleaming in the subtropical sun... .

She noticed her personal assistant, Lawrence, fanning himself behind Michael's back. She realized that Jennifer was standing behind her in a chemise that whipped the imagination into frenzy.

"Okay, Jen, I think we're down for today," she said briskly, throwing a robe around the brunette's shoulders. "Law, give her a hand, will you?"

Yvonne watched Michael as Lawrence and Jennifer left. To his credit, his eyes never wavered from hers, even when Jennifer "accidentally" dropped the robe in front of him.

Yeah right, she thought, eyebrows arching. She knew Michael wasn't a saint, and decided to prove it. "Jennifer's my best fit model."

"Really."

"She seemed to like you."

He just shrugged, as if models falling over him were an everyday occurrence. It probably was.

Curling her toes into the carpet, she again forced her hands from her hair. The man was downright infuriating with his noncommittal replies. "I can give you her number," she offered, just to force the issue.

Again he shrugged. "What's the matter, Michael?" she asked pointedly. "Surely models are your type?"

Golden, his gaze held hers. "Women are my type, Yvonne," he responded dryly. "How about you?"

Her jaw dropped. Surely he didn't think … ? His sudden, enigmatic smile caused her face to flame. She all but ran to her desk, seeking refuge behind the smooth surface. Opening the mini fridge, she removed a bottle of water.

"Why are you here?" she wondered. "Do you want to make me feel worse than you did Friday?" She opened the bottle and took a sip. The chill of the water refreshed her overheated senses and she closed her eyes, swallowing more.

Somebody groaned.

Her eyes popped open. Michael was staring at her, looking as if he was about to pass out. Knowing how dehydrated a person could get after exercising, she retrieved another bottle from the refrigerator.

"Want some?"

"Excuse me?"

Why did he look so surprised? She gave the water bottle a shake. "You look a little parched. Would you like some water?"

He accepted it, rolling it across his forehead before opening it and putting it to his lips. Something inside Yvonne went full throttle as she watched him down the water, head tilted back, eyes closed, throat flexing with every swallow.

Any thoughts of masculinity she had would be irrevocably tied to Michael. All-American male, international man, heavenly angel, Eros personified; he was all that and a bag of chips. This was a man she could design an entire wardrobe for, and enjoy every measurement-taking, pattern-cutting, fit-modeling moment of it.

"Boxers or briefs?" she murmured.

"What?"

A bark and a scream filtered into the room. A huge German shepherd raced in, Lawrence close behind. The dog sat at Michael's feet, his tongue lolling from his jaws.

"I take it that he belongs to you?" Yvonne asked, glad for the interruption.

"Yep. This is Cutter," he informed her, adding, "he's not very friendly."

"I can attest to that," Lawrence said, folding his arms. "He damn near scared Jennifer to death."

Yvonne smiled at the divine retribution. "He doesn't look mean to me," she declared. She squatted until she was eye level with the shepherd. "Hi there, Cutter," she said, holding out her hand, palm up. "You're gorgeous, but I'm sure the girl dogs tell you that all the time."

The large shepherd licked her palm then butted it in an obvious entreaty for a pat. Laughing, she complied. She soon had the animal on his back, legs in the air and grinning with joy as she scratched his belly.

"It doesn't take much to please you, does it?" she asked. "I bet your master spoils you rotten bringing home steaks and yummy leftovers from all his dates." Was that a twinge of jealousy in her voice? Hoping that Michael hadn't heard it, she quickly continued. "You know, if I got a dog, I'd want it to look just like you."

"Why don't you?" Michael asked.

She looked up. "Why don't I wh…"

Her voice stammered to a stop. He was standing right beside her, and from her vantage point, she got a good look at his legs, and his shorts, and…

My God.

Her nails sank into Cutter's fur, drawing a whining protest from him. She quickly turned her attention back to the shepherd. "W-why don't I wh-what?"

"Get a dog. Especially since you live alone."

Her hand stilled. She wanted a dog, more than he knew. She and Vette had always wanted a puppy. But their dedication to skating had left little time for other hobbies. Now, she didn't dare bring a life into her home. She couldn't take the risk.

"Well, sometimes I have to fly out on a moment's notice," she said, hearing the lameness in the excuse and mentally cringing from it. "It certainly wouldn't be fair to the pet, and Lawrence has his hands full taking care of me. I couldn't ask him to take care of my pet too."

She gave Cutter a final pat and got to her feet, stepping away from both of them. "You live around here?"

She was deliberately changing the subject and realized he knew it. He didn't call her on it though, for which she was grateful. "I live closer to Virginia-Highlands. Usually Cutter and I jog through the neighborhood, but on weekends we go to the park. He likes to Frisbee."

He looked at her. "If you're done, why don't we go to the park? It's a gorgeous day out. We could pack a picnic. I make a great humble pie."

Hesitating, she occupied herself by straightening the pins and designing implements scattered on her desk. She didn't want him to get the wrong idea about their relationship, such as it was. But he was clearly trying to make amends, and it was a pretty day out.

Lawrence rescued her. "Actually, I left plenty of food in the fridge. And you were waiting on a call from London."

Michael wasn't easily put off. "Then we can picnic on your deck," he suggested. "I have some questions about the boutiques I hope you can answer."

Well, if they were going to talk shop … Michael put his hands up in a harmless gesture. "I promise, I won't bite." Unless you want me to, his eyes added.

A feeling that could only be described as ornery had her digging her toes into the carpet. She would prove to Michael once and for all that he didn't affect her. "You're going to have to cook," she warned him. "I can only make microwave popcorn."

"And not very well," Lawrence added. At her cutting look, he grabbed some files and headed to the door. "I think I'll enjoy the weather too, while I have the chance. Do you need me any more today?"

She really didn't want to be alone with Michael, but she couldn't begrudge her assistant time off. "No, just pick me up tomorrow at eight. I want to make the rounds before noon."

Lawrence left, leaving an awkward silence. Michael cleared his throat. "Why don't you show me your kitchen, and I'll prove what an excellent cook I am."

"Okay." She led him through the dining room and into the kitchen, Cutter trotting along behind.

"Does Lawrence drive when the girls are over?" he asked, looking in the refrigerator.

She put her teakettle on a back burner of the stove, showed him where the utensils she never used were, then got out of his way. "Law is loyal, but even I wouldn't ask him to ferry around fifteen teens. I rent a van and driver for the weekends with the girls, and if Law's not around, I have a Volvo in the garage. Course, I only drive on sunny days."

Michael didn't have to ask why. Anyone involved in an accident would be leery of getting back on the road. "Let me know if you need help driving your charges around," he told her. "I can handle one of those big vans pretty well. I used to drive a shuttle bus during college for extra money."

She flashed him a grateful smile. "That would be great. Jeff sometimes chaperons with me, but he's been making a lot of trips to New York lately. We have a couple of field trips planned, and we could use all the volunteers we can get."

"No problem. You just let me know when." He made himself at home in her kitchen, making a teriyaki chicken stir fry as she let Cutter into her tiny backyard. They passed the meal in companionable conversation, and she showed her appreciation for his culinary skills by cleaning her plate.

They discovered common interests in movies and music, differences in reading material, and an almost fanatical devotion for karate movies.

In fact, the more they talked, the more she found they had in common. They could be great friends, she thought wistfully, the way she and Jeff were good friends. If only Michael wasn't trying to sabotage it by bringing sex into it.

Is that such a bad thing?

The thought came to her mind unbidden, spoken in a tone of voice she hadn't used before. It had a purring, hungry throb to it. Just look at him. The man was born for passion. He looks like some Mayan fertility god, all sunkissed and sensuous. And for some reason he wants you. Who cares if he's not going to want tomorrow? You don't, either.

Besides, do you really want to be an eighty-year-old virgin?

Michael caught her staring at him. "Do I have sauce on my chin?" he asked, grinning.

"You're a dangerous man, Mr. Benjamin," she said solemnly. She wasn't trying to be sarcastic; she was simply stating a fact.

"Why do you say that?" he wondered.

Her gaze never wavered. "Because you're too beautiful for your own good, and you know it."

"And that makes me dangerous?"

She shook her head. "No, the fact that you use it as a weapon makes you dangerous."

The boyish grin slid off his face. "You are the only woman I know who thinks of me as dangerous," he managed to say. "Or as a weapon."

"You're right," she agreed. "Most women probably only see the superficial things in you. The kindness that opens a door, holds an umbrella, volunteers his services to make her life easier. The looks and the charm and the sex appeal. Most of them probably don't see the hard shell that you have locked in place around yourself. They know you love women, but they don't realize that you hate them too. Or at least, they don't see it until it's too late."

Stunned at her outburst, Yvonne bit off the rest of her words. She'd said enough already. He looked momentarily stunned, and she wondered if any other woman had ever nailed him to the wall like she had. She doubted it. Waiting for him to get mad and storm out, she told herself she would be glad if he did.

But he didn't. A smile spread across his face, a smile she distrusted immediately. She knew she was in trouble when he got to his feet and moved behind her chair, trapping her.

"So you're into pyschoanalysis as well as everything else, Dr. Mitchelson?" he asked, his voice a silky whisper. "I'm not the only one here who's dangerous, you know."

His hands slid along her arms to her shoulders, stopping at the pulse that beat frantically at the base of her throat.

"You, my sweet, are extremely dangerous." His breath was warm and sinfully delicious on her earlobe, his voice hypnotic. "The way you worked that water bottle earlier— do you know how erotic that was? It was enough to kill a man. Being around you is like being near a human lightning rod. Little shocks zing through me whenever I touch you. I know you're going to electrocute me, but I keep coming back anyway. Because, even though your mouth is telling me you don't want me, your eyes, your body, even your heartbeat, is begging me to take you."

He nuzzled her neck, extracting a tiny squeal from her. "Tell me I'm wrong. If you can."

Lord knows she tried. She shook her head repeatedly, tried to distance herself from him, but the chair held her trapped.

Like a tiger stalking prey, he moved in front of her, so close she could differentiate the shades of gold in his eyes. He smiled slyly. "Sweetness, you are not a convincing liar. I think it's time to show you just how much I absolutely don't hate you." He closed the fraction of space between them.

His lips slanted on hers, demanding a response. She slid her eyes shut, shuddering as his fingertips touched her cheek like a brand. When his tongue reached out to lick teriyaki sauce from her lips, she wanted to scream at the rush of heat that poured through her.

Instead she moaned, her hands snaking around his neck and into his hair. With a groan, Michael pulled her out of her chair and pressed her against the closest wall. Their t-shirts were flimsy barriers to their sensitized flesh. Her nipples were hardened bullets against his own, her mouth open and hot on his.

Unrestrained need coursed through her as she returned his kisses. She had craved this, this ability to touch another person and be touched in return. He was right. She was begging for this. Now, giddy with ravenous desire, she melded herself to him, devouring what he offered.

When she melted against him, Michael nearly buckled from the force of his passion. Her hot center wasn't even an inch away from him. All he could think about was being inside her, plunging into the moist heat she generated until they both screamed with release. He leaned against her until his arousal was firmly pressed into the juncture of her thighs. She whimpered, but didn't pull away.

Inwardly, he groaned. For someone who wanted nothing to do with him, she was all over him now. He decided to give her what she wanted.

His hands cupped her breasts through her T-shirt, brushing the pads of his thumbs over the distended tips. He replaced his hands with his mouth, lightly grazing each nipple with his teeth. She was moaning uncontrollably now, and trembled in his arms as he ground his hips against hers. The thin fabric of her leggings and the thinner material of his shorts didn't shield her from the imprint of his arousal. If it weren't for the fabric, he would be inside her now.

Obviously, he was close enough. Within moments she exploded in his arms, shuddering as she succumbed to orgasm. She pressed her open mouth against the base of his throat, holding on to him for dear life.

Breathless himself, he waited for her to recover, fighting to control himself. It was all he could do to keep from coming. As it was, the front of his shorts was more than a little sticky. My God, she burned him alive and they were both fully dressed! What would she do to him without the barrier of clothing?

He set her down abruptly and moved away, desperate to put some distance between them. He had wanted to show her just how dangerous he was, but the tables had been turned. Yvonne was the dangerous one. She forced him to lose control, to give instead of take. And he didn't like it one bit.

Still shaken, he looked at her. She leaned against the wall, looking so delightfully tousled that he was consumed with the need to sling her over his shoulder and take her to bed. The urge to have sex with her was so strong that he took a step toward her and had to restrain himself. He balled his hands into fists. What the hell was she doing to him?

"What—was that-what did you do to me?" Her gulping breaths pushed her breasts against the constraining fabric of her T-shirt, causing his erection to jump painfully.

"You don't know?"

Still looking dazed, she shook her head. "I-I didn't expect that. I feel wired, like I've been electrocuted."

"Lady, if you think that was something, wait until we're skin to skin!"

That instantly sobered her, he could tell. She pushed off the wall and nearly sank to the floor as her knees buckled. "N-no," she stuttered.

She took a deep breath and tried again. "Th-that was ... that was inexcusable. We should just forget it, pretend it never happened. I-I'm not going to-to be with you like that."

If he didn't know better, he'd swear she was blushing. "Why? Because I'm white?"

She was surprised by the question. "It has nothing to do with your color."

"Then I don't get it. We're both past the age of consent, Yvonne. There's nothing wrong with us getting together. In fact, it feels damned right. You're going to discover that some things are as inevitable as the tide. It's no longer a question of if. We are going to be together. I'll leave the when up to you."

He grabbed his keys and whistled for Cutter. The shepherd bounded through the patio into the kitchen, looking at them with curiosity. "Let's go home, boy. Yvonne's had enough excitement for one day."

He turned to face her. She still clung to the wall. "By the way, I wear boxers."

CHAPTER SIX

"Mail order?" Yvonne stared at Michael. She and her partners were meeting with Michael and Thom in the office of her Buckhead boutique. Jeff was also there, in his official capacity as financial advisor. But they might not have been in the room for all the attention she paid to them.

Michael had left her in a puddle on her kitchen floor. It had taken two days to recover, but seeing him now was causing her system to go into overload. There was no doubt now that he was attracted to her, just as there was no doubt that her body was clamoring for his. But was he what she needed?

Girl, please. Do you need chocolate? Just because you don't need something doesn't mean you don't want it.

That voice had gotten louder with each successive hour. Now it was screaming a chant: Violets are blue, roses are red, let that man take you to bed! Just the thought of him made her nipples constrict uncomfortably. Her face flushed with memories; then she realized that she had been silently staring at him for at least a minute. What were they talking about? "You want to create a mail-order catalog for Your Heart's Desire?"

"Hear me out on this," Michael urged. "You agree that expansion is what we're after for Desire. It's a fresh face, and no one's really challenged the Big Two in a while. Why not expand exponentially? Instead of getting a few hundred new customers in Atlanta, why not a few hundred thousand across the country?"

82 *SERESSIA GLASS*

Yvonne exchanged glances with Angela and Gwen. They had been with her since before the first store opened. They alone knew the full scope of Yvonne's master plan. Desire was like a baby to them; they wanted their child to grow up and become President.

"But isn't there a proliferation of lingerie catalogs already?" Jeff wanted to know. "Why should Yvonne add Desire to the pile?"

"Because her boutiques are more than lingerie," Thom answered. "And that's how the catalog would present it: 'Indulge your heart's desire'. Couple that with the new Web site, and generating business is almost a sure thing."

"Nothing's a sure thing," Jeff, the voice of reason, said.

"Well, I've got to admit, I like the new design of the Web site," Angela cut in. "You feel like you're entering a private boudoir." She looked at Michael. "I would never have pegged you as a computer geek."

Michael gave her a small bow. "We have many talents at Better Business Concepts," he said. "And our number one talent is making small businesses grow."

"I would have to expand the private label," Yvonne mused, toying with an idea she'd had for months. What better way to launch it than in a catalog?

"Our label has been outselling the other lines three to one in the last quarter," Gwen, the marketing guru and resident psychic, informed the group. "I've been telling Yvonne that the time was almost prime for expansion."

"Reality check," Jeff interrupted, holding up his hands. "Say a catalog is the next step for Yvonne. That's got to be an extremely expensive undertaking. You can't just paste a few photos on construction paper and say 'voila'. You have to hire models, photographers, someone's who's experienced in producing catalogs. How much would launching this thing cost?"

"Rain on my parade, why don't you?" Yvonne said, leaning forward. "But my financial advisor has a valid point. What sort of capital will I need to start this endeavor?"

Thom and Michael looked at each other. "That's the hard part," Thom admitted. "You will need an initial amount to cover production. You will also need enough inventory for orders, a warehouse to store it, people to answer order requests…"

"Those bridges can be crossed when we come to them," Yvonne interrupted. "We can sell current overstock from the stores on the web site, and that should give us an idea of what type of market we're reaching. Tell me how much I need to produce a catalog."

Michael told her.

Silence filled the room. Everyone directed their gazes to Yvonne, who rose to her feet. Her expression was neither shocked nor disappointed, but thoughtful.

Jeff knew that look. "Yvonne … "

She crossed to her computer, her hands flying over the keys. "Jeff, come here." When he stood beside her, she pointed to the screen. "Here are the operating budgets for the stores and the print shop."

Her hands danced over the keyboard, accessing graphs and charts. "Here are the investments you've made for Gemini Enterprises, not including the restaurants, and the investments you've made for me. Here's my monthly income. Add in my personal bank accounts and one I call my 'CYA-Cover Your Assets-Account' that you didn't know about, and this is my current net worth."

"Damn, Vonne!" Jeff burst out before he could stop himself. "I didn't know you were bringing in that much!"

"Yes." Her tone was dry. "Uncle Sam loves me." She shut down the screen and they rejoined the group. "I can back any loan Gemini Enterprises may need from my personal accounts, but it wouldn't hurt to bring in a few investors. It could work."

Jeff leaned against the edge of the desk. "Even so, as your financial advisor I have to make sure you understand the risks involved. No offense, Mike, but she stands to lose a lot of money if this doesn't fly."

"Or make a lot of money when it takes off," Michael asserted. "I intend to do a lot of groundwork before I even suggest incurring the first expense. But more than that, I am so convinced that this is the necessary next step for Your Heart's Desire's growth that I am willing to invest in it personally."

No one, not even Thom, was prepared for that disclosure. "You'll do what?"

"I'd like to invest, as a limited partner, in the catalog division of Your Heart's Desire and in Desire Online," Michael stated clearly. "I'll take shares in the company in lieu of my part of BBC's fee for consultant work, and I'll invest from my personal funds. That's how strongly I believe in this. As a very smart individual once said, dreams are worth the risks." His gaze settled on Yvonne.

She gave him a brilliant smile, acknowledging his words. "There is something wrong with the idea, however."

Everyone paused. She saw Thom and Michael exchange wary glances. "The only thing wrong is that I didn't think of it first," she said petulantly. "It's perfect. Launching Your Heart's Desire nationwide via catalog and online. Absolutely perfect! Angie, it looks like I owe you a raise."

"Then you accept the idea?" Michael asked.

"The idea, and you as my partner," she answered mildly, but Michael thought he caught a flicker of more in her eyes. Before he could read it, she turned away.

"Vonne, if we're going to do a catalog, you need to launch it in a big way," Gwen said.

"Do you have any ideas?"

"Actually, I keep seeing a runway in my head."

"Like a fashion show?" Thom asked.

Yvonne felt a surge of energy. "A fashion show would be perfect!"

"We are headed for prime time!" Angela declared. "Look out, Frederick's Secret!"

Everyone laughed. Yvonne got to her feet. "Ladies and gentlemen, you are witnessing the birth of a new era for Your Heart's Desire. And to celebrate, my new partner is taking us to lunch."

Gwen sidled up to her as the others filed out. "You may not want to know this, but I had a dream about you last night."

Yvonne's breath caught. Was something bad about to happen to her? "Wh-what was it about?"

Reluctance colored Glen's features. "Remember, I don't positively swear by my dreams until the third night, and ones like this ... well, I usually dismiss them. But the dream was so strong, so real ... "

She looked away, and Yvonne was surprised to see her coloring with embarrassment. "I don't think I should tell you. I don't want to influence you one way or the other."

Yvonne thought she was going to scream. Grabbing her partner by the shoulders, she all but yelled, "Gwen, for the love of Mike, what did you dream about me?"

"Sex, and lots of it. I think you need to go buy some condoms, girlfriend."

Three weeks later, the birth of Your Heart's Desire's catalog was proceeding at a frenetic pace. Angela and Gwen took over the daily functions of the boutiques, leaving Yvonne to concentrate on designing. She met with the handful of artists who designed her greeting cards and advised them of her catalog plans. They in turn recommended several photographer friends to her, and gave her preliminary designs for the runway show. While she wanted a polished quality to her work, she was always looking for new talent. Michael had agreed, and there were now twenty portfolios piled on the desk in her home office.

So far, he was taking his role as partner very seriously. He interviewed the photographers and catalog experts, then passed his selections on to Yvonne for final interviews and approval. He was also fine-tuning the Website, taking Yvonne's concepts and making them electronic reality.

He began stopping by the townhouse a few times a week, where the majority of the catalog plans were being formulated. But soon he was actually working in her office, taking over the computer. And her kitchen.

Of course she didn't mind; she only used her kitchen for water and coffee. Michael had informed her that cooking helped him think. Obviously he was thinking a lot, because she never had home-cooked meals so good. Unless she was in someone else's home.

Yet she had to admit she enjoyed Michael's presence in her home. They worked well together in her spacious office, he working on her computer while she designed. And boy was she designing. Ever since that day in her kitchen, designs were spilling out of her creative consciousness at a phenomenal rate. And she had to admit, they were sizzling, possessing a vibrant passion they hadn't before.

It was Michael's fault. His kisses and caresses had created a hunger she had never experienced before, desires the romance novels she occasionally read only hinted at. Even now, just thinking about his touch caused her nipples to harden instantly, painfully.

She wished with all her heart and soul that Gwen's dream would come true. She wanted him so very badly. But those damned scars held her back. If Michael rejected her because of her scars, she would die. So she kept her thoughts to herself and her showers cold.

Michael tried to keep his thoughts on work, but it was almost impossible. His desire for her hadn't slackened with time; if anything, the hunger he felt for her grew. It was now a ravenous, stalking beast, waiting to be freed.

He still didn't understand why she had refused him. It had nothing to do with color. She had said so herself. Her attraction to him was undeniable, as was her response. He knew he could make her scream. If she would stop thinking about it and simply let it happen, they could make magic together.

It was time to bring the situation to a head, so to speak. Tonight was the night. Usually, Yvonne's assistant stayed until Michael left, which lately had been stretching past ten or eleven at night due to her night-owl tendencies. He was determined to wait Lawrence out tonight, then launch a sensual assault that Yvonne would be powerless to escape.

"Hey, Boss," Lawrence called, breezing into the office. "Jaime's outside waiting for me, so I thought I'd knock off for the day."

She turned to him with a smile. She was wearing a lime green wrap blouse that was cut so low over her breasts Michael thought she was in danger of spilling right out of it. "That's fine, Law. I think everything's under control. Since you worked late today, you can come in late tomorrow. I'm going to the Buckhead store in the morning, so I'll bum a ride from Angela."

Her assistant touched her arm in what to Michael was an extremely intimate way. "Are you going to be all right? I can stop by later." He pointedly didn't glance in Michael's direction.

"I don't pay you to worry about me. Well, maybe I do, but you don't need to worry about me tonight. You left enough food for me to eat on for almost a week, all my plants are watered, and my alarm is set. You have fun. And tell Jaime I said hi, and congratulations." She steered him to the door.

Michael waited until he could speak without snarling to ask, "Lawrence finally leave on his date?"

With a sigh, she stretched in a way that set his blood boiling. "Yeah, tonight's a big night for him and Jaime. It's their third anniversary."

"Did you pick out something nice for his wife?"

"Wife?" She looked at him strangely. "Law doesn't have a wife."

"Okay, his girlfriend, then."

She frowned. "Girlfriend? Law doesn't have ... oh." She erupted into laughter. She collapsed into a chair, looked at him, and convulsed with more laughter.

The only reason he didn't stop her was because her laughter caused her blouse to move in ways that should be illegal. He gave himself ample time to admire the view before he asked, "What did I say that was so funny?"

"Jaime isn't Law's girlfriend. Jaime is a guy."

Michael finally understood, and felt a little sheepish in the bargain. "Oh, I thought he..."

"So did Angela." She sat up. "Angela hired him because he's intelligent, considerate, has a great sense of humor, and makes a great cup of coffee. In short, she thought he was the perfect guy for me. We had a big laugh over it—especially when she caught me fitting Law for a gown."

Michael decided he'd bite. "A gown?"

"Law wanted me to design a gown for him for one of his drag shows."

He could feel the headache starting but asked anyway. "Drag shows?"

"Yeah. He does a show a couple of nights a week at a club downtown," she explained helpfully. "He saw a picture of me in one of my skating costumes and wanted a reproduction made for him. My designing background was in skating costumes. Didn't I tell you that?"

"No, I definitely think I would have remembered that." He groaned heavily, and she came over to him.

"Are you okay?"

With a grimace, he pushed away from the computer. No, he most definitely was not okay. "Headache, backache, eyeache—it's a small price to pay for basking in your presence."

"I know you're not calling me a slave-driver," she teased. "You're the one who's been sitting down for the last few hours."

Without warning, she cradled his head in her hands. He stiffened, surprised to find himself getting an eyeful of smooth caramel cleavage, jasmine-scented and lace-framed. His continual state of semi-erectness suddenly went full-tilt into a raging hard-on. And then she started working on his head.

"Your problem is improper positioning," she informed him, her tone brisk. Her fingertips moved with assurance over his scalp. "Poppy, my old skating coach, told me a lot of body strains are preventable if you hold your body correctly and naturally."

With a grunt, his eyes slid shut, the sensations and the sights almost overwhelming. Did she even realize that her blouse was gaping open and his nose was almost touching the purple lace of her bra? "And I suppose your coach taught you to give a massage like this?"

Like an expert masseuse, she started kneading his shoulders, her hands strong and sure. "No, my physical therapists taught me this," she replied, apparently unaware of the tiny shocks she was sending through him by the thousands. "Now those were real slave-drivers. I was in P.T. for six hours a day for over a year. I think I was sixteen when I left the hospital for the last time."

Aroused and relaxed at the same time, Michael hung his head as her hands kneaded his spine. Any moment now, he was going to purr. Or squeal. He idly wondered what those small hands would be like massaging his bare back, his chest, his...

As if sensing his thoughts, Yvonne hastily stepped away from him. From the expression on her face, he knew she was blushing. "I almost forgot. I have a present for you."

"A present?"

"Yeah." She was grinning now, excited. "It's upstairs." She tugged on his hand. "Come on."

He let himself be led upstairs. While he had never been invited to someone's bed in quite this way, he did consider Yvonne a present he wanted very much to open.

A cherry four-poster bed dressed in burgundy and hunter green dominated the master bedroom. A large cheval mirror stood next to the walk-in closet, and a small sitting area was grouped near the window.

She went over to the bed, where a large box in Desire's colors lay. "This is for you," she said, putting the heavy box in his hands. "It's not much," she hurried to add, "just my way of saying thank you."

Intrigued in spite of himself, Michael took the box, sat on the edge of the bed, and opened it. Inside was a black robe of velvet so smooth it felt like silk. The collar and cuffs were banded in deep gold silk. Inside the collar, instead of a tag, the initials "YM" were embroidered in gold thread.

She made it. From what he had learned about Yvonne's private line, this robe could retail for a couple hundred dollars, if it was mass-produced. But she had made this for him with her own hands, and that made it priceless.

"Can you try it on?" she asked into the silence, her pixie-like face filled with concern. "I had to guess at the measurements."

Rising to his feet, he put the robe down and pulled his shirt off. He barely heard her soft exclamation, torn as he was between flattery and jealousy. Flattery because she had created this masterpiece for him in his favorite colors without asking what they were. Jealousy because he was sure she had more than her share of unclothed men in this room and had given every one of them a robe like this. Did Marco, Jeff, Nicolas, and the dozens of others have such an addition to their wardrobes?

Trying to squelch the irrational anger his thoughts had surfaced, he slipped into the robe. It fit him perfectly. It was very smooth, warm as flannel as it wrapped about him.

It took a moment to find his voice. "When did you have time to make this?"

Like a nervous hummingbird, she flitted around him, smoothing the robe about his shoulders, straightening the cuffs and collar. "I can't usually go to sleep until after two or three in the morning," she explained. "Do you like it? Maybe this material is a little extravagant, but it reminded me of you."

She didn't tell him how she agonized over each stitch, her senses assaulted with the image of how it would look on him, how it would feel to slide it off him, to run her hands over his chest, his arms, that perfectly shaped rear ...

Embarrassment caused her ears to burn. "You hate it!" she burst out, reaching to snatch it off his shoulders. "It's too personal, too flamboyant—I should have made a stupid tie! What the hell was I thinking of?"

He caught her hands. "It's beautiful, Vonne. I certainly don't deserve anything like this."

"Yes, you do," she whispered. "You remind me of velvet and silk. You're smooth, decadent, and just begging to be touched."

"Yvonne ... "

His eyes and voice warned her to stop, but she didn't. She couldn't. She ran a hand down his lapel. "I thought a lot about what you said. There is something between us, something that's alive and-and hungry. I knew it that first day. It scared me. But after what happened in my kitchen ..."

Her breath grew ragged. "After what happened in the kitchen, I knew I couldn't hide from it any more."

She looked up at him, her hands flat against his bare skin, feeling his heartbeat burning her palms. "You've awak-

ened something in me that I've never felt before. Common
sense tells me I should run screaming from you, but I
can't."

Another deep breath, then the plunge. "I want you,
Michael. I want your touch, your kiss, but ..." She
foundered.

With his forefinger, he lifted her chin until she stared
up at him. "You're afraid," he whispered, surprise and
wonder in his eyes. "Of me?"

She nodded. Might as well get this over with while she
could still out-think the desire. "Because you're perfect and
beautiful, and I-I'm not."

His laughter was low, husky with what she hoped was
desire. "Lady, you may not be perfect, but you're perfect for
me."

"I've got scars!" she blurted out.

"Scars?" he repeated.

She nodded. Turning away from him, she slowly
unzipped her skirt, letting it fall to the floor. Taking a deep
breath, she lifted the hem of her blouse and turned back to
him. "Scars."

She wore thigh-high stockings and purple and black
lace panties. On her right side, from abdomen to lower
thigh, was a network of fading scars.

Slowly, he reached out and touched her. She shivered
but didn't back away. Some of the scars were surgical, neatly
etched across her skin, but most came from trying to crawl
out of the twisted remains of her parents' car.

"Is this why you've been putting me off?" he softly
asked. "Because of your scars?"

When she nodded, he took her by the hand, leading her to the cheval mirror standing near the closet. She dragged every inch of the way. "No, Michael. Please don't."

But he was implacable, standing her before the mirror, moving behind her to close the trap. "Look."

Reluctant, she did, her eyes immediately going to the ugly marring of skin. She hid the scars behind her hands. For the first time in ten years, she thought she was going to cry.

"No, not there." His arms encircled her. "Look here."

His hands slid up her arms, the difference between his sun-warmed skin and hers the difference between honey and maple syrup. Softly, like a whisper, he slipped the straps of her lacy bra down her arms, freeing her breast to his gaze.

The intake of breath he made caused her eyes to rise to his in their reflection. Even reflected by the mirror, she could feel the heat of his gaze on her skin. The apparent hunger caused desire to flare and pool between her thighs.

Slowly, so very slowly she thought she would die, his hands lifted to cup her breasts, their fullness overflowing his palms. The touch of his fingertips on each sable peak caused them to tighten and swell, deliciously painful. A low moan left her, unable to remain trapped, and her head fell back against his shoulder.

His breathing, deep, excited, flowed over her shoulder. "Do you feel what you do to me, Vonne?" he asked, his whisper demanding. He closed the distance between them, his erection pressing against the small of her back and burning her through the layers of fabric that separated skin from skin.

Oh yeah, she could feel it all right, but she wanted more. Her want must have been evident, for he stepped away long enough to shuck the remainder of his clothes then wrapped his arms about her again, drawing her as close as he could without entering, his eyes sliding shut with pleasure. Hers followed suit, the sight combined with the feel causing sensory overload. The pool between her thighs began to trickle.

His hands moved to her breasts again. "Open your eyes sweetness. Open your eyes, so you can see how much I want you."

Compelled by the huskiness of his voice, Yvonne dragged her eyes open. One hand continued to tease her nipples while the other swept down, peeling the purple scrap of fabric away from her moistness. After she stepped free of them he pressed her rump against him again with the flat of his palm on her stomach. The feel of his erection pressed between the cleft of her cheeks nearly buckled her knees.

Low, hoarse, his groan stole through her. "God, you're beautiful." The stark hunger of the words impelled her to believe. "I've wanted to touch like this, to be with you like this, from the day I met you."

She couldn't form a single, solitary thought. All she could whisper was his name. Every thought, every atom of her being, concentrated on the sensation of his body on hers.

When his lips touched her neck, her knees unhinged. All that kept her upright was the bulge at her back and the implacable hand on her stomach. "Don't you go fainting on me," he admonished with a throaty chuckle. "We're just getting started."

"I can't help it," she moaned, need pulling words from her. "You're making me melt!"

If at all possible he swelled even more behind her, hot and insistent. "Not yet. But you will."

He continued to plunder the exposed sweep of skin from her ear to her shoulder. She continued to burn, the moisture at the apex of her thighs becoming a stream.

Then his hand slid down her stomach.

Stomach muscles clenched as she forgot how to breathe. Still, frozen yet melting simultaneously, she watched the slow progression of his hand to the dark nest of curls below. The hidden berry began to quiver in anticipation. When his palm brushed over her, her whole body began to tremble. When his fingers found her, her hips bucked outward, rising to meet him.

Coherent thought fled. All that mattered was the seeing and the feeling. She couldn't tear her eyes away from his hand—she would be forever addicted to his hand—as it delved into her, turning the stream into a river.

Moving sinuously behind her, he branded her with his hot, heavy length. "That's it, Vonne. Let it go. Give it to me."

And give she did. The river became a flood, cresting over his fingers. Arching back against him, her hands gripping his thighs, she gasped, groaned, and shrieked her release, her pleasure so pure it nearly did him in. It took every atom of willpower to stop, to dampen the overwhelming urge to lift her and drive into her then.

Gathering her limp form in his arms, he crossed to the bed and deposited her in the center, leaving her long enough to conduct a frantic search of his pockets for the elusive foil packet. By the time he returned to her, she'd regained her senses, propping herself on one elbow, her concern over her nearly nonexistent scars gone.

He ripped open the foil with fingers slick with her essence and clumsy with need. Before he could put it on she reached out, cautiously, curiously, to touch the tip of his penis.

The fire in her touch caused him to jerk as more blood rushed into the head. Her fingertips rubbed the moisture on the tip, the prerelease that threatened to become a raging flood. He gritted his teeth as she breathed with wonder, "You're beautiful. Michelangelo's David has nothing on you."

And then she gripped him.

Baseball. Paint drying. *War and Peace*. He tried to think of something, anything, other than her hot little hand wrapped around his pistol, primed and ready to explode.

His groan had her snatching her hand away. "Does it hurt?"

"No." He sounded as if he'd just run a mile, uphill, into a headwind. "But if you touch me again, I'm gonna explode in your hand."

"Oh." Her startle dissolved into a smile. All too sure of herself and her power. He unseated her simply by reaching out and brushing a knuckle against the hidden nubbin of flesh between her silky brown thighs. Sighing, she collapsed against the pillow, panting and ready.

So was he. Quickly he rolled the sheath down, then covered her, her legs flanking his. Just at her entrance he paused, wanting to savor the moment, this mad heated hunger about to be appeased.

She shifted beneath him, restless, a curious mix of trepidation and lust warring on her face. Lust won as she pulled him down for a kiss that was a voracious clash of lips, tongues and teeth. Her breasts pressed against his chest, teasing his nipples with each breath they took. Her heat, laden with the scent of her recent climax, engulfed him, drugging him. Inviting him. One last breath and he entered.

Hot, tight. Too tight. His mind registered the meaning a second before her sharp inhalation confirmed it.

"God ... Vonne?" Her name was strangled out of him, and he made to withdraw.

"Don't. You. Dare." She clamped her legs about him, drawing him deeper into the liquid tunnel of her sex. Drowning him. Unable to withstand the sensual onslaught, he surrendered.

He rocked against her, embedded to the hilt. A sound almost like a purr issued from her throat as he pulled out slowly and just as slowly flowed back.

She closed her eyes against pleasure so exquisite she couldn't breathe. "Open your eyes," he urged her. "I want to see it when you come."

Her eyes snapped open and she was pinned by the molten gold of his gaze. They moved together, seeking and finding the perfect rhythm. Passion flared like a volcano between them, making them wild. Her nails scored his back for purchase as his powerfully erotic thrusts pressed her relentlessly into the mattress. One hand—that warm, wonderful hand—slipped between their colliding bodies and unerringly found her sensual center.

The touch proved devastating. Yvonne suddenly lifted off the bed. "Oh, oh Mi…"

Her voice choked off as her body exploded in orgasm. He surged against her one final time. Dimly she heard him cry out and she wrapped her arms around him, bringing him with her into a glorious, light-filled world where everything was … perfect.

CHAPTER SEVEN

"You look awful." Michael raised his eyes, his head still cradled on his palms. Thom leaned in his doorway, a mug of coffee in his hand and a quizzical smile on his face.

"I feel like awful," he muttered, suppressing a groan. "Actually, I feel like the stuff you get on the bottom of your shoe and you don't know what it is. Why don't you get me a cup of coffee and tell me something I don't know?"

Thom thrust a steaming mug under his nose. "This is the first time in five years that you've come in later than 7:30, you haven't shaved, and I would swear that's the same suit you wore yesterday. What's up with that? Or should I say who?"

Michael gulped down the scalding liquid, ignoring the pain in his tongue. "I screwed up, Thom."

"Well, you're not exactly bounding with grace this morning, but I expect we can teach you some manners."

He shook his head furiously. "No, I mean I messed up. Big time. The queen of mistakes."

Immediately Thom sobered. "A client?"

Michael nodded miserably.

"Which one?"

"Yvonne."

Thom's eyebrows shot up. "Yvonne?" he repeated. "But I thought the two of you were getting along fine—despite the fact that you've been treating her like a brick wall lately. Yvonne wouldn't cancel a contract over that!"

"She hasn't canceled. Not yet, anyway. Besides, I was only acting like that to protect myself!"

"From what?"

"From her."

Thom sat on the edge of Michael's desk. "She was hitting on you?" he asked, incredulous. "I mean, I know that's a common occurrence for you, but Yvonne doesn't seem like the type."

"She isn't. Wasn't. She told me she just wanted to be friends. I thought I could accept that. I thought I could be close to her and keep my cool. But she burned me. She burned me good."

"Mike, make some sense, please. You were at the townhouse last night—"

"And this morning."

"Oh my God." Thom stared at him, looking as stunned and shell-shocked as he felt. "You and Yvonne ... " he let the question trail.

Miserable, Michael nodded. "I had a headache—don't laugh—and she gave me the best massage ... " He told Thom about the robe. "One thing led to another and we ended up in her bedroom." He put his head in his hands again. "Jesus, I don't even remember what it looks like! I feel like an idiot!"

Memories swamped him. He'd awakened just before dawn, pleasantly surprised by the dark shoulder and black curls that filled his view. Yvonne lay mostly on her stomach with her nose pressed against his ribcage, her left leg hiked up between his. He smiled to himself as he wondered if she knew she snored.

He remembered looking at their intertwined legs. The difference between their skin tones was not night and day. More like afternoon and evening. His was a tawny olive gold, hers a warm caramel.

It was beautiful, looking at their different shades. And, he was honest enough to admit, the difference was a turn on. Making love with Yvonne had been intoxicating, mind-blowing, addictive …

And wrong as hell.

Thom folded his arms and regarded him unsmilingly. "I don't have to tell you I told you so, but I knew this would happen someday. Mr. Casanova, who has to have every woman he sees, finally comes across an irresistible prize. She's pretty, self-made, only wanted your friendship, and has an eternal tan. I'll bet you couldn't wait to notch your belt with that one."

Michael got to his feet. "I know what you're getting at Thom, and I don't like it. It was good old-fashioned attraction that made me interested in Yvonne, not her color. I've had dreams about this woman since the day we met!"

"That's somewhat reassuring, Mike, but you're still in dangerous waters here."

"I realize that," he answered, starting to pace. "Romancing a client is against our code of ethics!"

"I didn't know you had ethics when it came to women," Thom cracked.

"This is different. Yvonne is different."

"Okay, so you have some morals—maybe," Thom conceded. "But, knowing your history, I'm sure she didn't run from you. Then again, knowing your history, I'm surprised she didn't."

Michael glowered at his partner again. "She could have stopped me, several times, but she didn't."

He sighed heavily, reluctant to share too much of his night with Yvonne, as if it would cheapen it somehow. "And I ran like a scared rabbit this morning. God knows what she thinks of me now."

"What difference does it make?" Thom demanded, apparently deciding to play devil's advocate. "After all, that's your modus operandi, isn't it? You didn't care what Diedre thought, or Alexa, or Susann…"

"Yvonne is different!" Michael cut in. "I can't explain it. She's just more real." And a virgin.

That had been a surprise. Especially for someone pretty, single, financially secure, and with more male acquaintances than female. She was a lingerie designer, for Pete's sake! Her business was built on sex. Who would have thought she was a virgin?

It explained a lot of things. Why she had run from him after their first kiss. Why she had been so shaken when he had her against the wall in her kitchen. But why had she changed her mind?

Thom emptied his mug and glanced at his watch. "Well, Mike, we're partners, so I can't order you around. But I am going to remind you of a few things.

"Gemini Enterprises is a gold-mine for us. The Your Heart's Desire catalog is just the beginning. We get the right people to attend the runway show and we'll have international attention. We have the possibility of making this boutique a national chain. Yvonne's success is our success. Think of the attention Better Business Concepts would garner. And the bottom line is, we can't afford to lose another account. Our credibility would be shot."

"I know." Michael sighed heavily. Thom was saying everything he'd told himself for the past few hours. No matter what, they needed Yvonne's business. If she decided that she never wanted him to set foot in her company again, that would be the price he'd have to pay.

"I have to see her. I can't not see her."

"I didn't think you could," Thom said quietly, and he realized he'd spoken aloud. "You know, Mike, this is the first time I've seen you so bent out of shape over a woman since Beth died. Could it be that your personal ice age is coming to an end?"

"Don't even think about it, Thom. There's no way in hell that I'm going through that again." I don't need that kind of pain.

He drew himself up. "Well, no use in delaying the inevitable. I'll let you know how it turns out. Wish me luck."

Thom walked out with him. "I do. Besides, if you lose Your Heart's Desire, you'll have to tell Brianne yourself."

"That's a fate worse than death. Don't worry. I'll make it right."

Somehow, he had to find a way. Because all he could think of, all he could see, was Yvonne in his arms. He'd go insane if he couldn't have her again.

"You did what?"

Yvonne dropped her sketches and rounded the desk. "Angela, will you hush? They'll think I'm killing you back here! And if you don't lower your voice, I will!"

"I told you!" Gwen exclaimed. "I told you about the dreams I was having about you and Mike Benjamin. I didn't have one last night. There's only one thing that puts that kind of stupid smile on a woman's face, and I didn't have to dream it to know!"

"Gwen!" Yvonne wasn't sure how much she believed of Gwen's "listening to her ancestors", as the older woman put it, but she sure did spice up a party.

Her partners sat in the office's seating area, looking very much like excited puppies. Arriving to pick from the plethora of sketches to put to pattern, they found her daydreaming over a particularly sexy drawing with an insipid grin on her face. It didn't take much prodding for Angela to get the whole story.

The important part of it, anyway.

Angela leaned forward. "Girl, you are lying! I can't believe you sat in the car with me on the way over here and didn't say a word."

"If you believe Gwen, it was inevitable," Yvonne said, hunching her shoulders defensively. "Besides, it's not like he's butt-ugly."

"He is fine—for a white man," the operations VP agreed reluctantly. She jumped out of her seat again. "I can't believe it. You and Mike Benjamin did the wild thing!"

"Angela!" Yvonne blushed, but her grin was back. With a quick look to ensure that the door was closed, she added in a stage whisper, "But if I had known sex was gonna be like that, I would have started sooner!"

Angela's jaw dropped. "You gave Mike Benjamin your virginity?"

"Oh, come on!" Yvonne exclaimed, suddenly feeling very uncomfortable. "I'm twenty-eight years old! What was I going to do with it—have it bronzed?"

She flopped down in her chair. "And what's the big deal about it being Michael that I gave it to?" she demanded. "He's male. I'm female. We're the same species, for goodness sake! You don't have to sound so shocked, like it's taboo or something!"

Gwen deftly moved Yvonne's sketches away as the latter pounded her desk. "Hey, you know it's nothing but good news to us, Boss," she said soothingly. "I mean, we were a little worried about you, and I'm not talking about stagnant creativity. After all, you never even talked about a relationship before. We didn't know if you were saving yourself for marriage or sainthood or what."

"Well, I wasn't," Yvonne muttered darkly, tapping a pastel pencil on the edge of her desk. "I just never met anyone I wanted to take a risk on."

"Until now." It was a statement, not a question.

The grin was back. "He absolutely lit my fire," she said conspiratorially. "And it wasn't a match either. It was a flame-thrower!"

They shared a laugh and attempted to get back to work. Angela handed Yvonne a bottle of fruit juice and popped cans of soda for herself and Gwen. "Are you okay?"

Yvonne flipped to a clean sheet on her easel, kicking off her heels to get comfortable. "I'm a little stiff, but otherwise I'm okay ... oh. Yeah, we were protected. Even though we didn't plan what happened, Michael was prepared. Thank goodness."

She paused, a faraway look to her eyes. "He told me I was beautiful."

Gwen made notations on one of the sketches. "Well of course he did. You are beautiful!"

Yvonne shook her head. To herself she could never be more than cute, and on good days, pretty. But when Michael had looked at her last night, when he touched her abdomen, she had felt like the most beautiful woman in the world. "He said that even after he saw my scars. He didn't even mind them."

Angela picked several of Yvonne's sketches and passed them to Gwen, who sorted them into maybe, maybe-not piles. "So that makes him really nice or really smooth," she said dryly.

Discomfited, Yvonne picked several colored pencils from her tray and stuck them in her hair. "Do you have something against Michael in general, or is it just the fact that I slept with him that's bothering you?"

Angela couldn't quite meet her eyes. "Well … "

"Angie, we're friends as well as partners," Yvonne said softly. "Just say it."

"All right, Mike Benjamin is the last person I thought you'd wind up with. I didn't think you went for his type."

"I wasn't going for any type. I'm still not."

"So what are you saying? That it was a one night stand?"

"I'm saying I don't know." And she didn't. Michael had gone before she awakened. She didn't know if she felt relief or disappointment that he wasn't there. She definitely had no idea what he felt, if he felt anything at all.

She told herself that it didn't matter, didn't bother her. If things were business, only from here on, that was just fine with her. More than fine. The problem would be if Michael wanted more than that one night. He would be wanting more than she could give.

"What are you going to do now?"

"There's nothing to do, Angie," she said absently, carefully drawing a flowing sleeve, focusing her mind on designing. "We had a great night last night. He's still going to do marketing for us, and I'm going to continue to mine this creative surge I'm in. I'm not going to put more into it than that."

I'm not stupid, she thought.

Angela, who considered herself Yvonne's best friend, folded her arms and grunted. Her opinion was clear.

"That's enough," Yvonne said testily. "Even if it we wanted more, I don't have time for an affair, involvement, relationship, whatever the hell you want to call it. I'm trying to run two stores. I have to create enough designs for a full line—and have either of you forgotten about the fashion show that's supposed to launch the catalog in two months?"

She ripped she sheet from the pad, letting it fall to the floor, needing the angry sound of it to punctuate her mood. "Between finishing these sketches, making prototypes, choosing which ones should go into the catalog, dealing with the restaurants, my volunteer work, and everything else, you tell me where and when I have time for a relationship!"

Angela stared at her, stunned. Yvonne couldn't blame her. She'd heard her voice rise a few octaves and decibels, and her face felt as if it were on fire. She never, ever lost her temper, and never with her partners. In a struggle for composure she closed her eyes and counted to twenty in German.

Gwen broke the awkward silence. "Come on, Boss," she said gently, putting an arm around Yvonne's shoulders. "Me and Angela, we've been with you since the beginning. We just want you to be happy, that's all."

Yvonne turned back to her easel with a sigh. "I know, Gwen, Angela. Thanks." God knows she didn't want to yell at Angela, but her partner had no right asking questions she hadn't asked herself yet!

"I know I don't have to ask you this, but I'd really appreciate it if this stays just between us and the four walls."

"Uh, Yvonne … " Gwen's voice was nervously high.

"Guys, I am over this conversation! I don't want to talk about it anymore!"

"Then perhaps you'd like to talk to me."

Suddenly a dozen butterflies executed double axles in her stomach, and she turned around slowly, willing the mortification from her face. How long had Michael been standing in the doorway?

My God. Did I really make love with this man last night and survive? He's friggin' huge!

But she knew it wasn't a dream, not the way her body suddenly came alive. She had spent the night in his arms, enjoying her first uninterrupted sleep in years. That alone made last night one she would cherish, even if he decided to walk away now.

Gwen and Angela left quickly and quietly, for which Yvonne was eternally grateful. Michael closed the door behind them and leaned against it, his eyes unreadable. He looked tired, as if he didn't get much sleep. Was it from making love or pondering ramifications? She wasn't sure if she wanted to know yet.

Awkward with the silence, she went to her desk, reaching for her juice. "Would you like something to drink? I keep my little fridge stocked for everything."

"Why?"

Yvonne turned to stare at him in confusion. "Why would you like something to drink, or why do I keep my fridge stocked?"

He pushed off the door and moved toward her. The expression on his face was relentless and unforgiving, and she backed up until she ran into her easel. He took her by the shoulders and drew her to him until they were nose to nose. "Why didn't you tell me you were a virgin?"

Her mouth gaped open. "You're angry," she said, surprise coloring her tone. "Why are you angry?"

"Why didn't you tell me?"

She felt her face erupt in flames. "Did I-did I not do okay? I mean, I've seen it happen in movies and read it in books, but it's not really like that in real life, is it? It's more sweaty, for one thing, but the way it felt—they don't even come close to describing it—"

She was rambling, she knew it, but she couldn't stop. Not with the way Michael was staring at her as if she'd just flapped her arms and flown around the room. He finally stopped her stream of useless chatter by putting a hand over her mouth.

"Last night was your first time," he whispered, incredulous.

With her mouth still covered with his hand, she simply nodded. He sighed. "Why didn't you let me know?"

"Mhmph." She looked pointedly at his hand. When he moved it, she said, "There really isn't a way to bring that up in polite conversation, and then I thought that if I told you it would ruin the mood or you wouldn't go through with it, and I really wanted you to keep going…"

His hand clamped back over her mouth. "I couldn't have stopped if you'd held a gun to my head," he answered, "but I would have been more—hell, I don't know!"

He expelled an exasperated breath. "I've never been with a virgin before. These days, you kinda assume that anyone over sixteen's been with at least one other person before you came along. I can't believe you're a virgin."

Why couldn't he get past that? Her heart thumped, painful, and she removed his hand. "I know, it's the joke of the century. Designer of sexy lingerie, owner of boutiques that cater to romance, still a virgin at twenty-eight. Wouldn't they laugh if they knew?"

"I'm not laughing, Vonne. I'm just … That's too precious a gift, and I feel like a bastard for taking it from you."

She didn't know what to say to that, afraid that anything she could say would make things worse.

Finally he ran his hands through his hair, then simply stared at her. "Why did you pick me?"

The bewilderment in his voice had her wincing inwardly. "You picked me, Michael," she reminded him. "Still, it was time, don't you think? How can a designer of sexy lingerie not know what it is to have sex? Besides, every time you touch me, I seem to melt."

She stared up at him, willing him to understand. "And there's something in your eyes, something that told me you wouldn't hurt me. And I knew for sure when you didn't turn away when you saw how ugly I am."

His eyes widened. "Ugly?"

She felt her face flame. "I-I know the scars are a big turn-off. There are days when even I can't stand them. The doctors didn't think I could have survived another surgery, so they stayed. So I understand if that is one of your reasons for not wanting to continue this."

"Your scars have nothing to do with it. You're beautiful despite them, and you're beautiful inside because of them."

Warmth rushed through her at his words. "Thank you."

His eyes darkened as he brushed a lock of hair from her cheek. "Ah Vonne, don't do it."

"Do what?"

"Put me on a pedestal. I'm not the type of guy for that. I'll only fall off." Reluctantly he let her go, and put the desk between them. "Uhm, about last night ... "

She sat in her chair, folding her hands in her lap and studying them intently. "Last night," she repeated slowly, trying to find the right words. Were there any?

"Is this the part where you tell me how much you appreciate working with me, and we should keep it strictly professional and pretend that last night never happened? Or is this the part where you tell me that you're assigning someone else to take your place on my account?"

"Look, Michael," she said quickly, before he could interrupt, "if you want, I can pretend that last night never happened—or I can at least try. But I can't say I'm sorry it happened. I enjoyed it too much."

"You did? I didn't hurt you?"

A decidedly feminine smile of satisfaction welled within her as she remembered exactly how he didn't hurt her. "Not at all. So don't you ruin last night by having morning-after regrets. If that's the only time, so be it, but leave me with a good memory, all right?"

"Next time will be better."

"Next time?"

His eyes bored into hers. "I can't forget last night, Vonne, and I don't think I can go a day without seeing you."

Her body surged at his words. "Me neither."

"But I've got to be honest with you. I'm not looking for a commitment."

Her knees nearly shook with relief. "No commitment required, Michael. We enjoy each other professionally and personally, and when the time comes, we part friends."

He stared at her as if he was disconcerted by her answer. What did he expect her to do—pout and plead? She never pouted, and the only thing she had ever pleaded for was denied her.

She hurried on. "And I think it would be better to keep it between ourselves. I think Jeff would have a fit. That 'big brother' mentality of protecting my honor would definitely kick in."

Jeff would probably have more than a fit, Yvonne knew. He had warned her away from Michael more than once. If he discovered that his best friends were sleeping together, all hell would break loose.

She wasn't going to tell Jeff. It wasn't his business anyway. Besides, she could handle this situation. She knew she would never have love and marriage and all the bells and whistles that came with them. Glorious passion with a handsome, intelligent man was the next best thing—and the best thing for her.

His arms circled her waist and he stared down at her, his expression ambiguous. "All right," he finally agreed. "We take each day as it comes, no regrets, no worries."

His lips brushed hers, just a passing whisper of touch. They returned, infusing her with desire that caused her insides to dissolve into a pool of liquid passion.

Panting, he broke away. "I've been wanting to do that since I walked in."

"I've been waiting for that since you walked in," she answered breathlessly.

"Can you take a long lunch?"

"Food's the last thing on my mind."

He held her close. "I'm not talking about food."

She knocked her day planner off her desk. "What do you know, my calendar just cleared!"

CHAPTER EIGHT

"Gemini Enterprises, Yvonne Mitchelson speaking."
"Vonne … " "Michael?" she sat up straight. "You sound awful!"

His voice came weakly over the line. "I don't look so hot either. Think I'm comin' down with something."

"Sounds like you've already got it. Have you taken anything for it?"

"I can't even move, much less make it to the drugstore," he mumbled. "I just wanted to tell you I wuddn't be comin' by today."

"Slacker," she chided. "If you wanted a break, there are easier ways than this. Why don't I pick up something for you, and some old-fashioned soup, and drop it by? Then if you have any ideas, you can run them by me. That way, you won't feel so guilty about taking the day off."

A sneeze answered her. "I don' wanna impose. The models need to be interviewed…"

"I think work can survive without me," she cut through his protests. "Besides, Law's getting a thrill out of telling these models whether their bodies are useable or not. So stop protesting! I'll be there in about half an hour."

"'Kay," he answered meekly, sneezed, thanked her, sneezed again, and hung up.

Replacing the receiver, she rang for her assistant. "Law, I'm going to be out for a while," she told him when he appeared.

"Does this have something to do with 'Mr. Under-the-Weather'?" he asked, handing her an invoice to sign.

"As a matter of fact, Michael's not feeling too well, and I thought I'd take him some medicine. We don't have anything too pressing, do we?"

Law put his hands on his hips. "You mean besides all these ten-cent table dancers thinking they're the next 'Supermodel of the World' and making unnecessary demands? No, there's nothing pressing."

She laughed despite herself. "If anyone can handle them, you're the one."

They headed to the door, Law pausing long enough to snag a gym bag by the stairs. "It's a beautiful day, Boss," he told her as he handed her the keys. "Not too warm, not too cool. And the roads aren't too crowded at this time of day."

In other words, perfect driving weather. "What's in the bag, Dad?"

"A set of sweats, some kinky lingerie, and flavored oils."

"My God, Law—are we that obvious?"

He assistant propelled her out the door. "No one else suspects a thing. Okay, Estrella the cleaning lady knows too, but only because she empties your bedside waste-basket. Don't you think it's time to consider a sponge?"

"Law!" Embarrassment almost sent her through the driveway.

"Hey, if I had a man like that, I'd be all over him like divas at a PRIDE parade."

"You do have a man like that." She did her ritual walk around her car, checking for signs of wear. She could feel her heart speeding up as she got in, and forced herself to calm down by adjusting the seat and mirrors and securing her seatbelt. "Law, I'd appreciate it if—"

"What do you think you pay me for?" her assistant asked in mock indignation. "Of course I'll run interference for you. We'll keep this just between us girls."

Impulsively, she threw her arms around him. "Thanks, Law. What in the world would I do without you?"

"Not have nearly as much fun, I can tell you that. Now go on, get out of here before we do something stupid like start crying. I'm not wearing waterproof liner today." He shut her door and waved her off.

With a laugh and a grateful wave, Yvonne started the car and drove off. She stopped at the supermarket for medicine, orange juice, ingredients for a gumbo, and fresh fruit. Approximately thirty-five minutes after she hung up the phone, she rang Michael's doorchime.

She heard Cutter bounce down the stairs and scratch on the door, barking loudly. Michael didn't come to the door, so she found the spare key in the well of a cobweb-covered lantern light on the doorpost. Carefully balancing her purchases, she let herself in, noticing that the alarm wasn't engaged.

"Michael? It's me," she called up the stairs, pushing the door shut with her foot.

Cutter bounced around her feet, happy to see her. "Hi there, boy," she greeted the huge shepherd, depositing her bags on the oak foyer table. "Daddy's not feeling well, huh? Well, let's go upstairs and see how he's doing."

The shepherd whined, scrambling ahead of her to the master bedroom. It sat directly above the living room and boasted its own fireplace. It was a masculine room, tastefully decorated with solid pieces of darkly stained hardwood. There was no question, however, that the cannonball bed dominated the large room. It was king-sized, dressed in navy blue and gold stripes, and boasted a definite hump in the middle of the bed.

She pulled back the covers. Michael was asleep, his breath rattling in his lungs. His hair spilled over his forehead in wild curls, and thick stubble shadowed his cheeks and chin.

He was gorgeous. She sat on the bed beside him, feasting her eyes. How is it, she wondered, that guys can look so cute when sleeping and women looked like zombies? In slumber, his features were relaxed, open. There was even a degree of vulnerability in him, something that she had not expected to see.

She reached out to touch his forehead. It was scalding. Her other hand gently shook his shoulder. "Michael, wake up. It's Yvonne."

He groaned and rolled over, slitting his eyes. They were watery, bloodshot. "Vonne ... " his voice faded hoarsely.

"You're right, Mr. Benjamin." She gave him a tender smile. "You do look like hell."

"Kick a man when he's down, why don't you?"

"I didn't know you were into the kinky scene," she teased. "But let's get you well before we try the whips and chains."

She went downstairs, Cutter trailing after her. Michael's house was a two story, three-bedroom brick traditional, and if she remembered correctly, had a full basement. What one man and a dog needed with all that space, she hadn't a clue. The living room had a slight Texmex flavor, with a bare floor, bleached pine furniture, and a Navaho rug under a driftwood table. She went over to the ficus trees framing the fireplace, and was pleased to find they were real.

"A dog and real plants," she murmured to herself. She turned to the shepherd. "Hey Cutter, wanna go out?"

Cutter bounded out of the room. She followed, through a big kitchen to a door that let out onto a spacious deck. After letting him outside, she retrieved her bags and started the gumbo, trying to convince herself that this domestic scene wasn't more than it was.

It had been nearly a month since they became lovers. There were times when they went days without seeing each other, and there were times when they couldn't go two hours without needing to be together. Yvonne was proving to be a quick study in lovemaking, more than making up for her inexperience with enthusiasm. Their times together were nothing less than explosive.

But when they were with others, they maintained a polite casualness that made them seem no more than friends. It wasn't that they were keeping their relationship secret; in Yvonne's opinion, everyone she knew was a little too interested in the subject of her love life, or apparent lack thereof. She really didn't want anyone to offer advice or opinions when it came to her and Michael.

And honestly, she didn't want the sympathy she would be lambasted with when the relationship ended.

There was no way she entertained any illusions about her relationship with Michael, as he had none. Neither one, for their own reasons, wanted a commitment. For Michael, it had something to do with his late wife. Yvonne didn't know the whole story, except that his wife had died in an accident. She had never dared to ask him about it. Perhaps he felt that he could never love anyone the way he had loved her.

That was perfectly fine with Yvonne. If Michael still loved his late wife, he would never love her. And if he didn't love her, he wouldn't care that she would never, ever love him.

Michael rolled onto his back, waiting for Yvonne to return. When he had called her, as sick as a dog, it was with the secret hope that she would rush over and take care of him. The fact that she did was not lost on him.

In just a month, he was addicted to her. And it wasn't just the sex. It was the way she belted out disco tunes when she had a creative surge. The way she never said anything negative about anyone. The way she inspired everyone who worked for her, from her partners to the guys in the print shop. The way she smiled.

Her smile brightened a room. She was as magnanimous with her smile as she was with her encouragement. But there was a smile she reserved for him alone, one full of secrets and promises, one that empowered and enchanted him. He found himself anticipating it. He lived for her laughter, existed for her smile. The thought left him shaken.

She returned, bringing medicine and orange juice. Dressed for work, the teal power suit with an ivory camisole concealing her cleavage seemed at odds with her caretaker touch. She helped him sit up, stuffing pillows behind his back. Her hair swung across his face, and he wondered if she smelled of jasmine as she always did.

"Do you mind telling me how you caught this bug?" she demanded, sitting beside him. "You were fine yesterday!"

He leaned his head against her shoulder. "Don't know," he coughed. "I just woke up this morning feeling like I'd been tossed into the back of a garbage truck. My head hurts, my nose hurts, every muscle aches, I'm hot, I'm freezing, I'm exhausted, and if I cough one more time, I think I'm gonna bust a rib!"

She stifled a laugh, but couldn't wipe the smile from her lips. Michael knew he was sounding petulant, but damned if he could do anything about it.

"Are you sure it wasn't Elaine Mulholland?" she asked. "You worked with her yesterday."

Ms. Mulholland, a stunning redhead straddling forty, was head of a computer information company. She also seemed to be president of the Michael Benjamin Fan Club, an idea, he knew, that alternately amused and irritated Yvonne.

"Well, maybe," he admitted with a sneeze. She stiffened, and he hastily added, "But I go jogging with Cutter every day, so I could have picked it up anywhere."

She rose, retrieving a box of tissues and pouring him a glass of juice. He reached up and caught hold of her jacket, getting her attention. She stared down at him, her tortoiseshell eyes warm and concerned. For a quick, tortured second his throat clogged with emotion, not congestion.

"Did you drive over here by yourself?" He knew she hated driving with a passion that bordered on phobia.

"You needed me," she answered simply.

He closed his eyes, feeling undeserving of a woman's attention for the first time in his life. "Vonne." He swallowed. "Thank you for coming over. I appreciate it. I really do."

Her eyes crinkling at the corners as she smiled again, "You should," she answered in mock seriousness. "I'm hardly the domestic type. This is quite a stretch for me. But I couldn't let my partner suffer. You work better healthy." She moved to the door.

"You're not leaving, are you?" he asked, panic making him sit up.

"Not for long," she assured him, returning to push him back into the pillows. "I'm going to slip into something a little more comfortable, maybe pick up a few videos."

"Are you going to stay?" Yvonne had never stayed the night with him.

Her eyes were unwavering. "If you want me to."

He did want. Very much. That was the problem. "I do—I mean, I want you to stay."

Cool and comforting, her hand cupped his cheek. "You get some rest, because when I come back, we're going to put you into a hot shower, get you dressed, and make you eat something."

"Eat?" His stomach lurched in response to the threat. "I haven't eaten since lunch yesterday. Just the thought of eating makes me want to puke. I can barely breathe, and you want me to eat?"

Yvonne put her hands on her hips. "Don't argue with me, young man, or I'll spank you!"

"You promise?"

She laughed, and he warmed in response. "You're sick in more ways than one," she grinned, pressing her lips to his forehead. "Take some of this medicine, and get some sleep."

He looked at the bottle and shuddered. "Ugh—I can't swallow this disgusting stuff!"

She chucked his chin with a knuckle. "Drink it and I'll scrub your back for you."

He immediately turned the bottle up.

By the time she returned, he was much improved. Yvonne scrubbed his back as promised—fully dressed and standing outside the stall, to his disappointment.

When came out of the bathroom, he discovered that she'd got a small fire going for ambience, more than warmth, and was feeding Cutter chopped steak. A tray sat on the nightstand. It was filled with rolls, a brimming bowl of soup, and orange slices.

"You're spoiling him rotten, you know," he informed her, tossing his robe on a nearby chair and climbing back into bed. "The way you keep feeding him, he'll start to think he's human."

"I can't help it. He looks at me with those eyes, and I just melt."

"What about my eyes?"

She appraised him like one of her designs. "Well, they're kind of rheumy. I'm not melting at all."

"Gee, thanks."

"Of course," she added in that throaty way she had, "you do make me melt in other ways. But enough of that." She settled the tray over his legs. "Since you're congested, this should help."

She popped a video into the VCR and crawled up beside him. She was in her favorite loungewear: leggings and an athletic team T-shirt, and both hugged her curves gratefully.

"What kind of soup is this?" he asked, spooning up a huge spoonful. He shoved it in quickly, willing his mind away from Yvonne's body. Heat blossomed in his mouth, and his eyes watered as he began to cough.

"Chicken gumbo, my mother's recipe. It's slightly spicy."

"Slightly?" His words were strangled as he gasped for cool air. "I thought you couldn't cook."

Yvonne took her own heaping spoonful and swallowed. She didn't even blink as the blazing bite went down. "Mom's family is Creole. They've lived in and around New Orleans for two hundred years. My sister and I learned how to cook gumbo before we could walk. His isn't my best though—I had to cheat on the roux. Gee, Michael, can you breathe? Here, suck on this orange, it should help."

It was the coldest, sweetest orange he had ever tasted. And she was right. The spice was loosening his congestion.

He lay back against the pillows, closing his eyes in contentment. It had been a long time since a woman—any woman—had taken care of him. In fact, the last time he had been so thoroughly coddled was when he was eight and had chicken pox. And no woman besides his mother had ever nurtured him like this, without a hidden agenda.

How macho it would have been just to ride out the sickness, how masculine to not need to be taken care of. To hell with being macho, he thought to himself. Inside every man was a little boy wanting to be coddled by Tyra Banks.

But this, this nurturing, was the kind of woman Yvonne was. She didn't make any demands on him beyond those necessary for her company, and she probably wasn't going to. When he went days without seeing her, she didn't get angry and didn't interrogate him about his whereabouts. She didn't even demand monogamy from him—but there was no way he was going to risk their relationship with other women. Not even with the models she was forcing him to interview. By the same token, she didn't give him a detailed explanation of her absences either, especially those that took her out of the state. It was refreshing to know that such a woman existed.

It still boggled his mind that a woman like Yvonne could be unattached. He would have thought that she'd been really burned by a bad relationship, but she'd never had one. He still couldn't believe that. A few scars couldn't be the reason.

But sometimes scars went more than skin deep. He knew that as well as anyone. Although he had no physical scars, his heart was so covered with scar tissue it was dead. And he didn't want anything, or anyone, to resurrect it. Didn't he?

Yvonne must have sensed the exact moment his thoughts spiraled downward. Gathering the remains of their meal, she set the tray on the dresser then moved on the bed until her back was against the headboard. "Put your head here," she ordered, patting her thigh.

"I think I'm a little too congested for that, sweetheart."

She punched him playfully on the shoulder. "That's not what I had in mind," she told him, putting his head on her thigh. "This is."

With the index and forefingers of her hands, she ran a light touch up the bridge of his nose, following the curve of his eyebrows. He relaxed instantly, melting beneath the soothing caress.

He stared into the fire, conscious of his head in Yvonne's lap and Cutter curled at his feet. He was conscious, also, of the rightness of the image.

It did feel right, being here. In fact, very few things had ever felt so right. So far, she had been nothing but a positive influence on his life. She had helped with some of his other clients and breathed new life into his heretofore-latent artistic talents.

And Cutter liked her! His dog, who had never even pretended to like any woman Michael brought home, became puppy-stupid whenever she was around. He dreamed of a lazy day, with Cutter chasing butterflies as he lay Yvonne down in soft flower-laden grass ...

"Tell me about Beth."

Surprise lifted him out of his reverie. He was still in bed, his head pillowed in Yvonne's lap, receiving the most relaxing and arousing scalp massage of his life. He had just decided to flip her on her back when she popped her quiet question. It had the effect of being plunged into ice water.

Firelight played across her features, making copper highlights in her hair. She deftly avoided his gaze, a small, it's-no-big-deal smile on her face.

"Why do you want to know about her?" he wondered, one eyebrow raised in suspicion.

"Well ... " her hands fluttered nervously now, tracing his ears, eyebrows, lips, collarbone. "I mean, I know the past is the past, but she had a major impact on your life, and, well, I was just curious." This was said defensively, leaving Michael to wonder if the flush on her cheeks was from the fire or another source.

With a little jolt, he toyed with the idea of Yvonne being jealous, maybe not a lot, but envious nonetheless. And she would only be jealous if she cared for him more than just a little, right?

He started to smile, then frowned. To talk about Beth ... It was still a touchy subject with him, and he had spent more than half his twenties trying to forget the past. Resurrecting it was the last thing he wanted to do.

Yvonne took his hesitation for refusal. "I apologize, Michael. I didn't have the right—there was no call to ask you about that. Besides," she added brightly, "that's way behind you anyway. Right?"

Belatedly he realized his silence had embarrassed her. "Vonne, it's okay."

She scrambled to her feet. "I think I'm going to take these dirty dishes to the kitchen and get some vanilla coffee," she announced. "I'll bring you some of that chamomile tea, okay? Be right back." She fled for the kitchen, Cutter following.

Michael rolled out of bed and went to the fireplace, cursing under his breath. It was wrong to be rude. Her curiosity about his late wife was as innocent as it was valid. She didn't know the can of worms it represented. Besides, she didn't put him off when he asked about her finances or history, and he had been rather blunt about it.

Still, he hadn't talked about Beth and her effect on his life in years. Jeff was there through it all, and Thom had come along right after. And yet, they didn't know the whole story. Maybe it was time to tell his version, the true version, of the story. Maybe Yvonne was the person to tell it to.

He heard her cautious step behind him and was angry with himself for making her uncertain. She dropped awkwardly beside him, setting the steaming mugs on the floor beside her. "I let Cutter out the back door. I hope that's all right."

He replaced the poker in its stand. "Yeah. He's got his own door to come in and out."

She fidgeted with her cup, and Michael bit back apologies. "Okay, we still have one more video to go. It's got the Wayans brothers in it."

"No, I think we'll just talk for a while."

She took a deep breath. "I think this will be a good year for the Falcons."

He laughed briefly at her attempts to change the subject, a movement of his shoulders, nothing more. "I want to talk about Beth."

"Michael, you don't have to," she protested. "It's none of my business, really…"

"I need to talk about it."

He toyed with his mug. "It's hard to find a place to begin," he said after a lengthy pause. His voice was barely above the crackling of the fire. "There's so much to tell …

"Beth was the epitome of clichés. She was Homecoming Queen, captain of the cheerleaders, National Honor Society, Beta club: the blonde-haired, blue-eyed girl next door. She was a star, even in our first year in high school. She had a personality like a magnet. Jeff, Beth, and I became the Three Musketeers because we were the anchors of the ever-changing popular circle. I guess that's why everyone started pairing us off, even though I suspected she liked Jeff—there weren't, aren't, many girls who don't.

"My parents were bowled over by her. She fit in perfectly with the plans they envisioned for their only child: valedictorian, Harvard law, marriage to the perfect girl, joining the family firm. It was often that I'd come home from football practice to find Beth already there, making plans with my parents.

"I went along with it, overlooking a lot of things, because by that time I thought I was in love with her. She was like sunlight: beautiful and warm and necessary, but dangerous in large doses. Of course, I didn't learn this until it was too late.

"I did go on to Harvard, and Jeff got a full scholarship to North Carolina. Beth opted to stay in Atlanta, working in my mom's interior design firm while learning how to be the perfect little wife. Although she wrote me letters, I didn't see her except for breaks. The wedding was planned for the summer before my senior year."

He stared into the fire, his mind years and miles away. "During the summer before my sophomore year, Beth got pregnant. Of course I did my duty; we were married before fall semester. It was a big adjustment to make, and it put tremendous strain on both of us. Beth lost the baby two months after we were married."

His grip tightened on his mug, and he swallowed audibly. "I told myself it was for the best, that we weren't ready for parenthood, but I was devastated. Beth behaved as if her miscarriage never happened, hitting all the campus parties. I couldn't understand why she wasn't grieving like I was, and it drove a wedge between us.

"Everything changed after that. I threw myself into studying, but it didn't feel the same. I realized that I wasn't living my life; other people were living it for me. I felt trapped, as if I was being pushed into a corner. I realized that all my life, no one had ever asked me what I wanted. What I wanted was to be my own boss, to start my own company, make my own way."

His expression became grim. "Stupidly, I thought Beth would go along with it, or at least understand. But Beth wanted everything. She liked the nice little package I represented: big house in a ritzy neighborhood with a couple of nice cars in the garage. She wanted the prestige of being a lawyer's wife. And she wanted to have her cake and eat it too."

Pained by the memory, he closed his eyes. "Since my future was becoming uncertain, Beth decided to move higher on the food chain. About six months after her miscarriage, I caught her in bed with another man, a med student."

He dimly heard her dismayed exclamation, but his mind was miles—years—away. He hunched over and continued. "I dragged the guy from the bed and threw him out the front door, tossing his clothes out the window. Beth had the nerve to tell me that it was my fault that she cheated on me, that I had ruined her plans by not going to law school. I was supposed to be her ticket to bigger and better things. And then she dropped a bigger bombshell: she had faked her pregnancy to make sure I would marry her. She had been using me all the time, and fool that I was, I didn't even realize it."

Silence. The finality in his voice was evident, but there was more, much more to his story. Yvonne knew it too because she asked, "What happened?"

"I killed her."

Yvonne flinched as if she'd been slapped. He died a little inside, knowing she would never see him the same again. But she needed to know that he wasn't a good person; his character was a fabrication.

She reached out, clasping his hand in hers, compelling him to look into her eyes. "I don't believe you," she said quietly, and the conviction in her voice undid him.

"I threw her out on a dark and stormy night." His laugh was shaky, humorless. "Sounds like something out of a gothic novel, doesn't it? But I didn't care. At that moment,

I wanted her to die—I wanted her to be as hurt as I was. I hated her as I have never hated anyone in my life. She used me. My family, my money. She stole a part of my soul.

"I had forgotten that the brakes were bad on her car. I was supposed to fix them, but money was tight. A few hours later the police came to my door, telling me that Beth had died in a seven-car crash. A part of me was grieved, but I was also relieved. It was like I'd been granted my freedom after being imprisoned."

He raked a hand through his hair, hating himself for telling this story, but needing to release it. "A couple of days later, the coroner who performed the autopsy told me that Beth had been three months pregnant. That's when I got angry—hell, I got furious. It didn't matter if it was my child or not. I hated her for dying, for taking an innocent life, for putting blood on my hands.

"No one knew the truth, and I didn't bother enlightening them. I learned my lesson, though. I learned to be a taker; I would never be taken. No woman will ever use me like that again. No one has, and no one will."

Silence. Even the log in the grate had ceased popping. He was aware of Yvonne sitting beside him with her eyes fastened to his face, numb with disbelief. He shouldn't have told her. No one had been able to understand his rage and anguish, and he had kept it to himself until it festered inside him, eating him alive. It felt good to purge the bitterness from his soul, but now his pain had poisoned her.

She would leave him now. He told himself he was glad.

When he turned to look at her, the expression of horror on her face shriveled his soul. "So now you know my dark secrets, the reason I've been called a heartless bastard by more women than I can remember."

He released her hand and she gasped in relief as sensation flooded back into it. "And now I've hurt you. I suppose you hate me." He turned away.

Yvonne stared at his profile, saw the way his jaw worked. He was still in pain, pain so great it was a living thing in the room with them. She had asked for this, asked him to bare his soul to her. The least she could do was ease some of the hurt.

Gently, silently, she cupped his face in her hands and turned him to her. How easily she saw the anguish and anger in his eyes, and the need. She recognized the need, for it mirrored her own: the need to be forgiven.

With the pads of her thumbs she drew the moisture from his cheeks then kissed each one. "I don't hate you, Michael," she whispered. Like a benediction, she gently covered his lips with hers.

He shuddered, then grabbed her in a bruising kiss. When his hands roamed over her, blindly seeking the solace that was old as time, she opened her arms and offered it freely. Desperation underlined his every move as he stripped their clothes away and dove into her. She yielded to him willingly, soothing him with her hands, her words, her body.

Afterwards, remorse set in. "Oh, God, Vonne, I didn't mean to—"

She pressed her fingertips to his lips. "Sshh," she breathed. "You don't have to say anything. Not to me."

Holding him in her arms, she soothed him to sleep. He quickly fell into an exhausted slumber, leaving her with her private battle.

Stunned, shaken, wrung-out. That's how she felt because of his story. He wasn't averse to commitment because he still loved his late wife. He hated her, and God help her, Yvonne almost hated her, too.

How could someone be so cruel to a man so caring? It had happened a decade ago, but it was still fresh. He was wounded, scarred just as she was.

Yvonne was no stranger to pain. Living with hurt for the past fifteen years had made her sensitive to the pain of others. With the sensitivity came a need to comfort, to care and console, that hadn't been readily available to her all those years ago.

Even after the dark hour passed and the clock chimed three, sleep still proved elusive. Michael had achieved a measure of peace, and she was glad to help him gain it. In her mind, easing someone else's pain staved off her own hurt, hurt she would carry to her grave.

The agony and terror she had felt when she learned that her family was gone and that she would probably not walk again was always just below the surface, feeding the insomnia she'd suffered since the accident. The guilt and anger over being left behind were her constant companions.

Uselessly she wondered what it would be like to be free of the pain and grief, to find release the way Michael had. She couldn't imagine it. She had carried them too long, so deeply rooted inside that she knew she would never be free of them. Guilt and anger were as much a part of her as her limbs. Even if Michael were there to help, it wouldn't be as easy for her to achieve peace as he had. But she wouldn't put him through that. He didn't deserve that kind of hell.

But Michael wouldn't be there. She knew that for a certainty now. He was once bitten, permanently shy. His late wife had taken his heart and ripped it to shreds. He would never give anyone the opportunity to do so again.

He would leave her now. She had forced him to be vulnerable, forced the scalding tears that dampened her shirt. She had pushed him out of her own curiosity, and now he would push her out of his life.

She told herself she was glad.

She finally fell into a fitful sleep, her dreams punctuated with images of Michael smiling and waving to her as she sped off into a dark and stormy night.

CHAPTER NINE

It was Girl's Night Out, the fourth Saturday of the month. The management staff of each Your Heart's Desire gathered at Yvonne's townhouse for a quick meeting before joining Atlanta's teeming nightlife.

The pace of her life had been so hectic she had nearly forgotten about it. Yet even with the signature line going into full production, and sets for the show being finalized, her thoughts kept straying to Michael.

Neither of them had mentioned what had happened when she spent the night with him. The next morning, both had dressed quickly and gone their separate ways. Even later, when they were together, they were awkward with each other. The sex was still as good as ever, but there was distance between them now, and she didn't know what she could do to bridge it.

She believed that she had embarrassed or belittled Michael by forcing him to tell her that story. He had been reluctant to share it, and with good reason. He obviously thought he was beyond goodness after what happened between him and Beth. Yet Yvonne knew there was goodness in him, lying dormant under years of disregard.

He thought she should leave him. She didn't have to hear the words to know that he was waiting for her to run. If she had common sense, she would have left and been relieved. But common sense had left her the moment she let him touch her.

"Men are dogs!" Kourtney announced upon her arrival, flopping into the booth in disgust.

"Thank you, Barbara Walters," Angela retorted, watching as the striking redhead reached for an unclaimed beer. "Tell us something we don't know. And get your own beer!"

Grateful to have her thoughts interrupted, Yvonne waved a credit card in the air, snagging a waiter's attention. "Be a sweetie and start a tab; we're going to be here for a while."

They were all silent as they watched him walk away. Law swung back to the group. "If that man was a dog, he'd be a boxer. He's built like a brick wall!"

"Nah, he's a poodle," LaShun, from the Gwinnett boutique, corrected. "Great little ass but not a thing upstairs."

Several of the ladies, laughing, spoke up to argue the point. "No, wait a minute," Angela broke in, "Shun's got a point. And it's a good one. Sometimes you just need a little stud puppy, someone to make your friends jealous, make you see fireworks in bed, and change a flat tire. When I want a reasonably intelligent conversation, I talk to you guys."

"Isn't that a little sexist?" Terri wondered, her almond-shaped eyes filled with concern.

"Okay, okay," Angela conceded, taking her beer back from Kourtney. "I can change my own tire, and oil, and antifreeze. But it's a hell of a lot sexier watching a man sweat over it than me!"

"Why shouldn't we be sexist?" LaShun wanted to know, moving so the waiter could set up another round of drinks and a heaping platter of buffalo wings with extra celery. "At this very moment, there are thousands of guys all over this city doing the exact same thing we are."

"She's got a point, Terri," Yvonne pointed out mildly. Her role was strictly that of referee, first round drink buyer, and designated driver. Sometimes, though, she couldn't help putting her two cents in. "I think we deserve to be a little sexist."

"After all, timid women we're not, and if a man's a dog, a man's a dog," Aimee chimed in. Another pair of tight jeans caught her eye. "And that one's a Great Dane!"

They erupted into laughter, the center of attention on the deck. They always were when they got together. Seventeen women and one honorary sister of various shapes, sizes, and ancestry, united by the simple fact that they were women, and sometimes, all men are dogs.

"So what kind of dog is Rob, Kourtney?" Terri wanted to know.

The manager of the Buckhead boutique shook her head angrily, red curls flying. "He's a mutt, a no-good, crazy, mixed-up mutt!" she spat decisively.

"Uh-oh," everyone said in unison, passing knowing looks around the table. Kourtney was having man trouble. Again.

"No, I take that back," she added. "He went to Georgia, so he's a bulldog—bullheaded and stubborn. As if my opinion doesn't mean anything—"

"Sometimes it doesn't," Lawrence, ever the smart aleck, observed. Kourt threw him a dirty look and stole his beer.

"Regenia," Yvonne cut in quickly, "what about Pete? If he was a dog, what kind would he be?"

Regenia's hazel eyes gleamed beneath her Halle Berry bangs. She and Pete, a Georgia Tech linebacker and aeronautical engineer, had been dating for over a year and had just moved in together. "Pete? He's a cocker spaniel," she replied without hesitation.

"I ain't touching that one," Shun said, rolling her eyes in exaggeration.

They laughed again, enjoying the warm night and the company of friends. Their waiter returned, to appreciative glances from the table. They ordered another round of everything and a collective sigh went up as they watched his rear disappear into the crowd.

Just then, a convertible full of guys pulled up to the intersection, hooting and barking at them. "We don't need further proof of men as dogs than a carload of them with their tongues hanging in the breeze, now do we?" remarked Lisa from South Dekalb dryly.

"Be nice," Yvonne chided gently. "They're pulling in."

"Hey, maybe the next round will be on them." Shun's eyes twinkled.

Kourtney shot her an evil look. "Is that all you do, scheme a man to buy you a drink?"

Shun gave her a wide-eyed look. "What else are men good for, besides money and sex?" She went off into the crowd, some of the others trailing after.

Angela sighed. "That girl, I swear ... " she upended her drink. "And don't you know, she's the one who'll get all the attention. Proof-positive that men's brains are not in the upper part of their anatomy."

A chorus of "Amens" littered the table. Kourtney pressed on. "I mean, it's almost like you have to be a bitch for the guy to be happy. I'm not a bitch—well, not most of the time, anyway—and I keep getting stomped on! It's like if you're a nice girl, nice guys run like hell."

"Girls Night Out" was definitely turning into "Man Bashing Night", Yvonne noticed. Some of the others were getting on Kourtney's bandwagon.

"That's because they think you want to lead them straight to the altar!" Aimee, from South Dekalb, snorted. "Right, like I've got time for marriage! Between working full time at the shop and pulling a full load at State, where can I fit in taking care of a husband?"

"And you can bet your ass he'd expect you to wait on him hand and foot," Kourtney added. "Like Rob, the little worm!"

"Oh, don't even go there!" Angela dove back in. "If you both work outside the house, you both work inside the house. The Dark Ages are over. Hello!"

Several hands snapped their fingers around the tables. Kourtney, president of the Man Bashing Club, summed it up. "Men seem to think that everything wrong is Eve's fault, and men are blameless. But who here thinks Eve was listening to a female snake? Nah, it was male, and women have been falling for snakes in the grass ever since!"

Everyone exploded into laughter, leaning back in their chairs and holding their sides until tears came. Terri wiped her eyes. "Show me a good looking, sane, straight, single man with a decent job and a willingness to be in a real relationship, and who's not dead or in jail, and I'll show you a cheesecake with no fat or calories!"

They laughed, but Regenia surprised them by saying, "I hope you're going to have that recipe at our next meeting."

They gawked at her. "You know someone like that? And Pete doesn't count."

Regenia gave them a wide grin, tossing her gorgeous, shiny, to-kill-for dark mane. "I know two."

"Two?"

"Well, who are they?"

"Why have you been holding out?"

"'Fess up, girl."

Regenia's grin was like Garfield's after he kicked Odie off the table. "Actually, they both belong to our dear boss Yvonne."

Yvonne choked on her Diet Coke. Angela and Lawrence helped her wipe her skirt, which was unfortunately leather. "Who-who belongs to me?" she demanded when she could speak again.

"Well, there's Jeff Maxwell—"

"They're practically brother and sister!" Angela protested vehemently.

"We are brother and sister, at least in spirit," Yvonne assured them. "He doesn't belong to me!"

"Then you don't mind leasing him out to the rest of us?" Aimee asked. "That man is beyond fine! He's smart, and he has money! I'll fight anyone here for him. Hell, I'd give up chocolate!"

Everyone nodded, agreeing to the seriousness of that commitment. Everyone knew, if you can't have sex, you have chocolate. Some were running ruts into the floor before the Godiva counter at Lenox Square.

"Yeah, but what about Yvonne's partner, Mike Benjamin?" Regenia slyly asked.

If the tables weren't animated before, they sure were now. Everyone had an opinion.

"Chief, you gotta admit, he's the finest specimen of a man since Adam, and God made him personally."

"He's got the face of an angel."

"And the body of a devil."

"The man screams S-E-X."

"He's a walking orgasm."

"And those eyes!" Suddenly there was a dreamy-eyed chorus signing the praises of one Michael Benjamin.

"So, Chief," Angela asked slowly, "if Mike was a dog, what kind would he be?"

"Yeah, Boss," Lawrence chimed in. "Give us the complete 411."

Suddenly Yvonne was the center of attention as a dozen pairs of eyes swung to face her. She didn't like being put on the spot, but knew they weren't going to let up.

She shot her second-in-command and assistant a dirty look, but both smiled benignly behind their drinks. "Well ... " she licked her lips nervously. "He reminds me of Cutter—that's his German Shepherd."

"You met his dog?" Kourtney demanded, stunned. Yvonne nodded hesitantly. "Well, you certainly didn't meet him at the shop. That means you've been to his place!" They waited expectantly for confirmation.

Yvonne glanced uneasily around the table. Even Angela was staring curiously at her. She hated being the center of attention; hanging in the shadows and watching everyone else fence was more to her liking. She sighed. Better to get it over with. "He has a beautiful old house in Virginia-Highland, near Piedmont Park," she answered, feeling like a witness at a mob trial.

"He isn't gay, is he?" Aimee wondered.

"Absolutely not!" Yvonne spat before thinking. She instantly regretted the outburst.

"And do we know this from personal experience?" Regenia asked silkily.

Open up floor, open up and swallow me now. She was glad it was dark; she had a feeling even her hair was blushing. "We've, uh, talked." Lawrence choked on another wing. "He didn't even know Law was gay—and Law did everything but rent a billboard."

"I didn't know Law was gay either," Angela pointed out.

"That's because your radar hasn't been used in so long, it's rusted," Lawrence cracked.

"Don't make me snatch that wig off your head!"

"Excuse me, ladies," Kourtney cut in, "but some of us are trying to pump our boss for information. Does he have a girlfriend?"

"How much money does he make?"

"Why don't you jump on that?"

"Yeah—he can't keep his eyes off you!"

"Like he'd jump your bones if you'd let him!"

Angela finally bailed her out. "Hey—isn't that one of the guys from the Braves?"

The group stood en masse.

"Where?"

"That man has the finest ass in baseball!"

"There he is!"

They departed like a fire drill.

"And to think, these women are responsible for a couple of million dollars in sales," Yvonne sighed. "And as for you two—putting me on the spot like that! As if I'm ready to tell everyone about me and Michael!"

"So you are still dating him," Angela surmised. "I'm amazed that you've been able to be so discreet about it. Gwen hasn't even had a dream about you two."

"That's all thanks to me," Lawrence boasted. "After all, I am 'The Law'." Both women gave him an oblique look. "I think I'll go make sure our girls stay out of trouble," he said, taking the hint and leaving.

"I don't know if you can call it dating," Yvonne finally said, her tone brusque. "Let's just say we're business partners who happen to sleep together occasionally."

Angela snorted, tossing her auburn bangs. "You make it sound so clinical."

"Well, what do you want me to say? That we're lovers?"

She leaned back, trying to distance herself from the conversation and the tumult of her emotions. "That's way too emotional. I'm not ready for that. And neither is Michael."

"How can you be so sure?"

"He told me."

She gave Angela a capsulated version of her conversation with Michael. "Basically, he adamantly swore that he'd never let another woman use him like his wife did. He'd never let anyone get close enough. Which is fine with me. I'm happy with the way things are."

Happy was a relative term, however. She felt like a fool for delving into his past when it was clear that if he'd wanted to tell her, he would have. What terrified her, however, was the thought that he would want her to share her past in return. It would be fair, and it would keep their relationship even. But she wouldn't, couldn't do that.

She looked around the deck. The majority of the crowd was single, college-age, and clean-cut, carefully cruising the night for whatever gratification they could scrape from the sexually frightening 00's. She wondered how many "love connections" made in this environment lasted after last call wore off. Not many. What glittered like gold at night usually turned into a fool's mistake in the morning light.

Angela leaned towards her. "You know, when I first declared independence from Richard, I bought a king-sized bed for my apartment. I went to college; then I got a queen-sized bed because the other was too big for me alone. Now I work for you and even though it's the best thing in the world, I find myself looking at bedding sets again. I'm beginning to think my next bed will be my final resting place."

"Angela … " Yvonne didn't know what to say. Her friend had infrequently talked about the oppressive nature of her ex-husband, whom she finally divorced five years ago. But she couldn't be suggesting that being with him was better than being alone?

Before she could open her mouth, Angela spoke up. "Who was the last person you were close to?"

"Poppy," she replied, referring to her former skating coach. She'd lived with his family after the accident and still visited them. "You know that."

"Outside of family."

"Jeff."

"Jeff is your 'play-brother', as you say, so he doesn't count."

Yvonne's brow furrowed. "What about the girls?"

"You're a mentor to them."

"You and Gwen."

Angela smiled. "We've shared a lot of dirt, but it's been mostly us digging the dirt while you sweep it up; but we still fall into the business category."

The frown deepened. "Then I don't get what you're driving at."

"You're so used to it that you don't even see it!" Angela exclaimed incredulously.

Yvonne began to simmer. She did not, under any circumstances, like people talking about her. It made her feel paranoid. "See what?" she demanded irritably.

"How alone you are."

She didn't deny it, but she did argue it. "You make it sound like a crime, or a disease. I happen to enjoy my solitude."

"I'm supposed to believe you like being lonely?"

They had this conversation too many times. "Being alone doesn't mean being lonely, Angie. My life is full. You know that."

Angela nodded. "With the girls, the catalog, with your suppliers, running the stores, handling the financial interests of Marco's and Creole, creating new designs. You always claimed you were too busy to find someone. Well, now someone—and a fine someone, for a white boy—has been dropped into your lap and you still claim to be too busy for a relationship!"

Feeling the pulse of a headache coming on, Yvonne rubbed her forehead. "Angie, I just told you that Michael doesn't want a relationship."

"He doesn't want a woman using him," her partner corrected. "Big difference. And regardless of what his brain is making his mouth say, that man is deep into you. Real deep."

"How can he be deep into me? We're as different as night and day—literally. Our relationship, if you want to call it that, has no future. We both know that."

Angela's gaze was probing. "Is that what you believe, or what you hope?"

Yvonne stared into the pile of bones before her, unable to remember eating so many. Absently she calculated the amount of exercise she would have to do to compensate, but her mind was reeling from the idea that Michael might care about her more than she knew.

The idea terrified her.

"You've been living in a bubble since you lost your family and your uncle," Angela continued gently. "You've never let anyone—not me, not Jeff, not even the girls—get close to you. We've known you for years, Vonne, yet you're still a mystery to us in a lot of ways. For nearly fifteen years you've been piddling along behind this cute little fence that guards you from the rest of the world. You've got a golden opportunity to break down that fence now, with Mike.

"Both of us, because of our pasts, have been alone. Maybe that's true for Mike Benjamin too. But the past is meant to shape the future, not dictate it. Don't let another fifteen years go by before you realize that."

Yvonne peered into the dim light, meant to provide ambience, but was actually a shield to conceal what would be unacceptable in the cruel light of day. She received the impression that all these people, tiny cells in the body of life, were passing her by while she sat. It made her feel old and out of sync.

Perhaps Angela was right. Maybe she was hiding behind a fence. That was the only way she knew how to stay safe and sane. Because if she remained alone, she would never have to worry about being lonely. And the one thing she had promised herself on the plane to Atlanta a decade ago was that she would never be lonely again.

"Michael has been commitment-free for years, Angela," Yvonne tried to explain. "I can understand that. I even feel relief about it. The fact that he's commitment-phobic suits me just fine. I don't make demands on him and he doesn't make demands on me. It really is the best way for us. Things are perfect the way they are."

So why did everything feel so wrong?

CHAPTER TEN

It was midnight when Lawrence finally returned Yvonne to her townhouse. She rarely stayed long with her bunch. Despite the camaraderie she had with all her associates, she knew they wouldn't let loose with her around. Even though they knew driving inebriated would get them fired, she still worried about them. Tonight, her thoughts were mostly focused on Michael.

Kicking off her heels, she went to the massive mahogany audio cabinet and punched in a blues CD. That proved too depressing, so she switched to Mozart, slumping into a heap on the couch. Even with the lively symphony in the background, the silence still hung around her shoulders. It was that damned conversation with Angela. Hell, it was that damned conversation with Michael, too!

She had been content, as content as possible. For a dozen years she had been alone, with only her work for company. It was an arrangement that suited her. Until now.

Now, she realized just how empty her home was. Maybe even her life. Running Desire and her various other business interests were her life. Any emotional highs she needed came from her outings with her protègèes.

But that was before sex.

Before sex, her life fit into a neat, ordered pattern that fluctuated only with the retail seasons. Before sex, her life was a Chanel suit; now it was something from Gautier. It was like not knowing you were allergic to chocolate until you actually ate it.

Thanks to Michael, a whole new world had been opened to her. Now she knew what it was like to be intimate with someone, to be laid bare. Literally. She knew what closeness was. Hell, she knew what a multiple orgasm was.

And now she knew what it was like to spend a satisfying evening out with her staff and want nothing more than to go home and get laid.

The door chime interrupted her reverie. Cautiously she approached it, wondering who would be ringing her bell this time of night. "Who's there?"

A loud, joyful bark answered her, and she flung the door open. "Cutter, what are you doing here?"

Michael lounged against the doorframe, darkly handsome in black jeans and shirt. "He missed you," he explained, nodding at the big shepherd staring rapturously up at her. "He kept barking and yowling and wouldn't stop until I agreed to bring him over."

Of course, Michael wasn't about to let her know that he wasn't able to get to sleep, wondering just how good a time she'd had during Girl's Night Out. He also didn't tell her he had been driving through her neighborhood since ten o'clock, waiting for her to get home.

She squatted in the doorway, the big shepherd almost lying in her lap as he eagerly licked her face. "I've missed you too, boy," she laughed. "Thanks for bringing him over."

She looked up at him. "Well, are you going to hold up my doorframe all night, or are you gonna come in?"

"Since you put it like that, I'm gonna come in and not leave until the sun is up and all your neighbors can see me." He shut the door and turned, finally catching a full view of her dress. "Is that all you wore tonight?" he roared.

Nearly tripping over Cutter, she spun to face him. "What's wrong with what I'm wearing?"

"What you're not wearing is more like it."

She wore a halter-necked mini-dress of supple turquoise leather with a deep back and an even deeper front. It was designed to accelerate the pulse of any male within a hundred yards. It was doing a damned good job of it, in Michael's opinion.

"We always dress up for Girl's Night Out because we never know where we're going," she explained. "We went clubbing after all the calories we packed on eating. Besides, this dress has been hanging in my closet for months, begging me to wear it when it got warmer. But if it will make you feel better, it has a little matching jacket that I wore. Still, it was a big hit."

"I'll just bet it was," he snorted, picturing hordes of men salivating over her. The image made him want to kill.

"So were you," she told him with a smile before sauntering into the living room.

Intrigued by the casual remark, he followed her. She half-sat, half-reclined on the black leather couch, her hair, now loose, flowing over the arm and glinting in the light from a sleek torchiere.

He admired her decorating sense. The room had a Far East feel, from the gold rug with black accents and the lacquered horn chair to the black marble fireplace and the gold Oriental screen backing the loveseat. Plants, a bonsai on the mantel, a couple of trees, and several floor plants scattered throughout softened the black and gold profusion.

The room, indeed, most of the townhouse, looked right out of a decorating magazine. Yet there was something lacking, some esoteric essence that makes a house a home. In fact, the only rooms in the house that held anything close to vitality were the office and bedroom.

He moved to the couch, lifted her legs, and sat down, draping her legs across his lap. "Why was I a big hit?"

She raked her hands through her hair, then stretched. "Well, Kourtney launched an 'all men are dogs' campaign, and they wanted to know what kind of dog I thought you'd be. When I told them about Cutter, they pressed me for the complete 411 on you."

"They did?"

"Oh yeah. They seem to believe that you and Jeff are the only two stable, sane, straight, single, unimprisoned, living men in the world. And since you are basically 'new meat', they were extremely interested in you, Mr. Benjamin."

The thought of Yvonne's people sitting around dissecting him made him uneasy. Especially if Kourtney and Aimee were in on the discussion. They were relentless. He took one stockinged calf in his hands and began to knead the muscles. "What did you tell them?"

"I gave them the 'full Monty' on you: gender preference, real estate holdings, credit rating, blood type, stuff like that." She grunted as he attacked the ball of her foot. "Have my muscles offended you?" she wondered.

"Sorry," he muttered, relaxing his grip. "Did you tell them about us?"

"Of course not," she answered, indignation evident in her tone.

"Why not?"

"It's none of their business. My private life is just that: private." She propped herself on her elbows, gazing at him. "Are you disappointed that I didn't?"

"No," he sighed. "It's just that—no, you're right. Your private life is private. Even from me."

"What?"

He grabbed her hands as she swung into a sitting position. "Vonne, we've been sleeping together for months now, and we've known each other a little longer than that. I know you love Belgian chocolates and funky jewelry. I know where each of your twenty-two moles are. I know when you get nervous, you start fiddling with your necklaces." He gently moved her hand from the ornate silver choker.

Yvonne felt her cheeks burn. "I didn't realize you knew so much about me."

"I know some," he agreed, "but not enough. For instance, why have you never talked to me about the single most monumental event of your life?"

The flush immediately left her cheeks. She knew what he was asking. "No," she whispered, curling her hands into fists.

"Yes," he answered just as softly. He leaned toward her. "Why don't you have any pictures of your family out? All I see are photos of the girls you mentor. What about your real family, Vonne? Surely you still have some photos from your childhood? Where did you live, who took care of you when you were growing up? Why are you so afraid of driving? Why do you leave town every three weeks like clockwork? Where do you go?"

"Stop it," she demanded, clamping her hands over her ears. Her voice was shrill, ragged. "For the love of God, just stop."

She surged to her feet, wrapping her arms about her in a futile effort to warm the cold place inside her where she hid her memories. It was a dark and lonely place that left her frightened and vulnerable. It made her keep a night-light on in every room. It made her unable to sleep until three or four in the morning. It was as voracious as it was cruel, that lonely place of memories. She never wanted to be that vulnerable and lonely again. "I-I don't want to talk about it. I can't talk about it."

Michael followed her to the fireplace. He stood close, but didn't touch her. "Not even to Gwen, Angela, or Jeff?"

Jittery, she shook her head. "They know how I lost my family—they couldn't help but know—but I never talked to them about it."

Careful, afraid of upsetting her further, he put his hand on her shoulder. What he wanted to do was take her in his arms, protect her from the monsters of life. He wanted her to trust him, and trust in him. "It's been a long time,

Vonne. Don't you think it's time to tell someone, to let it out?"

Yvonne had her necklace in a death-grip. The memories danced on the edge of her consciousness, taunting her, threatening her. She had spent almost half her life bricking away the pain of the past, remembering only what was safe to remember.

"You don't know what you're asking, Michael," she said in a strangled voice.

"Why are you afraid?" She shook her head mutely, unable to explain. "We're as close as two people can be, Vonne. If you can't talk to me about it, who can you talk to?"

No one. Jeff and Angela only knew parts of her past, and she intended to keep it that way. Only her coach, Poppy Calhoun and Auntie Grace, his wife, knew everything that had happened to her. She still couldn't talk to them, her surrogate parents, about it. And Michael ... Surely if he knew everything, he would leave running. She wasn't ready for that.

Gently, he tilted her chin, and she knew what he was going to say. "I thought it would take electrocution to get my story out of me, but all it took was someone willing to listen and not judge. Let me do that for you, Vonne. Don't you trust me?"

"It's not a question of trust," she managed to say. She couldn't even trust herself. Her own body betrayed her, swaying against him as if he alone could provide salvation. But her heart knew the truth. She was beyond saving.

Looking up into his face, seeing the concern in those damnable golden eyes, she felt her resolve weakening. "What happened—the accident—it's not something that's easy for me, not even all these years later. But if I can, when I'm ready, you will be the first one I talk to. Please, don't rush me on this, okay?"

"Okay," he promised, wrapping her in his arms. For less than a second she stiffened, then relaxed against him. She always did, instinctively, whenever he showed affection for her. There had been so many times when she'd had to hold herself apart, to protect herself against the need to touch. She had learned to live without the comfort of another person's warmth so well that touching seemed foreign to her.

Saddened, Yvonne closed her eyes. She knew she had disappointed him, and it caused an ache deep inside her. But she couldn't talk about the past. Even thinking about it caused the darkness and coldness to swirl around her, attempting to drown her.

But Michael was warmth, and Michael was light. If she could only become part of him, immerse herself in him, surround herself with his essence the way his arms surrounded her.

She pressed her mouth against the base of his throat. The pulse jumped to life at the touch of her lips, throbbing with energy. She rained kisses across his throat and jaw, tracing the heat in his veins. "You're so warm," she whispered, awed by the fact. "Even your hands." She kissed his open palms.

He shuddered. "It's because you're burning me alive." She fumbled with the buttons on his shirt, needing the warmth of his skin against hers. Desperation made her clumsy. "Help me," she whispered, frantic.

He obliged, shouldering out of his shirt and freeing her from the turquoise sheath. She wrapped her arms around his neck and melded herself to him, eyes sliding shut in pleasure as the heat from his heart pounded against hers.

Lifting her in his arms, he moved to the couch. She slithered off his lap to remove the rest of his clothing. Laying her cheek against his freed erection, she sighed dreamily. "So very warm."

She closed her mouth around him, bathing his shaft with her lips and tongue. He groaned as his head fell against the back of the couch. His obvious pleasure made her insistent, and only when he breathed her name in a harsh warning did she pull away.

She clambered into his lap, framing his thighs with her own. "Give me some of your fire," she begged against his mouth. "Burn me, make me feel alive."

He wrapped his hands around her waist and lifted her effortlessly. She poised above him for just the space of a heartbeat. Then he surged upward even as she ground down, simultaneous groans snatched from them as their heat combined in a volatile mix of passion.

Her hands splayed on his shoulders, she rose above him, her movements urgent. Need made her demanding. "More," she breathed, leaning into him, her nipples teasing his own. "Faster."

Obliging her, Michael slipped off the couch, putting her back against the carpet. He caught the backs of her knees with the inside curve of his arms, lifting her for his stroke. In one savage movement, he plunged deeply inside her, deeper than ever before. She screamed as the exquisite sensation boiled the blood in her veins, shattering her senses. "Yes! Oh, God, yes!"

As his name was ripped from her throat, Michael exploded into a thousand shards of light, answering her with a shout of his own. The release held them suspended for a moment outside of time, bonding them more strongly than vows ever could.

For a long while they lay still, senses, bodies, and heartbeats intertwined. He rolled until they were side by side, causing aftershocks to shoot through them both. He pulled away. "Sorry about that. Carpet burn wasn't what I had in mind."

He smoothed her bangs from her damp forehead, his fingers coming into contact with the tears she'd tried to conceal. "You're crying. Are you all right?" He pulled her upright.

"I-I'm okay." Breathless, she gulped air, fighting for control. She couldn't tell him how, at the height of their joining, she had no longer felt alone. Instead, she had felt completed, whole. The darkness and fear and cold had been banished, replaced by the warm glow of ... togetherness. She couldn't tell him how much she had needed him tonight.

Michael saw the shaken, wide-eyed stare and understood. Gently, wordlessly, he lifted her in his arms and carried her upstairs, enjoying the feeling as she snuggled against him.

He had every intention of tucking her in and leaving, but she surprised him by stretching her hands toward him. Her dark eyes shone with some unnamed longing. "Will you stay, just for a little while?"

She had never asked him to stay before. He couldn't refuse her, and discovered that he didn't want to. She needed him. Whether she wanted to admit it or not, it was true. And he was glad.

He slipped into bed beside her, taking her in his arms. She was silent a long time, and he believed her to be asleep. Then, "Do I really have twenty-two moles?"

"Sure do. Want me to show you?"

"Please."

He did, until languorous touching birthed desire. They made love again, gentle and slow. They explored each other, mapping each curve with fingertips and lips, unhurried by driving need.

Afterwards, he cradled her against his chest, stroking her back until she fell into a deep sleep. But sleep proved elusive for him.

With a light touch, he traced the faint scars that criss-crossed her from ribcage to thigh. Yvonne had been through so much pain, and she was still able to laugh and smile somehow. He could sense the sadness in her though, could see it in her eyes when she thought he was unaware.

He really couldn't blame her if she didn't want to talk about what had happened when she lost her family. Still, it hurt to think that she didn't want to share herself with him.

No, that wasn't really fair. She did share herself. She was able to reach out to people, especially those who were hurt. She always came into his arms willingly. More people than she realized called her friend. But there was a core in her that he couldn't reach, a painful part of herself she kept fenced off and fiercely guarded.

He wondered why it should upset him that she still kept parts of herself private. He hadn't wanted any strings between them; it was something they both agreed on.

But lately, he had found himself wanting more. Their conversations and creative times were becoming just as important as lovemaking to him. He didn't know if the idea frightened or excited him.

She snuggled under his chin, tucking her hands into his. "So warm," she sighed. "Feel good."

Gently he gathered her close. He remembered her saying once that she never went to sleep before the wee hours of the night. It was after three A.M. now. He vowed to do whatever it took to give her those full nights of sleep.

A feeling of protectiveness assaulted him so fiercely it left him breathless. God help him, he hadn't intended to have feelings so strong. He considered himself entirely too jaded and cynical for it. But Yvonne wouldn't use his feelings against him. She wouldn't manipulate him for her own gain, or make him jump through hoops to pander to her whims. Would she?

He pressed a soft kiss to her forehead. "You make me feel good too, Vonne," he whispered into the darkness. "Damned if I know what to do about it."

CHAPTER ELEVEN

"What would you like to drink?" Michael asked, lifting Yvonne onto a barstool. "See if they can do a virgin 'sex on the beach' rocky," she answered, blowing her bangs off her perspiring forehead. They had been dancing nonstop at the retro music club for half an hour. "If not, I'll take a virgin strawberry daiquiri."

He gave her a smile that caused her insides to jump. "A virgin version of sex on the beach, hhmm?" he murmured close to her ear. "I don't know about the bartender, but I could certainly arrange for your first time on the beach. You think about where, and I'll be right back."

The pounding blood in her ears nearly obliterated the sounds of disco music pouring through the speakers as she watched him walk away. He had convinced her to visit the club for a much-needed break from planning the fashion show, and she was glad they had.

She delicately pressed a napkin to her forehead, then adjusted the hem on her fire engine red mini-dress, the first outfit she had ever purchased for a man. Even though she adored lingerie and beautiful clothes, she had never thought of herself as a sexual being until Michael came along. The dress definitely made her feel sexy, even a bit risqué. But it was worth it to see his eyes nearly pop out of his head when he first saw her in it. They very nearly didn't make it out the door, and his efforts to persuade her to wear a coat over it were comical.

She thought again about her conversation with Angela days ago. She had told her partner that Michael didn't want a relationship, that they were both content to keep things superficial. But he'd surprised her by wanting to go way beyond superficial by digging into her past. She shuddered inwardly at the terror that had swept through her under his barrage of questions. Nothing would make her voluntarily divulge her history, certainly not someone who was temporarily in her life.

Strangely enough, she knew she would miss him when he was gone. No one stayed in her life for very long; it was a simple statement of fact. It didn't matter that it seemed as if someone had decided she shouldn't be alone anymore and had sent the perfect best friend. She knew her time with him was limited.

"Well hello, my sister!"

Yvonne turned and watched two men approach. "Funny, but my parents never told me I had brothers." She turned back toward the bar.

The two men flanked her, shoving other patrons aside. "We saw you when you came in," the taller of the two said. "I told J.T. that you were one together sister. Class, style … You have everything."

"Yeah," the other one agreed. "Except a brother on your arm."

Yvonne sighed. She knew something like this was bound to happen someday, but she certainly never expected a frontal assault. She had enough to deal with. She didn't need prejudice thrown into the mix.

"Like I said, gentlemen, I don't have a brother. Is there a problem with that?"

"There most definitely is a problem with that," the first one replied. "We have it hard enough as it is. Those people want to destroy us— don't you know that? And the best way to do that is by turning our women away from us."

"'Those people' aren't turning me away from you," she retorted. "Your rudeness is turning me away from you."

"You've been blinded by the white man!" J.T. spat angrily. "He's made you a goddamn sellout!"

Yvonne lost her patience with a biting laugh. "Oh, that's rich! You don't even know my name, and you're accusing me of being a sellout? I think it's time to take the gloves off.

"First of all, I'm not being blinded by any man, no matter what color he is. Second of all, I'm helping my brothers and sisters by donating time and money to after-school programs and community centers. And third, if you keep on bitching about being a victim, you always will be one!"

Her hands clenched and her voice dropped, quivering with outrage. "How dare you stand in the middle of a majority white club in a majority white neighborhood and accuse me of being a sellout? Tell me that you're Big Brothers to a few boys who have no hope, and maybe I'll listen to what you have to say. But to accuse me of selling out because my escort is white is too much! Just who's being blinded?"

She slipped off her barstool to stalk away, but was grabbed by the arm. "All that chump's got is 'the fever'," her unnamed accuser said. "He'll use you, just like his ancestors used yours. And when the fever's burned out, he'll toss you aside like yesterday's trash. He can't respect you because he can't understand where you're coming from. So don't even fool yourself about that, sister-girl. You're just an itch he wants to scratch, and you know it!"

J.T. pulled on his friend's arm. "Yo, Darien, he's coming back!"

Darien's eyes bored into hers. "Think about what I said. And believe it." They disappeared into the crowd.

Yvonne all but ran toward Michael. "It's hell trying to get a bartender's attention around here, but mission accomplished." He handed her drink over. His grin faded as he caught her expression. "Hey, what's wrong?"

She managed to swallow half of the fruity concoction before answering. "I'm fine," she brightly assured him. "Just a little tired. All that dancing."

He didn't look convinced. He stared at her, and Yvonne schooled her features into a calm expression. He scanned the crowd. "Those two guys I saw you with," he finally said, too casually. "Are they friends of yours? You seemed to be having a deep conversation."

By now Yvonne's hands shook so badly she dribbled a portion of her drink down her chin. "No! I mean, no, they aren't friends of mine. We were just discussing … politics. You know how opinionated I can be at times." She managed a weak smile.

He obviously wasn't buying it, but made no comment. "Why don't we get out of here? The air seems to be getting a little thick."

She readily agreed, and they left. But if she thought that was the end of it, she was sadly mistaken.

Yvonne disarmed the security system and walked into her townhouse, pausing to remove her heels. Michael followed, locking the door and turning on lights. He was silent. They both had been silent since leaving the club. The silence stretched between them like a crater around which they danced, each waiting for the other to fall in.

"Would you like something to drink?" she asked, heading for the kitchen. "Rumor has it I make a mean cup of coffee."

He stood in the center of the room, a brooding statue. "No, thanks."

Yvonne stared at him. He invaded her senses like a conquering army. He could have any woman he wanted, but he was with her. Why?

Suddenly afraid of the answer, she moved to the stairs. "I'm exhausted, I think I'll go on to bed. I'll see you tomorrow."

He moved in front of her, effectively blocking her escape. "I'm not leaving, not until we talk."

Her shoulders sagged. She knew what he meant, but still she played it. "Talk about what?"

He brought her closer, but she refused to meet his gaze. "You know about what. What happened with those guys?"

Yvonne tried to twist her arm free, but she might as well have tried to extricate it from concrete. "Nothing."

He pulled her closer until she was just inches away. "It was more than nothing, Vonne," he insisted. "Something happened. I can see it on your face. What were they talking to you about?" He paused. "It was about me, wasn't it?"

Panicked, her gaze skittered over his face. "They didn't mean anything. They just had too much to drink, that's all!"

Michael's jaw clenched. So those two bastards had said something, something that upset Yvonne so much she couldn't look him in the eye. And she was defending them!

His hands descended on her shoulders like clamps, holding her rooted. "Tell me what they said, Vonne," he ordered, a hard edge creeping into his tone. "They didn't like us being together, did they?"

Her shoulders jerked spasmodically. "No, they didn't," she answered in a small voice. "They didn't understand why I was with you. They said that you c-couldn't respect me because you don't have the same experiences I do."

Unconsciously, his grip tightened on her shoulders. "What else?"

Yvonne stared at his chest, conscious of its strength and solidity. She was overwhelmed with the need to press her cheek against that broad expanse and say it didn't matter.

But it did, and they both knew it. Yvonne didn't have to see his face to know he was getting angry. But if she continued, if she told him everything she had heard ...

"Michael..."

"Tell me. I want to know everything they said to you."

Defeated, she closed her eyes, unwilling to see his reaction. "They said that you were using me, that I'm an itch that you needed to scratch. A-and, when you got over the fever, you would dump me like yesterday's garbage, because that's what your people do to our people."

Silence. It was the type of silence that rings loudly in the ears, begs to be broken, and crawls agonizingly along.

A strangled sound, escaped him, his chin jerking as if she'd slapped him. She watched in horrified fascination as the olive color drained from his cheeks and was replaced by crimson. Oh my God, she marveled distantly. He's gonna explode.

She wasn't disappointed.

"Son of a bitch!" he burst out, causing her to jump despite herself. He pushed away from her to pace the room. "I don't friggin' believe this! I can't believe they even had the nerve to come up to you like that. I knew I should have popped their lights out when I had the chance! If I ever see those bastards again, so help me … "

He faded, aware that Yvonne had neither moved nor spoken. She stood forlornly in the middle of the room, her arms wrapped tightly about her.

"Vonne?" He stepped toward her, suddenly extremely cold.

She threw up a hand to stop him. "Do you think they were the only ones?" she demanded, her voice shivering with anger or tears or a mixture of both. "Two white women in the bathroom wanted to know why you'd pay me for a good time when they would do you for free! They thought I was a-a prostitute, Michael! Don't you see? It doesn't matter who they are. They're all saying the same thing!"

"And what is that?"

"That we don't belong together!"

Her words left him thunderstruck. "And you believe them? People who don't know us from Adam?"

Stormy eyes stared back at him. "You don't want a relationship, remember? You don't want to be used. You don't want to be needed. You just want to have a good, light-hearted romp. You and I both know this thing between us has no shelf life. After all, that's why we're together. And even if I-we- wanted more, we're too different. So quit your game. I'm not going to play along."

"Is that what you think?" he asked in barely restrained anger. "That I'm playing some kind of game?"

"Aren't you?"

Reeling, he spun away from her. "I don't believe this!" he exclaimed, thrusting his hand through his hair. "What the hell happened to make you think this? Things have been going fine between us. Now all of a sudden you can believe something like this of me?"

"What should I believe?" she cried, flinging her arms wide. "I've never experienced anything like this before! I was content. Hell, I was almost happy when I wasn't emotionally involved. And even if I wasn't content, at least it was familiar and I was accustomed to it!"

Eyes flashing with anger, she advanced on him. Her tone became accusatory as she jabbed a finger into his chest. "My life was going fine, and then—bam! There you are at the airport, intoxicating me with those debonair *GQ* looks of yours. How am I supposed to know what you want from me? I mean, really want?"

Incensed, Michael held his ground. "Know what I want? I want to be able to take you to clubs, movies, concerts—on a goddamn picnic—without you feeling uncomfortable, like we're doing something illegal!"

"I don't feel that way!"

"Don't you?" he retorted. "Why haven't you told Jeff about us? We went out to dinner with him and his date, and you wouldn't even take my hand! I feel proud to be seen with a beautiful, intelligent woman who is black. You seem embarrassed to be seen with me, you can't even admit to being with me, and now you've got it in your head that I'm playing some kind of game?"

The fight drained out of him as he locked his gaze on her. "Is that what you think, Vonne?" he asked her softly. "Can you really believe that of me?"

Yvonne opened her mouth to protest, but no sound came. She didn't know what to think. And how could she deny his words? Part of her wanted to dismiss her fears. But there was another part of her that wanted to believe it, was relieved to believe it, since it meant she could end this farce with him and be alone again.

Dazed from the realization, she slumped on the couch, putting her head in her hands.

"Jesus, Vonne," he whispered, the hurt so obvious in his voice that she winced. He sighed heavily, a defeated sound. "I thought we were beyond this. When I told you about Beth and you didn't run away, I thought we had something." He snorted sarcastically. "I guess that's what I get for thinking."

He turned away, then circled back. "Something happened to us. And I'm not talking about those idiots at the club. We were fine until I started questioning you about your past. You threw up a wall so fast I'm still dizzy. And now, now you want to take the word of people we don't know over mine. Are you trying to push me away?"

Mind constricted, she could only shake her head once, like a reprimanded child.

"Then what's the problem?" he bellowed, irate with her lack of response. "Will you talk to me?"

Yvonne struggled with the fear and confusion that threatened to suffocate her. Could she trust him? Could she let him into her world? Did she dare?

No, she didn't. Letting him into her world, really truly into her life, would be letting him into her heart. And that she couldn't allow.

Unfortunately for Yvonne, her silence struck Michael like physical blows. "It's pretty damned obvious that you don't trust me enough to open up to me. I can certainly take a hint."

She didn't, couldn't move, couldn't speak as he whistled for Cutter and took out his keys. "Since you're obviously not going to say anything, I'm going to leave before I say something I might regret."

He left then, the slamming of the door reverberating through her heart like it echoed through her home.

CHAPTER TWELVE

"Yvonne, either stop looking at that phone or use it!" Yvonne blinked rapidly. She was staring at the phone, and probably for the umpteenth time today. "I'm sorry, Brianne," she managed to smile. "I love this material. Can you get me a few hundred yards of this?"

Brianne laid the kente cloth on the desk. "You don't give a damn about the cloth," she said in her characteristically blunt way. "At least, not right now you don't. Have you created at least one new design in the past few days?"

Yvonne pushed back from her desk and stood up. "No," she admitted, tucking a strand of hair behind her ear. "I was too busy taking care of the girls. I haven't even thought about designing."

"The girls have been gone for what? Three days now. You haven't done a single new design?"

Yvonne shook her head. "No. My mind's been too cluttered."

Brianne swiveled in her chair. "May I ask why? On second thought, I'm not asking. I'm ordering you to tell me." Yvonne hesitated. Brianne leaned forward. "I'm a lawyer, remember? I don't violate attorney-client privilege, even with my darling husband. Besides, with Angela in New York, you need someone to talk to."

That was all the encouragement Yvonne needed. She told Brianne everything, leaving nothing out. The lawyer had taken Yvonne's notepad and scribbled notes on it. When Yvonne finished, they were silent for a moment. "Do you really think Mike is playing a game with you?" Brianne asked.

Yvonne leaned back in her chair with a tired sigh. "You tell me. You've known him longer. Is his reputation unearned?"

Brianne threw up a hand in surrender. "All right, so his past is less than savory," she admitted. "That doesn't mean that he can't change."

"Maybe you're right." Yvonne admitted grudgingly.

"Maybe?" Brianne echoed. "Yvonne, he's a changed man already. In all the years I've known him, I've never seen him act like this about a woman. You inspire him."

Yvonne toyed with the material. "Maybe I just inspire him to design new ways to torture and torment. I mean, what am I supposed to think about a man who swears he doesn't want a commitment, then plans to take my girls to Six Flags?"

"You should think that he wants to be a part of your life."

Yvonne shivered. "He doesn't. He can't. He has to have some other purpose. You know him better than I do. You know he hasn't stayed with one woman for more than a few months since his wife died. Part of me is glad of that, because it means I won't have to drive him away. But a part of me wishes he'd never leave."

"You want to drive him away?" Brianne asked, as if the idea was preposterous. And perhaps it was.

"He scares me," Yvonne whispered. "When I'm with him, I feel so many things. I feel like I'm breaking apart and being reassembled in a completely different way. I feel like he can shelter me from any storm. It frightens me how easily I lean on him when he's around. But when I'm not with him, it's like half my senses aren't working. All I can think of is seeing him again, getting that little jolt of recognition when he walks into the room."

"That doesn't sound like you want to drive him away," Brianne pointed out.

Yvonne returned to her chair. "I don't know what I want," she whispered. "It used to be so clear-cut: make my girls happy, make Gemini Enterprises a multimillion dollar company."

"What about making Yvonne happy?"

Yvonne waved her hand, dismissing the idea. "I haven't been happy in a long time. Oh, I've been glad, I've been satisfied, I've even been content—but happy?" She shook her head. "I don't even remember what happiness was like."

Brianne leaned forward, her dark eyes boring into the younger woman's. "I think what you're afraid of is the fact that Mike can make you happy. And he already has. But think about it. Is that really such a bad thing, being happy? Don't you think you deserve it?"

Yvonne lowered her eyes. She wished she could talk to Brianne, tell her everything. She had the feeling the prickly lawyer wouldn't offer cloying pity, something she absolutely detested. She'd had a lifetime of pity, a lifetime of guilt.

She firmly believed it was an accident that she survived when her family didn't. What happened afterward was proof of that. Why and how she had managed to survive the Dark Ages, she didn't know. She felt like she was living her life waiting for someone to realize their mistake. She was always afraid to enjoy herself too much, afraid to care too much, afraid to grow too attached. Her worst fear was to be stripped of everything she loved once more.

Maybe it was time to stop being afraid. Maybe it was time to stop believing she was cursed. "Maybe," she whispered. "Maybe I do deserve it."

Brianne stood. "No maybes about it," she said briskly. "If anyone deserves happiness, it's you and Mike."

"He does deserve happiness," Yvonne agreed. "But do you think that's necessarily with me? Do you really think he could want me in that way?"

Brianne looked at her in disbelief. "Haven't you looked in the mirror since you hit puberty?" she asked. "You're pretty— even with that haunted look in your eyes." She started to protest but the attorney cut her off. "I'm a prosecutor, remember? I know a victimized look when I see one. But getting back to Mike. Don't you notice the way he looks at you?"

She tried a nonchalant shrug. "I know I turn him on. I know we have great sex. But he said—"

"Don't think about what he said," Brianne advised. "Most men don't make sense anyway."

Yvonne smiled despite her mood. "But—"

"No. No more buts. You are good for him, and he's good for you. And I have a feeling he's sitting in his office as moon-eyed as you."

"Are you sure?"

"Doesn't my husband have to work with the man?" Brianne rolled her eyes and dragged Yvonne to her feet. "All right then. I want you to drive over there right now. I want you to march into his office, shut the door, and before he can say a word, take your blouse off. He won't care about a silly old argument after that. Oh, pick up a doughnut or two on the way."

"A doughnut?"

Brianne's smile was positively wicked. "You're a creative person. I'm sure you can discover lots of creative uses for a pastry with a useless hole in the middle."

Michael put the file down and rubbed his eyes. It was hard as hell to concentrate. All he could think of was Yvonne and how much he missed her. But he wouldn't call her first. After all, he wasn't wrong.

He sighed. You'd think he was the one with the problem, not her. Yet here he was, three days later, as hurt and confused now as he was then.

What was difficult about it, he wondered for the thousandth time. Yvonne either wanted to be with him or she didn't. And since she hadn't called or come by, that probably meant the latter.

Frustrated, he pushed away from his desk and began to pace. He couldn't accept the idea that Yvonne didn't want him. She couldn't fake the hunger in her eyes when he entered her, couldn't conceal the genuine pleasure of just being together. He made her happy, he even made her laugh. He was good for her. He knew it, why didn't she?

Their differences had never been an issue before. In fact, they had more in common than not, not the least being the similarity of their tragic pasts. They liked the same movies, the same restaurants. It was as if someone had decided it was time for him to move forward, to leave the pain of the past behind.

Unable to believe the path of his thoughts, he shook his head. But he had come to realize that even with Cutter there, his home—even his life—was empty. A vital energy was missing whenever Yvonne was not around. She had a way of lighting a room, of lighting his senses, that made her absences all the more poignant.

How could she think he was playing games with her? After all the time they spent together, after everything they had shared ...

Of course. Telling her about Beth had been the turning point. Yvonne had been uncomfortable with him after that, and when he started wondering about her past—a natural curiosity—she had backed away completely. Couldn't she understand his desire to know more about her? Surely she needed him as much as he needed her. Surely she knew that their relationship had already deepened beyond the boundaries they'd set for it.

A cold knot formed in the pit of his stomach as a new thought occurred to him. What if she knew how he felt? Maybe that was the cause of their problems. Maybe he was putting more and seeing more in the relationship than she did. Just the way he had with Beth.

"Hello, Michael."

Surprised, he looked up. Yvonne leaned against his now-closed door, stunning in a pale blue walking suit. He thought he heard his zipper creaking.

As casual as you please, she threw her briefcase on a chair, removed a bag of doughnuts, and started toward him. "Connie wasn't at her desk, so I let myself in," she said silkily, unfastening the gold buttons of her jacket.

"I also brought a peace offering. I hope you don't mind." She removed her jacket. "You don't have to meet with a client, do you?"

Speechless, he watched her drape the jacket over a chair. The bone-colored lace and sheer bustier she wore barely covered her nipples. He swallowed audibly. "No. Not for an hour."

A sensual goddess in the flesh, she stopped before him, one hand holding a fresh glazed doughnut, the other hand drifting to his zipper, which was opening on its own. "That should be enough time," she murmured. "Want to play ring around the rosy?"

He would never view a doughnut the same.

"You still haven't answered my question," Michael told her.

Yvonne, fully dressed again, looked at her reflection in a gold compact for any signs of icing. "What question?"

He took the compact from her. "Remember the conversation we had a few days ago?" he reminded her. "I asked if you were uncomfortable or embarrassed to be seen with me."

She rolled her eyes with a here-we-go-again sigh. "Michael, we just had the best sex ever! That makes your question irrelevant, don't you think?"

"I think it's a very relevant question, and I don't care how many orgasms you just had," he retorted. "You can't expect me to just fuck and forget!"

She winced at his choice of words then folded her arms. "I thought you had a meeting to go to."

"I lied."

Nonplussed, she stared at him. This was not going the way she or Brianne planned. She didn't know whether to hate him or launch herself at him again. "What do you want from me?"

"You know what I want. The truth. I want you to answer my question."

"The answer to your question is no," she said stonily, looking very much like a hostile witness in a trial.

He unfolded his arms and shoved away from his desk. "Then what's the deal? Why the hell is there this wall between us now?"

"Why can't you just drop it?" she asked, bolting from her chair.

Undaunted, he bore down on her. "Ignoring it won't solve it. We won't be able to go forward if we don't settle this. So answer me this question: do you think I'm using you?"

Yvonne was suddenly very interested in the pattern of Michael's carpet. She wondered what his cleaning crew would make of the stiff stain in the middle of it. She had come to his office to show him that she wanted to believe him, that she wanted to try to move forward. But the doubt she felt still lingered, and strengthened itself by feeding on the wounds her heart already carried.

"You know, the last time you didn't answer me I jumped to the conclusion that you did believe I was using you. Correct me if I'm wrong or tell me I'm right, but don't leave me hanging like this."

Yvonne stared at him. He just stood there, huge, strong, and vulnerable. At that moment, with blinding, earth-shattering clarity, she knew that she loved him. He made her complete, filled her heart and soul more than her twin had. She needed and loved him so desperately everything else paled in comparison. The knowledge filled her with agony and fear.

Tears crept from her eyes and the only answer she could give him was, "I don't know."

"You don't know?" he repeated, incredulous. Then his expression clamped down. "I see."

"No, you don't see!" she exclaimed, her heart pounding at his expression. But how could she explain the fear that lived inside her, a fear she had never shared with anyone?

Yet deep down she knew, if she could find a way to explain, Michael would be able to take the pain away, and she wouldn't have to be afraid, or lonely, anymore.

She became aware that he was speaking. "...thought we could trust each other, but I was wrong. And stupid." He turned away.

A lump jumped into Yvonne's throat and the fear enveloped her like a fog. "Mi—Michael, I ..." love you, she wanted to say, but her mouth couldn't form the words.

He shook his head, leaning against his desk as if for support. "It's strange, that you would accuse me of using you when it's actually the other way around. You're using me."

"Me?" she squeaked, filling with horror. "I'm using you?"

His smile was bitter. "The ironic thing is, you don't even realize it. First you were a friend, then a client, then a partner, finally a lover. When you needed a ride, I was there. When you needed business advice, I was there. When you needed liquid assets to expand, I footed the bill. When you needed creative inspiration, I gave it to you. When you needed someone to warm your sheets, I was there again. And yes, Yvonne, you used that, used me, to your advantage." He turned his face away. "Just like Beth did."

Numb with shock, she sank into the closest chair. Did he really believe that she was using him? And treating him as callously as his late wife did? Looking in his eyes, she saw the answer clearly.

Her heart sank, and with it, hope. He was right. All she had done was take from him: his time, his talent, his money, his body. What had she given him in return? A stupid robe he probably never wore.

The shock dissipated, to be replaced by anger. "How dare you pretend that you're an innocent party in this?" she seethed, getting to her feet as if preparing for battle. "You're not just a damned spectator in this farce!"

"What the hell are you talking about?"

She crossed the room, stopping in front of him. "I'm talking about the truth. That's what you're after, isn't it?"

"Of course."

"Well, I've got news for you, Mr. Righteous!" Her hand strayed to her hip. "We're using each other!"

He was off his desk like a shot, his eyes glinting. "Now, wait just a f—"

"Oh, don't look at me as if you're surprised," she cut in, her voice cold. "You've been getting revenge on the female population for what Beth did to you for the past ten years! You figured you'd pay her back, as if it mattered, like you were owed it.

"How many women have you had since Beth died? How many did you leave when they started falling in love with you? How many did you use and toss aside? Two? Four? One a month?"

She gripped her necklace so tightly her hand trembled. "Maybe I did use you—and I'm sorry as hell that I did. But it was a two-way street, sweetheart. Or did you forget that you now own stock in my company? Did you forget the ideas I gave you for BBC contracts? Did you forget that I gave you my virginity?

"While you're remembering all that, let me add something else. Did you forget how adamant you were about having a no-strings relationship? Did you forget that this is only about sex? Why should you care what anyone thinks of us? There is no us!"

She balled her hands into fists, fighting to keep the anger under control. But the anger felt good; anything was better than the anguish that throbbed through her. When she spoke again, her voice was flat and frozen, a barren wasteland.

"Since I'm answering your questions, Michael, answer a few of mine. How long were you going to toy with me? When were you going to tire of this game? How long before you dump me like yesterday's garbage?"

He was silent, and she knew he couldn't—wouldn't—give her any answers. The knowledge was like a knife in her heart, slicing open old scars. But there was one thing she could give him, the one thing he wanted most of all.

With an iron will that she'd utilized for years, she wrapped her wounded spirit about her. "You don't have to answer," she whispered. "I know you don't know what you want. Strings or no strings? Deep or superficial? I know, I'm asking a lot of questions. Questions you don't want to find the answers to. But I'll make it easy for you, Michael. Somehow strings got attached to this relationship, but I'm cutting them. Now."

She quickly gathered her belongings and walked to the door. "Don't forget to put another notch in your bedpost."

She was proud of herself. She made it all the way to the parking garage before bursting into tears.

CHAPTER THIRTEEN

Michael sat on his deck, a lukewarm, still full beer in his hand. The television was tuned to a basketball playoff game, but he wasn't aware of the teams, much less the score. Cutter lay at his feet, occasionally glancing worriedly at his master between dog naps.

Jeff was somewhere near Wall Street, schmoozing a very big client. It was a well-known secret that Angela was also in New York, meeting with several textile designers. They were due to return next week, a couple of days apart. Thom and Brianne had taken the weekend off in South Carolina to celebrate her victory in a major trial. He was keeping to his house, staying near the phone.

Just in case.

The "just in case" was Yvonne getting in touch with him to put the shattered pieces of their relationship back together. He had wanted to follow her when she left his office, but a client had come in, one he couldn't put off. By the time he was free, Yvonne had disappeared. She wasn't at any of the stores, the phones in her car and home went unanswered, and Lawrence, if he knew anything, was being extremely closemouthed.

He should have been relieved. He and Yvonne were getting too close. He had made a huge mistake, asking her for commitment. He shouldn't have let it go as far as it did, but he was like a man stranded in a desert, and Yvonne the only oasis.

He was alone.

A dejected sigh escaped him. He hadn't been assaulted by this kind of loneliness in years. Not since Beth's death.

He shifted in his chair, eyes staring blankly at the television. Would there ever come a time when he would not think of her? He had loved her, albeit unwillingly. He had loved her and she used him. And while her memory and his love for her had faded, the wounds his wife inflicted hadn't. He was jaded and terrified of giving his heart to another woman. He had done a remarkable job of avoiding emotional involvement and still getting what he wanted from them.

But the moment he'd laid eyes on Yvonne he knew he was in trouble. Against rationality, he had fallen for her. Hard. Like a ton of bricks down a greased hill. That was what really had him freaked. The ease with which he had allowed himself to be engulfed shocked him.

And scared him to death.

It was out of an instinctively male need for self-preservation that he had lashed out, accusing her of using him. He had wanted Yvonne to deny it, to alleviate his fears and set him on an even keel again.

But he had chosen an inopportune time. He realized that now. Obviously, she was unsure of the foundation of their relationship. She had needed reassurance too, and he hadn't given her any.

He wanted Yvonne to trust him, wanted her to admit that they meant more to each other than casual sex. He wanted her to share all of herself with him, not just her body. She had spurned every attempt he'd made to get close to her. Why?

Michael knew he wouldn't get any answers sitting on his deck. Somehow, he had to get through the walls she'd erected around her. To do that, he had to see her.

He called for Cutter and left, forming and discarding ideas as he went. The chirping of his cell phone startled him. "Hello?" he demanded breathlessly, hope constricting his lungs.

Hope died a quick death. "Mike Benjamin?" a female voice asked.

"Yes?"

The voice on the other end sighed with relief. "This is Gwen Cheveneau, Yvonne's partner."

The hairs on the back of his neck stood on end. "What's happened?"

"Nothing yet."

"What do you mean, yet?"

"I've been having dreams," Gwen confessed. "They aren't very straightforward. I see Yvonne surrounded by flowers, then darkness, in what looks like a cemetery, only she's trapped. The only one who can rescue her is you, if you choose to do it."

"I'm almost at her house now," he said, avoiding the question in Gwen's last statement. "Is she there?"

"I left her and Lawrence there about half an hour ago," she answered. "Mike?"

He pulled over, relieved to see Yvonne's Volvo in her drive. "Yes, Gwen?"

Gwen's voice was quiet. "No matter what she says, Yvonne does need you. I hope you'll be there for her."

"I'll try," he promised, and disconnected. Gripping the steering wheel, he sighed heavily. He wondered if he would be able to fulfill the promise he'd made to Gwen. He certainly hadn't done a good job of being there for Yvonne so far. Still, he would try.

Decisively, he exited his car and went up the walk, Cutter bounding ahead of him. Determination rang in every step he took. Even if she threw him out afterwards, things would be settled between them. One way or another.

Yvonne threw down her pencil and picked up her wineglass instead. Her nerves had been so frazzled all day that when Lawrence suggested Chardonnay to calm her down, she had readily accepted. Two glasses later she was still on edge, and not one new design had come to her.

She knew why. No matter how she concentrated, her mind always came back to Michael. The memory of how she had left him made her sick to her stomach. The fact that he didn't come after her made her sick to her soul. How was it that she had managed to fall in love, and with the one person she shouldn't?

His accusation that she was like his wife rang in her ears, burning her. It was obvious that he would never feel the way she felt, not if he could think that of her.

Weary in heart and mind, she reached for the phone. Whenever she was hurt or confused, there was one person she could call who could help her make everything better.

It rang beneath her hand. "Hello?"

"Yvonne! Thank God!" It was Melissa Calhoun, her foster sister.

Her stomach seized into a frigid knot. "Wh— what's happened, Melissa?"

"Vonne, oh God, Vonne—"

She knew what her foster-sister would say. "No…" It was such a weak sound.

"Dad … Dad had a heart attack during practice," Melissa was crying. "They tried t-to revive him but he-he didn't make it."

Yvonne closed her eyes as the pain assaulted her like physical blows. She shook beneath the tumult. "Oh, God, Melissa," she whispered. I should have been there, she thought to herself.

The receiver slipped from her clammy fingers. She unexpectedly felt very cold. Darkness swirled around her, threatening suffocation. Poppy, Poppy … Suddenly she was thirteen again, paralyzed with fear and pain and loneliness.

Sinking to the floor, she curled into a fetal ball, staring blindly ahead. James "Poppy" Calhoun had been more than her coach, much more than her mentor. He was her savior, her surrogate father. When everyone else, everything else, was gone, he had been there. His love—indeed, the love of his entire family—had gone a long way in helping her face the world again.

It wasn't even a week ago that she'd spoken to him. The conversation started as it always did.

"So when's my Birdie coming home to roost?"

"Poppy, you don't need me getting in your way or Jimmy's," she said, referring to his son, James Junior, who was assisting Poppy at the Meadowcreek Skating facility just north of Detroit. "Besides, all your skaters are better than I am."

"You could still skate on the professional tour. They ask me about you all the time. Look at Rory Flack Burkhart and Dorothy Hamill. Even Debi Thomas is thinking of putting her skates back on, and she's older than you."

"Poppy ... " She knew he always wanted her to achieve the final glory of Olympic gold, but after Uncle Reg died, her heart just wasn't into competition anymore. Now she only skated for exercise and the sheer joy of being on the ice.

"I know, Birdie," Poppy's voice intruded on her thoughts. "You're busy being a business bigshot and a Camp Mother." He paused. "Speaking of motherhood, how are you and that guy of yours?"

Yvonne had laughed at his none-too-subtle question. "Michael's fine, Poppy. We're getting along well— becoming the best of friends."

Poppy's snort almost made her laugh again. She could hear him muttering under his breath, "First guy she calls and talks about, and they're just friends."

Aloud he said, "Why don't you bring him up with you next week? Grace would like to meet him."

Meaning, Poppy wanted to take the measure of the man who had captured his Birdie. She remembered how he had been when Melissa brought Steve home the first time. It was a wonder he wasn't scared off.

"I don't know how his schedule is, Poppy, but I'll ask him." She didn't want to make any promises on Michael's behalf. She knew there wasn't a future for them, but she didn't want to tell Poppy just yet.

"Birdie." Poppy's voice became serious.

"Yes, Poppy?"

"I know you had to get away from Michigan. Grace and I, we didn't take it personally. But we—I—want you to know that we love you and we're proud of what you've done for yourself, proud you let us be a family for you. And when the time comes, well, I'd be honored to walk you down the aisle."

"Oh, Poppy … " Her eyes filled with tears. She had never known what they'd made of her abrupt decision to move to Atlanta. It felt good to know he wasn't disappointed that she didn't compete again.

As if reading her mind, he added on a lighter note, "And don't forget to bring your blades. It brings joy to this old heart to see you fly over the ice."

"You're not old, you can still move with the best of them," she laughed. "I love you, Poppy. I'll see you next week."

It was the last thing she'd said to him. There were so many other things that needed saying. Now she would never get the chance.

She huddled tightly on the floor, her mind a pain-filled fog. If she could just stay there, unmoving, perhaps the pain and cold and darkness would leave her bones.

Who was she trying to fool? The pain would never leave. The pain was a constant reminder that she had no right to hopes and dreams of love. Everyone she had ever loved had been taken from her. Poppy's death was fate's way of telling her that she had no right to be happy.

A cold nose bumped her shoulder; she barely felt it, she was so desensitized. She reached out blindly, wrapping her arms about the comforting bulk of the shepherd. Her breath wheezed in and out like a bellows. She concentrated on the sound, the act, for it kept the roiling darkness of her grief away. Breathe, breathe, how she longed to stop breathing.

"Yvonne?"

If Cutter was there, of course his master was as well. She didn't know why he was there, why she wasn't surprised that he was. "Leave me." Her plea was barely a whisper.

Michael sat beside her. "I can't do that, sweetheart," he gently refused. "I promised Melissa that I'd make sure you got home okay."

"I don't need you."

Michael closed his eyes, trying to fend off the pain her words caused him. "I know," he said tightly, "and I don't blame you for wanting me gone. I said some awful things to you, and I wish like hell I could take them back. I wish I could take your pain and carry it myself. I can't do that, but I can be here for you now. You don't have to go through this alone, Yvonne. Do you hear me? You are not alone."

She turned to look at him, and the desolate look in her eyes caused his heart to thump painfully. "I wish that was true," she said lifelessly. "I really wish I could make myself believe that."

"You can."

She took a deep breath, closing her eyes. She clenched her trembling hands into fists so tight her nails drew blood. He watched as she struggled to control her emotions, wondering how she could cope with the loss of yet another loved one.

She wouldn't be able to cope with this. She could feel her carefully erected defenses crumbling about her. It had taken her fifteen years to regain a sense of normalcy. Fifteen years to evolve from that sad, scarred teen that everyone alternately pitied and admired to a successful and outwardly serene woman. Fifteen years she'd spent erecting the barrier that kept the frigid darkness away, a barrier that had withstood the death of her uncle, her father's twin. Fifteen years, and now it was beginning to disintegrate.

Hands took her shoulders and helped her to a sitting position. Cutter licked her face until she absently petted him. She felt limp, like a forgotten ragdoll. Her movements were slow, as if she were drugged. She welcomed the dullness. Anything to keep from feeling. That way lay madness.

His face swam fuzzily into view. "Can you do this?"

No, she wanted to scream, but the feeling part of her was locked away. Instead she said, "Auntie Grace and Melissa need me."

Lawrence came into the room, carrying a suitcase. "I booked a flight for you, leaving within the hour," he said. "I'll let Gwen and Angela know where you are."

Yvonne got to her feet, her movements automatic. Lawrence handed the suitcase to Michael. "I booked the flight for two," he explained, his dark eyes bright with tears. "I'll take care of Cutter for you."

"Thanks." Michael turned to her. "Ready?"

No, she wasn't ready, she'd never be ready. She finished her wine, forcing her hand to be steady, her voice calm. Inside she was screaming. "Let's go."

They left Cutter with Lawrence and went by Michael's so that he could quickly pack a case. The trip to Detroit was uneventful. She spent the majority of the journey in stoic silence, giving monosyllabic answers to his questions. In fact, she didn't show any emotion at all until they got to their rental car.

"Where to?" he asked, putting their cases into the trunk.

She paused by the passenger door, her hand trembling on the hood of the car. "I want to go to my house first," she answered shakily. "If you don't mind driving, I'll give you directions."

"You have a house here?"

Yvonne nodded, not looking at him. She had a whole life here, one very few people knew about. By the cruelest quirk of fate, Michael was going to be made privy to that life. "My family's house, where I lived until the accident. We could go to a hotel, if you prefer."

Her tone was so polite it was stiff, and her back was defiantly straight. Somehow, Michael thought, he had to get her to bend. Yvonne needed to release the grief held hostage inside her before it consumed her. Perhaps, surrounded by mementos of her past, she could begin to exorcise her pain. Besides, he was curious to see the home were Yvonne spent the first thirteen years of her life. "I'd like to see your home."

The Mitchelson home was an imposing two story brick in the traditional style. For a long time Yvonne sat gazing out the window, clearly remembering parts of her youth. She had never spoken of her monthly trips out of town; he wondered if this was where she came.

Before he could ask her, she spoke. "My Uncle Reg made sure to pay the mortgage off so that I could keep it or sell it as I chose," she explained as she got out of the car. "I couldn't bear to part with it, and now it's my second home."

He retrieved their suitcases and followed Yvonne up the walk and inside. Hardwood floors gleamed up at them in a living room and den furnished in large oak pieces and earth tones, brightened by thick Persian carpets.

"It's a beautiful place," he said into the quiet, moving to a glass étagère in one corner of the living room. Its shelves were full of photos and trophies, testimonies of the full life the Mitchelsons had shared.

Yvonne's parents had been a beautiful couple; it was obvious that they loved each other, and their daughters, very much. There were photos of skating meets, Christmases, family reunions featuring the entire Mitchelson clan, and even photos of Mardi Gras.

The differences in Yvonne's houses were striking. This house, this rambling, four-bedroom structure, was where she truly lived. There was a vibrancy, a sense of home here, that the Atlanta townhouse didn't have. Michael could sense the ghosts of emotions past and present in every corner.

Yvonne appeared beside him, handing him a drink. "It was a long time before I was able to come back," she said softly. "Actually, I didn't step foot in this house for four years, not until after the Nationals were over. It-it felt like, once I could keep that promise to my family, I could let them go."

She straightened a small photo, swallowing audibly. "It was hard to decide what to do with everything. Even though Uncle Reg had boxed a lot of things up, I had to go through it all, and I had to do it by myself."

"I understand." And he did. Gathering Beth's things after she died had been an ordeal.

"Of course, during the Championships, Uncle Reg got sick," she said in a small, tight voice. She stared blindly ahead. "He died right after I got home. It was so damn difficult—Uncle Reg was my dad's twin. But I had Poppy. He helped me so much. He had three other championship skaters, but he always took time for me. Just last week, he told me I would always be a daughter to him, and he-he said, he said ..." She swallowed. "He said he would be honored to walk me down the aisle one day."

She trembled so violently she was in danger of dropping her glass. He took her drink away. "God, you're freezing!"

He guided her to the sofa, wrapping the afghan around her and making her take a hefty sip of his drink. "You need to rest, you've been through hell—"

She shook her head, her eyes wide and dry. "I can't. Auntie Grace and Melissa need me. I-I gotta go."

The shrill ring of the telephone interrupted her. Yvonne pulled free of his hold and answered it.

It was Angela. "Vonne, Gwen told me what happened. Are you okay?"

She sank deeper into the couch. "Fine. How are the negotiations going?"

"Screw the negotiations! I don't think anyone will mind if I cut them short to come to Detroit."

"There's no need for you to do that."

"But we want to be there for you!"

Yvonne sighed. Suddenly people who wanted to be there for her surrounded her, and all she wanted to do was be alone. "Angela, I appreciate it, but this deal is important. New York is where I need you, not here. Besides, I'll be spending all my time with Grace and the family."

As she expected, Jeff got on the phone. "Vonne, are you okay?"

If someone asks me if I'm okay one more time … Still, the concern in his voice almost brought the grief breaking through her barriers. Automatically she pushed it away. "I'll be fine," she assured him woodenly. "If you recall, I have more than enough experience with this sort of thing. I can handle it."

"You shouldn't be alone at a time like this."

Sighing, she closed her eyes. She wanted to be alone, needed to be alone. She didn't want anyone to witness the upcoming battle she faced with her fear and grief and the darkness that was always waiting, ready to pounce.

She looked toward Michael, who slumped in an armchair. He looked despondent. She wondered if it was because of their arguments or the circumstances, but she didn't have the time or the energy to figure it out. She had to get him to leave, but for now she needed him here, if only to keep Jeff and Angela away.

"I'm not alone," she finally said. "Michael's here with me."

There was a strangled sound on the other end. "Mike's there now?"

She felt Michael's intense stare weighing heavily on her, but ignored it. Now was not the time to tell Jeff about her relationship with his best friend. Besides, there was nothing to tell, since it was falling apart anyway. "Yes. He was at the townhouse with me and Lawrence when I got the call."

After a heavy silence, Jeff said, "Vonne, I know now is not the time, but I want you to promise to be on guard with Mike. He's my friend, but when it comes to women, he's not exactly a Boy Scout."

High-strung, she gripped the receiver tightly, her fingernails digging into her palm. "You're right, Jeff," she ground out. "Now is not the time. I really don't need a lecture right now."

"I'm sorry, Vonne," Jeff apologized, his voice roughening. "I can't help worrying about you. I love you."

A painful smile twisted her lips. "Ever the big brother, trying to protect me. But if you want to do me a favor, stay in New York with Angela. She's got my corporate card—take her to a show or something. I'll see you guys at home next week. Okay?"

Jeff sighed. "All right, we'll stay. Let me talk to Mike."

"I'm going to freshen up," she informed Michael as she handed the receiver over. She retrieved her case and her drink. "You can use the room at the top of the stairs on the left. Help yourself to anything in the kitchen, it's through those double doors."

Jeff wasted no time when Michael got on the line. "What are you doing there? Why did she choose you to go with her and not me or Angela?"

"She didn't choose me," he explained, wondering why he had to explain anything. "Like she said, I happened to be at her house when her foster-sister called. She didn't want me to come with her either, but I didn't think she should come up alone."

"Well, you can probably help her, since you've been where she is before," Jeff said grudgingly. "But if you hurt her, I swear to God, I'll … "

"Why would I hurt her?"

"You forget who you're talking to." Jeff's voice was cold. "I've seen you in action, remember? I know you haven't been out with anyone since that model left you. And I also know it's not your style to go this long without a woman. Yvonne's in a vulnerable place right now, and I'm warning you—"

"I have no intentions of hurting her." Michael interrupted, a hard edge creeping into his tone. "Right now, I want to help her get through the next couple of days."

Jeff was instantly contrite. "Look, Mike, I'm sorry. I just … oh, hell." He cleared his throat. "Is she really okay?"

Michael was wondering the same thing himself. "I don't know," he answered honestly. "She hasn't cried since she heard the news, not once. She's keeping everything bottled up inside."

"If she doesn't let it out, she's going to explode."

"I know that, but she's not talking to me."

"What did you do?"

Michael didn't answer. He didn't want Jeff to kick his butt from Detroit to Atlanta. Instead he said, "Have you ever tried to get something out of Yvonne when she doesn't want to talk? It's easier to break into Fort Knox!"

"I know. Believe me, I know. I'm just worried about her."

"So am I."

Jeff sighed. "Well, I-I'm glad … " His voice faltered. "I'm glad you're there. Take care of her for me, all right?"

"I'll do my best," Michael promised solemnly, and hung up. That made four people who had entrusted him with Yvonne's well being. It was ironic that he was the last person she wanted beside her. If she had her way, she would endure this as she had endured all her tragedies: alone.

Her whole life had been a struggle. If he could take some of the pain, bear it for her, he would do it gladly. But for some reason, she was pushing him away. He remembered how calmly she had tossed his words back at him, about not wanting to be used. He still needed to apologize for that. But would she accept his apology, or tell him to get lost?

"I'm going to Auntie Grace."

He looked up. She had changed into a muted navy ensemble, her hair loose about her shoulders. Her eyes had a dark, haunted look that chance had given her no time to erase. He knew he would give anything to make her smile.

He got to his feet and looped an arm around her shoulders. "Just consider me your shadow, with you every step of the way."

She looked up at him, her eyes dark but dry. "You don't have to do this, Michael. I'm sure there's a lot of stuff back in Atlanta that needs your attention."

Did she really believe he could leave her at a time like this, that he could leave her at all? "Nothing's more important than you," he finally said, his voice soft. "You need me."

It was true. She needed him as she had never needed anyone else. She needed his warmth and strength, needed the broad shoulders and large hands. She needed the soft timbre of his voice, the spicy musk of his scent, the golden glint of his eyes. She needed to believe he was here because he cared for her and wanted to protect her. She needed to keep him with her for as long as she could, and when he finally left, she would try to keep her heart from breaking.

She put her hand in his. "Thank you."

He gave it a reassuring squeeze. "You're always welcome, Vonne. Always."

CHAPTER FOURTEEN

The Calhouns lived north of Detroit, not far from the Meadowcreek Skating Facility they ran. Their residence was overflowing with friends and family members. Several were teens, all skaters, who greeted Yvonne with the warmth and awe of star-struck fans. She greeted them all politely, swimming through the mass of bodies with Michael in tow, until she came to the couch in the center of the room. Two women stood up as she ran to them, hugging them tightly.

Michael watched as people surrounded the trio, giving them comforting touches as they could. A minute twinge of jealousy snaked through him. Yvonne was right; she didn't need him. She had a massive support group of friends and family that obviously cared for her just as much as they did the Calhouns.

Then she was reaching for him, introducing him to her foster mother and sister. Grace Calhoun was a slender woman with the long legs and carriage of a dancer. Her dark hair was streaked with gray at the temples, the only indication of her age. Melissa, her daughter, was her younger mirror image.

"I'm glad you came with Yvonne," Grace Calhoun said. "She's spoken so much about you. It's a pleasure to finally meet you in person. I just wish the circumstances were different."

Yvonne began to apologize again. "I'm sorry I wasn't here, Auntie Grace ... "

Grace cupped her hands around Yvonne's cheeks. "There was nothing any of us could have done, Birdie. The attack was so sudden. We were at Meadowcreek when it happened. Jimmy was where he wanted to be, doing what he loved most."

She gave her foster-daughter a watery smile. "So don't berate yourself over this. Jimmy wouldn't want that."

"Okay," Yvonne nodded, swallowing audibly. Michael put his arms around her shoulders and she leaned into him gratefully. Grace looked from one to the other, missing nothing.

"Birdie, go talk to the girls. They were talking about having a memorial service at Meadowcreek after—the day after tomorrow. I think they can use your support. 'Lissa, will you get some more refreshments? I sent James Junior and Steve to the store, but I don't think they're back yet. Mr. Benjamin can keep me company."

They watched as the group of skaters engulfed Yvonne. Grace led Michael to a small den, away from the subdued crowd in the main room. She gestured him to the couch and took the seat opposite. "Tell me truthfully, how is Yvonne handling this?"

"Badly." He leaned forward, hooking his hand over his knees. "She hasn't cried, not once. I want to help her, but I can't even get her to tell me what happened fifteen years ago."

Grace nodded sadly. "It's hard for her to share herself. It's not because she's selfish—I'm sure you know how she donates much of her time and money to charity, something she learned from her mother. But she keeps her private self private."

"I know." He couldn't keep the bitterness from his voice, and felt guilty because of it.

As if reading his thoughts, Grace asked, "Would you like to see our photo albums?"

"I'd love too." He was starving for details of Yvonne's life.

For the next half hour Grace took Michael on a tour of Yvonne's life. He saw her as a five-year-old on ice, and as a thirteen-year-old junior champion beside her family and coach. It was eerie, seeing the little girl in matching pigtails who was her twin. It was obvious from the photographs that the sisters adored each other.

"Yvonne and her sister were naturals on the ice," Grace said. "They were an instant attraction on the junior circuit; there were only three or four other black skaters and no twins. When they swept the top spots at nationals, the future seemed bright."

She dabbed her eyes with a tissue, her hands shaking. "The accident happened the same night Yvonne won the championship. Jimmy and I had gone ahead, and the girls were coming back home with their parents. A tractor-trailer rammed into them, flipping their station wagon several times before it landed on its roof. Because it was a rural road, it was hours before someone discovered the wreckage. Yvonne tried to crawl for help, but between the wreckage and broken glass, her legs were paralyzed. She had to endure the sounds of her parents and sister dying before help arrived."

The blood drained from Michael's face. There was no way to imagine how Yvonne suffered that night. It was no wonder she didn't want to discuss it.

"The accident took a terrible toll on her," Grace said quietly as they flipped through the album. "Her life, her whole world, revolved around her family and her skating. Having both snatched away from her so cruelly ... it broke her."

Grace dabbed her eyes again. "I shouldn't be telling you this," she said, her voice warbled. "It's not my place."

Michael clasped her free hand. "Please, Grace, I need to know."

The older woman stared at him for an interminable moment, her blue eyes shiny with tears. "Yvonne is proof that a good heart can overcome almost any obstacle. But it wasn't easy for her. She was just a child, a poor, devastated little girl. Losing her family, and her ability to skate, she didn't think she had a reason to live anymore."

A chill went down Michael's spine as he realized what she meant. "No."

Grace nodded, her eyes filling with tears again. "She was extremely traumatized. Every night in her dreams she would relive the accident and wake up screaming. Her mental and physical pain was too much for her. In her mind, it was the best option, and she would be with her family again."

Michael was stunned. It was difficult to imagine the Yvonne he knew, the poised, successful businesswoman, as a frightened child contemplating suicide. "What happened?" he managed to ask.

Grace lowered her head, shredding her tissue. "Th-they placed her in psychiatric care, and sedated her to stave off the nightmares. She-she lost touch with herself, with everything. Jimmy and I, and her Uncle Reginald, took turns staying by her side, waiting for her to recognize us.

"Her mind, body, and heart were broken. Her body healed first. When the doctors told us that her paralysis wasn't permanent, we knew it was the lifeline Yvonne needed to come back to us. And slowly she did."

She ran slender fingers over a photo. "But she shut her heart away. There was so much sadness in her that it broke my heart. No child should have to go through what she endured. I knew we couldn't replace what she lost, but she and Yvette had spent so much time with us that we were the closest thing to an extended family that she had."

In a quiet voice Grace described the nightmare of physical therapy. "There were days when she came home in tears of pain and frustration, too tired to even eat. Yet she would still wake up each morning ready to endure it again.

"After about a year, she was able to walk unaided. She wanted me to teach her to dance, to be graceful again. I wanted to go easy on her, but she wouldn't let me. So I pushed her as I would any student. She fell down more than she stayed up, but she refused to quit. Finally, four years after she left the hospital, she was ready."

Grace turned the album toward Michael. Yvonne as an eighteen-year-old was pretty and determined, with eyes old beyond their years. Some of the pictures showed a tall, distinguished looking black man standing with her.

"That's Reginald Mitchelson. He was her father's twin. For a while, Yvonne had stayed with him and his family, but she decided it would be best to live with us. She never said, but I think her aunt and cousins were uncomfortable with her.

"Her uncle had cancer. He didn't want Yvonne to know until after the competition was over. But she qualified for the World Championships. When she was skating the performance of her life, he was lying in a hospital bed here, watching.

"She put her everything into that performance. It brought the house to their feet. She went straight to Jimmy; they were both crying. I don't think there was a dry eye in the facility. Some people actually booed when she only placed bronze, but it was more than we had hoped for. She said she was skating for her family and for Jimmy, to honor them."

Grace closed the photo album. "That was her last performance. By the time we got back home, her uncle was dying. He died two days later."

Michael took the album, flipping through the photos again. "She blames herself, for all the people she's lost."

Grace sighed. "Yes. And now she'll blame herself, for Jimmy." She swallowed hard. "We talked to her about a week ago. She comes home once a month, and she was supposed to come next week. We were hoping she was going to bring you along."

Michael looked at her in surprise. "She never told me that."

"I'm not surprised. It's hard for her to let anyone in. We thought she was determined to be alone. That's why we were happy when she mentioned you. We really wanted to meet the man who could make Yvonne laugh."

Grace's eyes glittered with unshed tears. "I think Jimmy would have liked you. You really seem to care about our little girl."

"I love her." The admission surprised him. "God help me, she's almost a complete mystery to me, but I do love her."

"I can see it in your eyes when you watch her," she said quietly. "Does Yvonne know?"

Michael shook his head. "I don't think she could. I just realized it myself. And there's been so much going on … "

Grace gazed at him evenly. "You know it's not going to be easy."

"I know." It wasn't easy now. "So you don't mind that I'm not black?"

Grace reached over and clasped his hand. "You love Yvonne. That means more to me than anything. But if I can give you a word of advice, it's this: Jimmy and I wasted four years after we first met. No one thought a hockey player and a ballerina could find common ground, much less fall in love. We had thirty-five glorious years together, but I would give anything to have those first years back.

"Yvonne has a natural ability to love; her tragedy has all but eradicated it. Give her time," she whispered tearfully, "but don't wait too long to tell her how you feel. Love is precious, and life is much too short."

Michael gripped her hands. "I know. And I will. Thank you for giving me some answers."

"Mom."

They both looked up when Melissa poked her head into the room. "What is it?"

Melissa's face was streaked with tears. "Yvonne. She's sitting in the dark in our old bedroom, just rocking back and forth and moaning. I tried to get her to talk to me, but she wouldn't. I-I think she's drunk."

CHAPTER FIFTEEN

Yvonne hugged her knees tightly, rocking back and forth on the floor of her old room. She was fighting a losing battle and she knew it. Agony battered at her paltry defenses, crumbling them inexorably. The agony and grief would soon give way to the cold and darkness of madness. Even now she could feel the icy fingers of blackness reaching for her, claiming her. Her only hope was to numb the pain as best she could.

She reached out, fumbling for the bottle beside her. A part of her mind screamed, demanding that she stop. The sane, sober part. But that voice grew smaller with each heartbeat.

A light came on, shattering the darkness of the room. She heard a sob, then someone was beside her. "Birdie, what are you doing?"

Auntie Grace. "I'm sorry, I didn't mean to kill him, I swear to God, I didn't mean for Poppy to die."

Her foster-mother's face swam in her vision. "Honey, it's not your fault."

"Oh yes, it is," she argued. "I love you and Poppy and Melissa and Junior with all my heart. I tried so hard to be good, so I wouldn't be a burden on you. I tried not to love you, tried to never tell you. I knew that if I did, if I told any of you how much I care, I would damn you. Just like Mom and Dad and Vette, I told them that I loved them, right before we got in the car. Just like Uncle Reg, before I was skating again. And last week on the phone, I told Poppy I loved him, and now he's gone."

Grace shuddered and buried her face in her hands. Melissa wrapped her arms about her mother. As Yvonne watched her foster-sister comfort Grace, she felt something inside her shrivel and die. The last of her hopes. She had frightened and hurt them, these people who knew everything about her and cared for her anyway, people she would gladly give her life for.

She reached out a hand, but was afraid to touch them. Afraid of being shunned and rejected. "Oh, Grace," she whispered in pain, "I-I'm sorry, I'm so sorry ... "

She moved away from them, only to bump into Michael. He put his arms around her. "Vonne, please don't do this to yourself. It's not your fault. It isn't anyone's fault."

Yvonne tried to crawl away from him, but he pulled her back. "Leave me alone!"

"I can't do that, sweetheart. I promised our friends that I would take care of you, and I intend to do it."

"I don't need your damn help," she protested in drunken belligerence. Unsteadily she rose to her feet. "I don't need anybody's help. And I sure as hell don't need you!"

"Like hell you don't!" he retorted angrily. "You're rolling around this damn room like some doped up college kid on spring break! Is this how you honor your parents and your coach?"

Yvonne stopped in the hallway. When she turned to face him, her features were livid with rage. "Don't you dare say a word about my family!"

He closed in. "What would your parents say, if they saw you screwing yourself up on the same crap that took them away from you? How would your sister or your coach feel—"

She slapped him. Hard. "Screw you!" she cried out in drunken fury. "You don't know, you don't even know!"

"I know you need to stop torturing yourself," he said. "I know you need to stop shutting out the people who love you and care about you—"

"I can't!" she cried. "I can't let anyone in. I don't want anyone else to die because of me. I can't have another death on my hands! I can't—I just can't!" She buried her face in her hands and slumped against the wall, one huge, strangled sob breaking free of her control.

His heart beat brutally against his ribs as he wrapped her in his arms. "It's going to be all right," he whispered into her hair. "I promise."

"Michael?"

He turned. Melissa stood just behind them, her eyes large and bright. "How is she?"

"Exhausted. I think she's sleeping," he whispered. "How's Grace?"

"Worried," she answered, her face drawn. "How could Yvonne ever think we could blame her?"

"She blames herself and assumes everyone else does too."

Melissa touched her foster-sister's arm. "She's wrong," she whispered, tears glimmering on her lashes. "I hope we can convince her of that. Will you take—"

"I'll take care of her," he promised for the umpteenth time. Strangely, it was getting easier to make that promise.

They managed to leave through the back door without incident, and he promised to call as soon as they made it back to Yvonne's house. He had to stop twice on the way, once to allow her to throw up, and once to convince a cop that he wasn't drunk or a kidnapper.

He needed convincing himself. Looking at her, he couldn't believe this was the same Yvonne Mitchelson he knew. She had always exerted such iron self-control. In meetings, with disciplinary actions, she was always calm, to the point of being downright icy. But tonight, it was like dealing with a volcano no one knew was active.

Night had fallen completely by the time he stopped in front of the house. He unlocked the front door before retrieving Yvonne from the car. Luckily, Yvonne's neighbors were either still out or asleep; no one saw him carry her inside.

"…Me down," she mumbled weakly. "No breathe … "

Gently he set her on her feet and she doddered toward the kitchen. "Wherz ev'rybody, wherz my drink?"

He moved past her and grabbed the vodka bottle off the counter. "No more drinks for you," he stated, pouring the remainder down the sink. "Don't you think you've had enough?"

"No," she answered, as if he'd just asked her to cart-wheel naked down the street. "Not 'till I forget. I don't wanna see or think or feel, just wanna sit inna corner and forget this day ever happened."

Abruptly she lunged for the sink, sick again. He supported her and held her hair back until only dry heaves escaped her. Then he wet a towel and wiped her face.

She pushed his hands away and moved away from him. "Leaf me 'lone!" she begged, heading toward the living room.

Aching over her, he followed behind, catching things she shoved out of her way. She flopped onto the couch, holding a pillow like a stuffed toy. "Go away," she pleaded. "I wanna be by myself. Is that so bad?"

"Yes, it is."

She squinted up at him, and gave him an empty smile. "Then screw you."

It was too much. "Dammit, Vonne!" he burst out. "Will you talk to me? Please?"

"Why? You just goin' to leave ennyway. You couldn't deal with what I'd have to say."

"Try me." He sat on the floor beside her. "I'm here, and I'm not leaving."

She stared at him owl-like, through a mass of hair and red-rimmed eyes. "Of course you'll leave," she insisted hoarsely, with the careful enunciation of the truly drunk. "Everybody does. Momma and Daddy and Yvette, they left me. Uncle Reg, he died right after the championships. Jeff will be so successful in New York that he'll move there. And my girls will grow up and go away to school and f-fall in love and forget all about me. Gwen's got her daughter and dreams of her own. And Angela, she's too talented to hold on to much longer, and she's half in love with Jeff anyway. Now Poppy's gone, and you..."

She pressed a shivering hand to her mouth and shuddered, breathing deeply. The moment passed. "I gave you my business, part of my company, my body. There weren't any strings attached, no expectations, because I remember, you told me, one night, that you'd never let anyone get close to you, not after what your wife did, so I said, okay, I won't read too much into this thing, I won't get greedy, I'll just make do with what you give me because I know, if I don't, if I hold on too tightly, it will all slip away, like everything else."

Tears poured down her cheeks, but she didn't notice or care. "And then I slipped up. I started loving you."

She gave a hollow laugh. "It wasn't supposed to happen. We were just supposed to use each other for sex. You had a built-in safety net: a white playboy opposed to commitment. I thought I would be able to be with you without needing you. But I fell in love with you anyway."

Her breath rushed in with a shuddering gasp. "Do you even know how much that terrifies me? Do you even know how I exist with a bubble around me just so I won't care too much? I don't want to love you! I don't need this torture."

She laughed again, a short, brittle sound. "Of course, it doesn't matter now. You think I treat you like Beth did. As if I wanted, or needed to hear that. I didn't realize you hate me so much. I feel like a fool."

"Vonne, I don't hate you," he said, his voice scrubbed bare with emotion. He reached out to touch her.

She looked up, and the depth of despair he saw in her eyes stunned him. "You should," she told him. "It would be safer for you if you did."

Cupping her cheek, he whispered, "I don't want safe. I want you."

Her eyes were wide with horror as she backed away from his touch as if he'd burned her.. "Oh God, I didn't mean to tell you!" she wailed, clapping her hands to her forehead. "I didn't ask for any of this! All I wanted was to die in that hospital bed. That's all I want—wanted ... "

She swayed, a frail weed in an emotional wind. "I-I don't feel so good. I wanna lie down—tired, so damn tired—"

He scooped her up before she hit the floor. She felt fragile and insubstantial in his arms, as if she would break if he held her too tightly. He forced all thoughts from his mind as he carried her to her bedroom and undressed her, pausing when he revealed her scars.

So much pain, so much guilt and anger and self-hatred. She would never be able to put the past behind her because she carried the tragedy with her every day on her abdomen and legs. And her arms.

Lifting her left hand, he removed her trademark bangle, pausing as his fingers came into contact with the raised smoothness of a scar. Drawn like a magnet to iron filings, his eyes dropped to her wrist. A dark brown scar marred it—not across, but straight up the vein. It was a cut that meant business.

Horrified, he staggered to his feet and back downstairs. He collapsed on the loveseat, fighting valiantly to control the tremors that shook him. He felt drained, ripped apart, and more frightened than he'd ever been. He had never seen anyone so torn apart by grief, and it unnerved him.

Yvonne had tried to kill herself.

The thought repeated in his mind like a child's nursery rhyme gone horribly wrong. She had tried, seriously tried, to end her life. If not for the timely intervention of Grace and James Calhoun, she would have succeeded.

Pieces began to fall into place. He understood now why she was so emotionally reserved, so reluctant to talk about her past. For her, the pain had never receded. It was still as fresh as if she had lost her family yesterday. Facing her foster father's death had resurrected the demons of grief and loneliness. She believed she was cursed, and that belief made her afraid to care. She didn't want to risk loss again.

A heavy sigh escaped him. He was afraid too. He had been afraid that their relationship was one-sided. The playing field was now leveled. Yvonne had said she loved him. She was intoxicated, her normal reticence fallen away. Had she really meant it? Was she even aware of what she said? And what was he supposed to do now?

Little more than a few months ago, he would have walked away without a backwards glance. A few months ago, he wouldn't have cared about what a woman was going through. A few months ago, he would have left at the first sign of trouble.

But that was then. Now, his thoughts began and ended with Yvonne. Now, witnessing her grief, he wanted to be the knight in shining armor and slay all her dragons. Now, remembering the look of utter loneliness on her face as she watched Melissa comfort her mother, made him want to hold her and never let go. Now, knowing her past, he wanted to make sure that nothing ever hurt her again. Now, having promised to look after her, he wanted to be strong enough to give her the strength she needed.

He had never felt this way about anyone, not even his late wife. This was real. Loving Yvonne meant dealing with her fears as well as her joys, sharing her tears as well as her smiles.

It meant making a commitment.

Sitting back, Michael waited for the sweating palms and heart palpitations that word usually caused him. There were none. Instead, his heart felt lighter and freer than it had been in years.

He loved Yvonne. Not just the designer, not just the businesswoman, but every facet of her personality, including the grieving thirteen-year-old orphan. He realized that, and he accepted it. Now, he knew, there was no turning back.

He just had to convince her of it.

A shrill cry jerked him out of his reverie. His heart in his throat, he took the stairs two at a time to Yvonne's room. She was sitting bolt upright in bed, her hand outstretched. "Daddy, that truck isn't stopping— watch out!"

Helpless, he watched as she curled into a tight fetal ball. "No, Momma, I don't wanna go! I wanna stay with you. Please don't make me go—I'll be good, I promise! Don't make me go!"

The tortured words galvanized him and he swept her into his arms. "They're all gone!" she cried. "Everybody's gone."

He tightened his hold on her. "I'm here, Vonne," he whispered, rocking her against his chest. "Everything will be all right, I promise. I'm here."

He wasn't sure how long he rocked her, how long he repeated the words, but finally he broke through her nightmare. "Michael?"

Tenderly he brushed the hair from her damp forehead. "It's me, sweetheart," he whispered.

"It's too dark," she whimpered. "No more dark."

Quickly he switched on the bedside light, and she sobbed in relief. Tightening his hold, he pressed reassuring kisses across her forehead, her cheeks, her lips. She clung to him, seeking comfort. Finally, her shivers subsided, and color returned to her cheeks.

Silently he asked for forgiveness for what he was about to do. She needed to get her demons out and if he had to push her to do it, he would.

Resting his chin on the crown of her head, he reached for her left arm. Too late she realized his intent. "No, please don't!" She struggled against him, but was too weak to offer more than a token struggle.

Implacably he turned her wrist over, revealing the ugly scar. She buried her face against his chest, broken. "Why?" she asked, her voice raw. "Why did you do it?"

"Because you need to talk about it."

"No, I-I can't … "

"I'm not going to judge you, love. I'm just going to listen."

She pushed away from him, shaking her head in denial. "I can't talk about it." Clutching her scarred wrist to her chest, she turned away from him. "I can't."

"Vonne..."

"Please, Michael!" Her voice was nearly shrieking before she wrestled it under control with obvious effort. She was visibly shaking, but her voice was calm as she said, "I need to be alone now."

He knew he had pushed her enough. Perhaps even too far. Calling himself all kinds of fool, he got to his feet. "I'm here when you need me, sweetheart," he said softly. "I'm not going anywhere. I mean it."

CHAPTER SIXTEEN

Yvonne opened her eyes and immediately started a jack-hammer in her brain. Her eyes began to water and she hurriedly squeezed them shut. Too late. Major construction commenced relentlessly.

Trying to get her bearings, she got out of bed and swayed into the bathroom, feeling her way with outstretched hands. She felt as if she had a hangover the size of Cleveland. A hangover?

Normally she avoided alcohol like the plague, having only a glass of wine with dinner when she ate out. But she was definitely hungover—that was easy to tell by the cardboard taste in her mouth and the lovely way the room spun. Why the hell would she binge?

The shower pelted her as she slumped weakly under it, struggling to remember her lost time. She had no idea what time it was— or what day, for that matter. Her throat was tender, her head was pounding. She felt nauseated and ravenous and drained. She must have retched her guts out. Then she realized that she had been completely naked when she awoke. Had she taken her clothes off? Was she at home when she did it?

She frowned as she scrubbed at her hair, making the headache more intense. She had a faint impression that Michael was mixed up in her lost time, which was stupid, because she hadn't spoken to him in three days. Or was it three weeks?

Michael. Did thoughts of him lessen the pain or intensify it? The memory of how she had left things with him made her want to retch again. He didn't deserve to be treated badly just because she was unsure of their situation. Then again, he wasn't exactly being an angel when she last saw him, either.

After a half hour she reluctantly stepped out of the shower, feeling refreshed if not rejuvenated. Drying her hair with a towel, she glanced in the mirror and paused. Her normally rosy glow had eroded to a faint yellow, making her face ashen. Her eyelids were puffy, her expression was haggard, and her eyes could go no higher than half-mast. A bulldozer, excavating right behind her eyes, joined the jack-hammer in her head.

She wondered briefly what old Dr. Kaufmann, her former psychiatrist, would think if he saw her now. More than likely he'd throw her back into the hospital and never let her out.

She froze. The errant thought triggered others, and she realized in horror that she was in Detroit, not Atlanta. Memories hurtled into her consciousness, nearly overpowering her with agony: Melissa's phone call, the trip home, the scene with Grace, her drunken tirade with Michael. The nightmare and the history and the confession.

"Oh God, oh God, oh God … " She sat heavily on the side of her bed, breathing deeply to stave off the tumult of her emotions. Poppy was dead. She had freaked out on Grace. She told Michael that she loved him. She had…

She had taken off her bracelet.

Groaning, she put her head in her hands. Stupid, stupid, stupid. How could she be so stupid?

She looked down at her bare wrist. The scar was still as horrible, and as jagged, as it had been fifteen years ago. A reminder that her life had once been so bleak, so unforgiving. Even if her other scars could be forgiven, this one she knew, could not.

Michael would leave her.

Panic welled up within her, and she bit back a hysterical giggle that was almost a sob. Falling apart. That's what she was doing. After fifteen careful years, her grip on sanity was slipping once again. She felt as if she stood on the edge of a dark, gaping chasm, and only one step kept her from oblivion.

There was a knock on the door and Michael entered, bearing a tray. She quickly retrieved her bracelet from the nightstand as he sat down, placing the tray between them. "I thought you could use some breakfast."

Breakfast? She couldn't think about food, not at a time like this … Her stomach rumbled in disagreement.

"Thanks." Her hands trembled as she accepted a cup of coffee and a slice of toast. She steadied them by sheer force of will.

She could feel his stare on her, gauging her. Judging her. Just as she was about to scream at him to stop, he asked, "How are you feeling?"

Grimacing, she put down her toast and placed her free hand against her forehead, massaging it. "Construction continues." Lifting her mug to her lips, she took a careful sip, grateful for the warmth flowing through her. "Did I make a complete fool of myself last night?"

"You don't remember?"

Mindful of the hangover, she shook her head carefully, hating to deceive him but needing the protection the lie offered. "Everything's sorta fuzzy."

That was true. Her brain felt like a hive of bees inhabited it. "I don't remember much after we got to Grace's. I can't believe I drank so much."

"You were understandably upset," he told her. "Grace and Melissa understand."

His hand touched her left shoulder, then slid down her terry-cloth-covered arm to take her hand. The robe slipped back, and the bracelet twinkled up at them.

As politely as possible, she snatched her hand back, burying it into her lap. She had to get him away from her, but God, she needed him so desperately. How could she make it through this without him?

The same way she made it through everything else. Alone.

"I'm sorry you got dragged through my personal life, Michael," she said softly. "I didn't mean for this to happen."

He pressed coffee-warmed lips against her forehead. "Don't worry about me. Right now, let's just get you through the next couple of days, okay?"

Before she could answer, the doorchime sounded. Who could it be? Unnerved, she set down her coffee and rose, but Michael forestalled her. "I'll get the door. You get dressed."

She murmured her assent, and Michael went downstairs. He hoped like hell it wasn't a reporter; plenty had called the Calhouns last night, and Yvonne wasn't in any shape to deal with them.

The woman at the door was chicly dressed, and impatient. "Where is she?" she demanded, pushing past him into the foyer.

Moving quickly, Michael shut the door and blocked the woman's path to the stairs. "If you mean Yvonne, she's upstairs getting dressed. Who are you?"

"I am Dinah Reeves Mitchelson," she announced, looking down her nose at Michael. It was an amazing feat, considering he was half a foot taller. "My Reginald was uncle to that worthless girl."

Dislike flowed through him, immediate and strong. Yvonne's aunt could have been beautiful once, but her face was pinched with bitterness and her eyes were cold. He folded his arms across his chest. "Yvonne's having a rough time of it right now. She shouldn't be disturbed."

"My niece is already disturbed," Dinah said cruelly. "Hasn't she told you that?"

It was all Michael could do to refrain from throwing the pompous woman out on her ass. "Look, I realize you're Yvonne's aunt, and if you've come to help her get through her loss, fine. But I would appreciate it if you'd lose the attitude."

The woman was suitably outraged at his effrontery. "How dare you speak to me that way?! Just who do you think you are?"

"Mike Benjamin, a friend of Yvonne's."

"Friend?" Dinah Mitchelson made the word sound dirty. "Of course you are."

Jaw clenched, he dropped his arms. "All right, I think I've had just about enough—"

Footsteps pounded down the stairs, and Yvonne rushed into view. "Hello, Dinah," she said breathlessly, pushing past him. She held her hands out to the older woman, who ignored them. "What are you doing here?"

"I heard about Calhoun, and I decided to see how you were faring," her aunt said. The lack of concern in her voice was painfully obvious to Michael. "Then this-this man has the audacity to be rude to me!"

"He's just concerned for me, Dinah," Yvonne said lamely. "I haven't been feeling well, and then I got the news about Poppy—"

"That does not give him the right to be rude," Dinah fumed.

Michael stood beside Yvonne, glaring at her aunt. "Neither does that give you the right to make disparaging remarks about your niece in her own home."

Dinah was aghast. "Are you going to allow him to talk to me this way?"

Yvonne looked between them, clearly indecisive. "Dinah, please, I-I've had a rough night. I have to get over to Grace's. Can I—can I come by later?" Michael looped an arm about her in a show of support, and was rewarded with a smile.

Dinah didn't miss it. "So that's how it is," she sniffed. "You do your level best to continue to bring shame to this family, don't you? First your own family, then your poor uncle. Now this!"

Her gesture took in their intimate embrace. "The Mitchelson clan is rolling in their graves, thanks to you! I certainly hope you haven't convinced yourself that you're in love with him. I'm sure you remember what happens to people you poison with your so-called love."

Michael felt Yvonne tremble before he heard her pained gasp, and his anger boiled over. "Okay, that's it!"

He moved toward her aunt, his stance designed to intimidate. "Yvonne needs your love and your support, not your snide remarks. If you can't be civil, you need to leave."

Dinah was clearly flabbergasted. Her mouth opened and closed several times before she found her voice. "I have never, in my life—!"

"Maybe that's your problem," he murmured for her ears alone. "You should try it. They say it has a very calming effect."

Dinah was so outraged she began to sputter. Grateful for the silence, he took her by the elbow and forcibly dragged her to the door.

"Fair warning," he said, his voice so low only Dinah could hear. "I am not going to let you blame Yvonne anymore. She's trying to live her life in spite of her loss. I suggest you do the same." He pushed her out the door, shutting and locking it firmly.

He turned to Yvonne. She stared at the door, her right hand gripping the silver cuff on her left wrist. Her eyes were bright with tears he knew she wouldn't let fall. Oh God, he thought, I've done it for sure.

"Vonne, sweetheart, I'm sorry. But that woman—"

"It's all right." Her voice was quiet. "A part of me knows she deserves it."

"Maybe you should have done that a long time ago."

She shook her head sadly. "I always hoped that we would mend fences. She blames me for Uncle Reg's death, and the fact that a lot of his last few months were spent ensuring that I would have some kind of future."

"Vonne, I'm sorry." And he was. Sorry that all he did was shove the old biddy out the door. What kind of a person laid a guilt trip like that on another? "But she still shouldn't treat you like that. It wasn't your fault."

Her eyes were haunted. "Dinah can't help the way she feels. The pain of losing Uncle Reg has been with her so long that it's hard to let go. Still, she's family. In her own way, she cares. Why else would she drive half an hour to see me?"

He had his own ideas, but saw no reason to voice them. He sincerely hoped Dinah Mitchelson took his warning to heart. Yvonne had been hurt enough. She didn't need to be hurt anymore.

Michael approached the hill slowly, captured by the sight of the forlorn figure huddled at the base of the tree. A huge headstone dominated the slight rise. He knew what it read even before his eyes made out the word "Mitchelson" with the names Robert, Sabrina, and Yvette inscribed beneath.

James Calhoun's graveside service had been poignant. Yvonne delivered a eulogy that had the gathering of friends and family alternately crying and laughing as she recounted anecdotes about the man who was her coach, mentor, surrogate father, and hero. Afterwards she had excused herself to Grace and the family and headed deeper into the cemetery, not stopping until she reached the rise.

She didn't acknowledge his presence as he stopped next to her. As if last night was just a dream, she had retreated into her stoic shell. He admired her strength, but he knew the pressure was building inside her, needing to be released.

He crouched beside her, watching as she straightened the already immaculate plot. Her expression was composed, but he could feel the pain and sorrow radiating from her in waves.

"I didn't get the chance to say goodbye."

Her voice was so soft he wasn't sure if she actually spoke or not. She kept her gaze riveted to the ornate headstone. He reached for her hand, not pressing her, giving her time to soberly tell the tale he'd already heard.

"I didn't get to say goodbye to Mom and Dad, or Vette ... By the time I regained consciousness in the hospital, they had already been buried. Poppy and Uncle Reg waited to tell me, until they were sure I would survive."

"It must have been devastating," he whispered, his free hand coming around her shoulders.

She looked down at her hand engulfed in his larger, paler one. "We, we were a very close-knit family," she said slowly, as if each word was a razor clawing from her throat. "Even though Dad worked long hours making the dealerships successful, we always sat down to dinner, they always told us a bedtime story, and they never missed one of our meets.

"And Yvette … my sister was my best friend. It probably sounds strange, but I could sense her in my head. We always used to finish each others sentences."

She stared unseeing at the headstone. "When they died, my identity died with them. I felt like a non-person, as if I didn't belong anywhere. But the hardest part of all was the emptiness in my head and heart, the utter loneliness of being incomplete."

He swallowed with difficulty. "That must have driven you crazy."

She turned look at him then. "It did," she said seriously. "It took a long time, almost three years, before I regained some sense of normalcy."

"But you had the Calhouns."

She nodded. "Poppy and Grace took me in after things didn't work out with my aunt," she replied. "They didn't try to replace my parents, but they loved me as if I were their own child. Thanks to them, I never gave up."

A broken sigh shook her. "And now Poppy's gone. The losses are so hard to take. I miss them so much … "

He pulled her close, stroking her hair, her shoulders. She trembled against him but remained dry-eyed

"Sweetheart, you need to cry, you need to let it out before it poisons you."

She shifted away from him. "I can't," she breathed in anguish. "I don't have any tears left. Besides, tears don't change anything. Tears didn't bring my family back. Tears didn't stop Uncle Reg from dying. Tears won't replace Poppy. I don't have any use for tears."

He started to protest, but she pulled away from him and rose to her feet. She stared into the iron gray sky, watching a bird's solitary flight. "I-I just wish ... " her voice trailed off.

"What?"

Yvonne shook her head. She wanted to tell him how desperately she yearned to stretch out on the cool, sweet grass and sleep forever, wanted to tell him how tired she was of simply existing, of struggling through each day.

She wanted to tell him that she loved him. But she didn't dare.

Those three words were a curse, coming from her. She had told her parents those words just minutes before the crash that stole them from her. She had whispered them to her Uncle before he succumbed to the cancer that ate him alive. And she had laughed them to Poppy less than a week ago, when she was making plans to visit. What would happen to Michael, if she told him how she felt? She couldn't risk it.

Yet when she looked at him, stared into those golden eyes that seemed to hold so much promise, she weakened. She ached to be held by him, ached to be engulfed by him. Ached to be made complete, to be loved by him. But she couldn't, and it left her so empty inside.

She stared down at the headstone then up to the leaden sky. "Everyone I ever loved was taken from me," she whispered. "Why? What's wrong with me? Is my love poison?"

Michael cupped her face with trembling hands. "No, sweetheart," he answered shakily. "Your love is the most precious, beautiful thing in the world. Grace and Melissa know it, Angela, Gwen, and Jeff know it, and so do those girls in Mentor Atlanta. They love you, and they know you love them. Don't be afraid of it."

She stared at him a long moment, her eyes bright with emotion. "I don't want to be," she confessed, "but—"

"No buts. If you want it, just say it."

His warmth encouraged her. "I-I want to be unafraid," she finally whispered. "I want the cold and darkness to go away, I want to feel the sunlight on my face and be glad to be alive. I want to live, not just exist."

She swallowed, looking away. "I want you. But you don't want—"

"What I want is to be with you." His words were warm, vibrant, ringing with sincerity. "I want to give you everything you want. I want to make you happy." He paused, and she gazed up at him, waiting. "I love you."

Her eyes widened with panic. "No, Michael—don't say that!"

"Whether I say it or not, it doesn't change how I feel," he informed her gently. "I know I haven't been the best with you lately, but I want to change that. Let me love you, Vonne."

Angry, she pounded her fists against his chest. "No. Can't you see what happens to people who love me? Look around you!" She flailed her arm around the cemetery. "Do you think I want this to happen to you? Do you think I could bear that? What would I do if I lost you?"

"Ah, Vonne," he whispered, holding her close. "It's not your fault; you're not cursed. Death is as much a part of life as birth is. Everyone hopes they'll be able to live a full life and die of old age, but that doesn't always happen."

He stroked her back, his touch infusing her. "I know it's hard, but you can't blame yourself. It'll eat you up inside. Believe me, I know."

Dear God, she wanted to believe him, wanted it more than anything. But the guilt and fear had haunted her for half her life. "I'm afraid," she confessed in a small voice.

"So am I," he whispered into her hair. "I'm afraid I'm going to make a mess of the best thing that's ever happened to me. I'm afraid that I'm going to ruin what makes you good and kindhearted. I'm afraid of the power you have over my heart. And I'm terrified that you'll never love me as much as I love you."

"How can you love me?" she cried. "I'm so-so broken."

"So was I," Michael admitted. "Beth took my heart and shattered it into so many pieces I didn't think it would ever heal. I thought it was dead. Then you came along, with your sweet smile. And you listened to me. You listened to me tell my story and you didn't judge me or blame me. I loved you for that. And I'll be overjoyed when you allow me to do the same for you."

The familiar panic welled in her chest, urging her to run as far and as fast as she could. She couldn't tell him. If she did she would lose him, and then where would she be?

He held her to him. "I'm not trying to pressure you," he whispered into her hair. "You'll tell me everything when you're ready. But I wanted to tell you how I feel, how I love you. Do you believe me?"

She looked into his eyes, reading the pain for her and the truth. There was only one answer. "Yes."

And then the tears came, and with them, release.

CHAPTER SEVENTEEN

"So what's keeping you busy these days, son?" Michael looked up from the steaks he was marinating. His mother, Amelia, rinsed salad greens in the sink. His father was out on the deck, lighting the grill. He had invited them over for dinner, knowing that his mother would eventually bring up her favorite topic of conversation: his personal life.

Tonight, all her questions were going to be answered.

"I'm doing a lot of work with a company called Gemini Enterprises," he answered. "Among other things, it owns the restaurant Creole and Your Heart's Desire boutiques."

Amelia Benjamin raised a cynical eyebrow. In her early fifties, she looked fifteen years younger, a testament, she claimed, to her Gypsy heritage. "I'm sure it's the boutiques, not the restaurant, that you're working on?"

He grinned lasciviously. "You know me so well."

Amelia sighed as she put the greens in the refrigerator. "I suppose you're going to tell me that you've hooked up with another model?"

"Actually, I'm seeing the owner."

"Then she's not after you for your money."

"Mom!"

Amelia refused to be apologetic. "Well, I don't want to see you getting used, son. You have a lot to offer the right woman, whenever you decide to look for her." She gave him a covert glance. "How serious are you about this one?"

"Serious enough that you're going to meet her tonight."

Her expression was so hopeful that he burst out laughing. "Does that surprise you?"

"What? The fact that there's a chance I'll become a grandmother before I'm sixty? Or the fact that my only child is serious about a woman I know nothing about?"

He kissed his mother's forehead. "I'm deliberately not telling you anything about her. I want your honest first impression." The doorchime rang. "That's probably her. Come on, I can't wait for you to meet her."

Yvonne eyed the late model Cadillac with trepidation. Michael didn't mention that he was having guests over. She certainly didn't want to impose on any business meeting he might be having. She had already taken up a lot of his time since the trip to Detroit two weeks ago.

Yvonne knew the main reason she had been able to survive without going off the deep end was because of him. He was like a rock, unflappable, unmovable.

It would have been so easy to slip into the crevasse her grief had made, to return to the old horror of losing everyone she loved. But he had been there, sitting with her in the house she had called home for the first thirteen years of her life. He held her hand as she walked through the pain of new and old losses. He held her when she cried, and he made her laugh when she needed to. He was her anchor and her protector and her strength. How could you not fall in love with a guy like that?

She was about to leave when the door opened, and she found herself staring at a female version of Michael. The older woman had the same golden eyes framed by thick black lashes, and her dark curly hair was pulled into a topknot held by cloisonné stickpins. She wore a raw silk tunic of green and gold batik over a bronze broomstick skirt and a funky pair of earrings Yvonne instantly coveted.

The woman blinked at her in surprise, then smiled and stuck out a hand. Several bracelets clinked merrily. "Hello, I'm Amelia Benjamin. And you are … ?"

"Yvonne Mitchelson." She shook the other woman's hand. "I'm sorry, I don't mean to stare, but Michael told me he was an only child."

Amelia Benjamin laughed brightly. "I like you already. Come in."

Michael came around the corner just as she stepped inside. "Hi," he said, giving her a quick peck on the cheek. "I see you met my mom already."

Her palms suddenly went damp, and her heart sounded like a drum corps in her chest. "Your … mom?" she squeaked. "She's your mother?"

His head swung from her to his mother and back again. "Didn't she introduce herself? This is my mother, Amelia Benjamin. Mom, this is the lady of my life, Yvonne Mitchelson."

Yvonne stared at the older woman, dumbstruck. Michael's mother. She had just met Michael's mother!

She was not ready for this! Luckily she still wore the rose-colored georgette dress she had worn to work instead of the T-shirt and shorts she had planned on wearing. "I-I…" I wish I could start this over.

"You're as surprised to see me as I am to see you," Amelia guessed, then leveled a glance at her son. "Women like advance warning for things like this, Michael. She thought I was your sister."

"She did?" He gave an impish grin. "Well, that's certainly a good way to earn brownie points." Yvonne glared at him, wanting nothing more than to elbow him in the gut.

Apparently Amelia did too, for she suited thought to action. She turned to Yvonne, shaking her head. "That boy. I swear I should have never taken him to Woodstock. The music must have rattled his brains."

Yvonne felt her mouth hit the floor, but was powerless to stop it. "You were at Woodstock?"

Amelia smiled. "Sure was. Both of them. Michael was barely a toddler for the first, but we sure had fun playing in the mud, didn't we?"

He nodded. "My earliest memory is listening to Jimi Hendrix's guitar."

Yvonne looked at both of them, aware of her head swinging like a spectator's at a tennis match. She knew her chin was dragging the floor, but was powerless to close her gaping mouth. And people thought she was crazy!

Michael must have seen the look in her eyes. "Mom's hippie days are behind her," he offered. "Now she's into New Age."

That earned him another elbow. "You keep it up, you're going to scare her off," Amelia told him. She took Yvonne's arm, leading her into the kitchen. "Why don't we have some tea while Michael and my husband Edward grill our dinner? We can get to know each other."

Amelia Benjamin was obviously trying to make her feel comfortable, which only unnerved Yvonne further. She looked over her shoulder at Michael. *Does she realize I'm black?* she mouthed to him.

He had the nerve to laugh. This time it was Yvonne who gave him the elbow to the stomach. "I'm leaving before I start to bruise. Enjoy your talk." He disappeared through the back door.

She immediately felt abandoned. Why was he doing this to her? His mother seemed like a nice person, but what if she was faking it, merely for the sake of being polite? Surely Michael hadn't introduced his previous lovers to his mother this way?

As if reading her thoughts, Amelia said, "You're the first one of Michael's lady friends he's wanted us to meet."

Flustered, Yvonne opened a cabinet and brought out two teacups, then retrieved her special herbal tea from the fridge. He could have warned her he was going to do this. She could have rented Guess Who's Coming to Dinner for research. "I-I don't know what to say. I almost feel like I should be apologizing to you."

"No apologies necessary. It's obvious that you're really special. I know for a fact that Michael doesn't let just anyone have the run of his kitchen."

Yvonne realized that she was indeed acting like she owned the place. She collapsed onto her stool at the breakfast nook, putting her head into her hands. "I'm not exactly making a good first impression, am I?"

Amelia filled the teakettle with fresh water. "Michael surprised us both. He didn't want either of us to have preconceived notions. What would you have expected if Michael had told you I still have one of his diapers autographed by Jefferson Airplane?" Yvonne's tea infuser clattered against her cup. "You see? Visions of hippiedom run through your head."

Yvonne had to laugh. "You're right," she admitted grudgingly. "That's not to say that he didn't deserve those jabs to the gut, though."

Amelia filled her own infuser with tea leaves. "Of course not. Just because he's right doesn't mean he has to know it." She tested her tea. "How did you two meet?"

Yvonne related the day in the airport, and the subsequent business arrangement. When she mentioned Jeff Maxwell, Amelia nodded. "Jeff's been Michael's best friend since high school. He and Beth used to come over all the time ... " her voice faded uncomfortably.

"It's all right. He told me about Beth."

"He did?" Amelia seemed surprised. "Everything?"

Yvonne nodded. "It wasn't easy for him. He still had a lot of guilt and anger over what Beth ... over what happened. Not that he let it show or anything. I was able to see it because I know what it's like."

She took a deep breath. "I lost my twin sister and parents when I was thirteen. I wore my anger and guilt like an invisible trenchcoat. We're helping each other through it, trying to put the past behind and move forward. It-it hasn't been easy, but I'd like to think we're doing okay."

Amelia gave her an inscrutable smile over the rim of her teacup. "You love him, don't you?"

Heat blossomed in her cheeks. She toyed with her cup, trying to marshal her thoughts and emotions. Did Amelia Benjamin want her to love her son? Did it matter if she didn't?

She took a fortifying breath. "I-I'll be honest with you. My ability to love was all but killed with my family. But since I've met Michael, since I've been with him, there's this sensation in my chest, something that's just as fragile as it is strong. It rules my every waking moment, yet I'm so afraid that it isn't enough. I don't love your son as much as I will, and probably not nearly as much as he deserves. But I care for him very deeply, to the best of my ability, and I hope that every day of the rest of my life brings a new way to show him how much I do."

Whoa. Did I just say what I think I said?

Amelia reached over to give her hand a gentle pat. "I can see the truth of it in your eyes. You're a good person, Yvonne. I'm glad my son found you."

Stunned, she sat back on her stool. Was Amelia Benjamin giving them her blessing? And what was she supposed to do with it now?

Amelia leaned forward. "There is one question that I'm dying to ask you."

Yvonne stared at her, apprehensive again. "Yes?"

"Can you tell me where you got that necklace?"

"Only if you'll tell me where you got those earrings."

The back door opened, and an older gentleman walked in, carrying a tray of grilled steaks and chicken. "Millie, Michael said something about a lady friend of his coming—" He broke off when he caught sight of Yvonne.

She got to her feet. The one word she would pick to describe Michael's father was distinguished. His dark hair had silver streaks at the temples, and the tall frame dressed in a polo shirt and khakis would have been more at home in a three-piece suit. His eyes, a clear, frosty gray, studied her even as he set the tray down. She could tell he didn't like what he saw.

She mentally squared her shoulders. It was all right if Michael's father didn't like her. She was just sleeping with his son, not marrying him. But she'd be damned if she would let him dislike her simply because of her color. He'd just have to find another reason to dislike her.

The meal wasn't a Grand Inquisition, but it wasn't a love-in, either. When dinner was mercifully over, she offered to help Amelia with the dishes. But Edward forestalled her.

"Actually, Ms. Mitchelson, I was wondering if you would join me in the living room."

Yvonne nearly dropped the plate she was holding. She gave Michael a pleading look. Get me out of this!

But he simply took the dish away from her. "Don't worry about Dad; he won't hurt you. I'll be in as soon as we clean up in here."

Yvonne was being taken out to slaughter, and she knew it. The knowing didn't make it easier.

She followed Edward Benjamin into the living room, where he turned on the television to a baseball game before sitting. He gestured for her to sit on the couch. "Mike tells me that he's doing some work for you."

She stared at Michael's father, not sure if there was an innuendo in the innocent remark. "Yes. His company has been a great benefit to mine."

Edward nodded. "Oh yes. You own that sex shop, Your Heart's Desire."

So the gloves were off already. Her chin shot up. He could demean her all he wanted, but she wasn't going to allow him to demean her company.

"I mean no disrespect, Mr. Benjamin, but the only people who call my stores 'sex shops' are those who have never been inside. Desire is more than sex. We offer books, greeting cards, event planners, workshops. My stores are for couples, spouses, anyone involved in long-term relationships, or anyone who wants to feel better about themselves. It's about love and romance, not sex."

"And what about your relationship with my son? What category does that fall into?"

Yvonne could feel her ears begin to heat. She was not going to go off on Michael's father, no matter how badly she wanted to. She would be civil, even if it killed her. "I'm sorry, sir, but I don't think that's any of your business."

He faced her, bringing the full brunt of his frosty-eyed gaze to bear. "I think it's very much my business, Ms. Mitchelson. I want to make sure my son is protected."

"Then you should have protected him ten years ago!" she burst out, and instantly regretted it.

But Edward Benjamin surprised her by nodding. "You're right."

"I am?"

Michael's father sighed. "My daughter-in-law, God rest her soul, was a gold-digger. She wanted the easy way out, and she didn't care whom she used or hurt in the process."

She couldn't believe her ears. "You knew?" she asked. "You knew what Beth was like and you let Michael marry her anyway? How could you do such a thing?"

"Because people should make their own decisions when it comes to love, for better or worse. And no one, not even parents, should try to dissuade them."

Yvonne had a flash of insight. "Is that what happened with you and your wife?"

He gave a wry smile. "As you may have noticed, Millie and I are as different as oil and vinegar. She's as full of energy as a lightning strike, and I know I have a tendency to be as dry and dull as stale bread."

"Well, uhm, I'm sure that's not really true, sir."

Edward laughed. "Don't be polite on my account, young lady," he admonished her. "I know I'm a stuffed shirt. Millie's a Gypsy through and through. Don't know why she fell in love with me, but she did."

"I think I know," she said quietly.

"Really."

"She saw in you what I see in Michael. Your honesty, and integrity, and strength. And obviously, your refusal to let the opinions of others influence you."

His laughter was warmer. "Very perceptive of you, Ms. Mitchelson. Our parents were dead-set against us getting married. Especially my parents. So we did what most young adults of the sixties did. We ignored authority and eloped."

"You did?" Somehow she couldn't imagine the man seated across from her being that reckless and daring.

He nodded. "Caused a great deal of bitterness that took years to heal. But Millie and I have had nearly four decades filled with love and adventure together that we never would have had if we'd given in to our parents' wishes. So I promised my son on the day he was born that I would never interfere in his decisions of the heart. For better or worse."

Was that a warning or a blessing? Yvonne wasn't sure, and she didn't really want to discover the answer. Why was she hoping it was the latter?

Edward Benjamin, having said his piece, returned his attention to the ballgame. "What's the score?" she asked politely.

He glanced at her. "You like baseball?"

Yvonne smiled. "I'll be a Tigers fan until the day I die, but I've learned to cheer for my adopted hometown's team."

Edward nodded. "Bottom of the ninth, one away, game's tied." He grimaced. "I can't believe he's sending this guy to the plate. He's having a terrible year."

Yvonne stared at the player in question. "I'll admit he's in a slump, but his lifetime average against this pitcher's pretty high. He'll take the first pitch, but if the next one's just off the outside corner, he'll connect."

Edward grunted. "We'll see."

Amelia Benjamin looked up from the dishes she was rinsing. "Do you think it was wise to leave them out there alone?" she asked worriedly.

"The Braves are on. At the very least, they'll ignore each other and watch the game. Besides, Cutter's refereeing."

Michael wasn't nearly as confident as he tried to sound. He was beginning to wonder if his plan was going to backfire. His father wasn't exactly bowled over by Yvonne. Dinner had been strained, though the ladies kept up a steady stream of chatter, especially when Yvonne discovered that his mother was an interior designer. He was glad that the two most important women in his life were getting along.

"I like her."

Michael swung around, surprised at his mother's words. "You do?"

Amelia handed him another dish to load into the dishwasher. "Of course I do. What's not to like?"

"She is black, Mom," Michael felt compelled to point out.

Amelia's grin was wry. "I noticed."

"It doesn't bother you?"

His mother turned off the faucet. "That's a question for you to answer, not me," she replied, drying her hands. "Do you love her?"

His reply was swift. "More than anything. I used to feel so dead inside, but now … She makes me feel complete."

His mother nodded, as if she already knew his intentions. "Love is the most important thing in a relationship, but you also need patience and understanding. A thick skin won't hurt either. Do you think you're prepared for this?"

He had thought a lot about that. Aside from that damned nightclub incident, he and Yvonne didn't have any problems when they went out. But then, Buckhead was on the progressive side.

"Mom, I'm prepared to be with Yvonne no matter what. We've already weathered some rough storms privately. I think we're doing okay together, and I'll make sure it stays that way."

"Then don't let her get away."

Michael grabbed his mother in a bear hug. "Thanks, Mom. Your vote means a lot to me."

"I can't speak for your father, but I'll do my best to persuade him." She smiled. "I can be very persuasive when I want to."

"I don't think I want to know—"

Yelling and barking interrupted them. Michael immediately threw down his towel and raced into the living room, fully expecting to see Yvonne in tears and Cutter chomping on his dad's leg.

He stopped short. They weren't arguing. They were laughing.

He turned to his mother. "Since when did Dad know how to give a high five?"

Amelia was just as surprised. "From beer commercials?"

Edward noticed his son then. "Where did you find this wonderful woman?" he asked, throwing an arm about Yvonne's shoulders.

She was clearly startled by the gesture, but her blossoming smile lit Michael's soul. He'd done the right thing, bringing them together the way he had. "Believe it or not, Dad, I found her at the baggage claim in the airport."

"Michael!" Both women wore identical expressions of indignation.

Edward Benjamin gave Yvonne's shoulders a squeeze. "Well, make sure no one comes back to claim her. She called the game perfectly. And she has season tickets to every sports franchise in the city!"

Michael groaned. "You shouldn't have told him that," he said to Yvonne. "Now he'll never leave you alone."

Yvonne's eyes were bright with emotion. "I don't mind," she said. "I'd be honored to take him to a game."

"Are you free Saturday?" his father asked eagerly, and with the ensuing laughter, Michael knew everything was fine. More than fine.

It was almost perfect.

CHAPTER EIGHTEEN

Yvonne was beyond tired when she finally pulled into her garage. Whatever had possessed her to plan a fashion show at the height of the wedding season, she didn't know. Record crowds had descended on the boutiques, and the private line was outstripping regular merchandise. Every other customer wanted to model for Desire, visions of snagging rock stars dancing before their eyes.

Coordinating the show was proving to be more than the migraine she'd imagined. The models, who were more than happy posing for the catalog, were skittish about wearing her designs on the runway—never mind that writers and photographers from fashion media around the country would be on hand, never mind that supermodels the world over had posed for pictures in less. The Your Heart's Desire staff, most of whom had never modeled in their lives, was being better sports about it. And Angela was positively giddy to be the centerpiece of the finale.

The show, to be held in the Egyptian Ballroom of the Fox Theatre, was already being touted as the must-attend event of the season in the local papers. Less than a month away, and Yvonne was looking forward to it. But lately she was looking forward to it being over even more.

She opened her door, then stopped, her mouth an "O" of surprise. The living room was bathed in the glow of at least a score of candles, filling the air with the scent of jasmine and sandalwood. Brahms' third symphony lilted gently in the background.

She unceremoniously dropped her briefcase and jacket, doing a slow turn about the room. Spying a pale sheet of paper on the couch, she quickly hurried over to retrieve it. Michael's bold handwriting scrawled across the page. "If you think this is something, look in the bathroom," the note read.

Wordlessly, she went into the guest bathroom. There were more candles, more music, a teapot, and a steaming bubble bath. On the vanity, next to the cordless phone, was another note.

"Something tells me you can use this," the note read. "Call me if you need your back scrubbed."

Without a doubt, she could definitely use this! She quickly stripped and sank greedily into the steaming bath. Water scented with herbs lapped over her stressed muscles, causing her to shudder at the practically orgasmic sensation it caused. It was sinfully, absolutely perfect.

She rose out of the water long enough to pour and taste a cup of tea. Another bone-deep sigh of contentment eased out of her. The tea was sweetened just right, the music was soothing, and there was no one to complain about the snug fit of merrywidows. She reached for the phone.

"You wonderful, perfect man!" she cried as soon as Michael answered. "You absolute angel!"

Michael's laugh was music to her ears. "I take it you like my gift?"

"You gorgeous, generous guy! You delightful, down-right delectable dude! You exquisite, exciting—"

"You're going to run through the whole alphabet if you keep it up!" he teased. "I thought you might like to be alone, but if you still need that back scrub, I'm available."

"I'd love a back scrub," she answered huskily.

"And if you're hungry, I've got your favorite dish—"

"Stuffed tenderloin?" Yvonne gasped. Suddenly her stomach rumbled to life. "I love your stuffed tenderloin!"

"And I even have your favorite fruit for desert—"

"Oh my God, you did not get fresh-picked blackberries! I love fresh-picked blackberries!"

"And what about me?"

She didn't even pause. "I love you. I worship the ground you walk upon. I grovel at your feet, you bodacious, beautiful—"

"If you keep that up, I'm going to have to turn my paycheck over to the cellular company," Michael replied. "I'll be there in five minutes or less."

Yvonne set down the phone and sunk back into the bubbles. She couldn't get over what he had done for her. How was he able to discern when she needed things like this? Was there any guy on the face of the planet as thoughtful, as kind, as generous —as gorgeous? Just when she got used to one aspect of him, he did something else that completely blew her away.

Like surprising her and his parents with that get-together. She understood why he hadn't warned any of them; given a choice, she much preferred his parents' honest reactions to their relationship. Amelia was a warm, free-spirited woman. They were rapidly becoming good friends. They even had a jewelry hunting expedition planned for next week. And once Edward discovered where her seats were located in Turner Field, she knew she had a friend for life.

The fact that his parents had taken to her despite their initial surprise touched her. She hadn't known how much their acceptance meant to her until they gave it.

Yvonne wrapped her arms about herself. Even if she and Michael broke up tomorrow, she would cherish the fact that she meant enough to him to be introduced to his parents.

"Oh, Michael," she sighed aloud, "I love you."

The words echoed in the bathroom, startling her. Had she truly, finally, said the words aloud?

But the earth didn't open up to swallow her, there was no clap of thunder, she didn't wake from a dream. The words were coming to her more easily, pushing out fear. She tried the words again. And again. And again.

She gave a whoop of joy.

Michael leaned against the door. Yvonne hadn't noticed him yet. She had her eyes closed, belting out "Joy to the World" at the top of her lungs. Badly.

He was more than content to watch her. It had been a long time since he'd seen her so free. Putting the finishing touches on the show was more fatiguing than Yvonne would admit, especially coming on the heels of the trip to Detroit, and meeting his family.

His heart thumped painfully in memory. She had been in so much pain, and he'd been powerless to do anything about it. Finally he just decided to be there for her, to offer her a hand to hold, a shoulder to cry on, a body to cling to. He would have danced across the Atlantic if it had made her smile, but all she needed, all she wanted, was him.

She had won his mother over with a simple misunderstanding, and the two were becoming friends. Her warm personality and her love of baseball had thawed his father faster than he thought possible.

He reveled in the elation he felt. Yvonne wanted and needed him. It was only a matter of time before she realized that she loved him with the same passion and intensity that he loved her.

And if he had his way, she would find out tonight.

"Joy—"

"Did I ever tell you how radiant you look when you're happy?"

Yvonne cut off in mid-bellow, her eyes popping open in surprise as she instinctively sank deeper into the bubbles. Michael leaned against the door, his arms folded across his chest. His easy smile soothed away the last of her fatigue.

"You've made me incredibly happy," she said softly. "Come here. I want to kiss you."

He knelt beside the tub. She leaned over and gave him the hottest, wettest kiss she could devise. Suddenly she was crushed against his chest, her hand snaking into his hair as she kissed him with all the pent-up love and desire her soul possessed.

"Whoa," he said a short time later as he slumped against the side of the tub. "I think I saw stars."

"Me too." Her voice was faint as she gasped for air. "Maybe it was from lack of oxygen."

"It's possible, but I think we should try it again, just to see."

She grinned eagerly. "Okay."

The second kiss was just as explosive as the first. She sagged against him, trying to catch her breath again. "Oh Michael, your sweatshirt is soaked," she exclaimed in dismay. "You're going to catch another cold."

"If I do, I'm sure Doc Mitchelson can whip up another batch of gumbo cure-all for me," he grinned. He pulled the wet shirt over his head. "Is that better?"

"Much." Her eyes gleamed as she feasted on his bare skin.

He stood and grabbed a robe off the doorknob. "I think it's time for you to get out of that cold water. You're shivering."

She stood, turning demurely away from his hungry gaze as he wrapped her in the terry robe. "It's not from the cold," she whispered.

He lifted her easily in his arms. "Is it because you're hungry? If you are, we can eat now. But if you aren't ... "

"I'll take door number two."

To her surprise, Michael went past the stairs to what she called her "green room": a glass-enclosed patio filled with plants, wicker furniture, and the prerequisite easel and drawing pad. The glass walls had huge rattan shades that could be rolled down for privacy.

He had been busy here too. The shades were all drawn, and more candles scented the air. In the center of the room was a pallet made of thick blankets. Beside it was an ice bucket with champagne, two glasses, and a bowl of blackberries.

"When did you do all this?" Yvonne was dumbfounded.

"This afternoon," Michael answered, setting her gently on the blankets. "I knew you'd be swamped at the stores, handling the final fittings before rehearsals start, so I set it all up while you were gone. Kourtney called me as you were leaving, and that's when I came in and lit the candles."

Yvonne blinked back tears. "I can't believe you went through all this trouble for me," she said in a small voice.

He hit a button on the remote for the hidden CD player, and the hypnotic, seductive beats of Enigma enveloped the room. "It wasn't trouble; it was a labor of love," he admonished her. "I wanted to pamper my woman, and this is the way I decided to do it."

My woman. She liked the way that sounded. "Thank you, you fantastic, fascinating fellow—"

His lips descended on hers, cutting off her words. "I'll buy you a thesaurus for your birthday, but right now, I want you to lie back and relax." He slipped the robe from her shoulders. "Sip a little champagne, eat a blackberry, and enjoy."

The sensual onslaught began with long rhythmic brush-strokes to her hair. Her eyes slid shut as she purred in contentment. "Umm, that feels good."

"It gets better."

He pushed her down until she lay on her stomach. Warm oil was poured onto her back and then his hands begin to knead her shoulders, the small of her back, her buttocks, her legs. The scent seeped into her soul even as the oil seeped into her skin, pervading her with tranquility and comfort.

She had never been pampered like this in her life. His fingers were magic, sending warm currents of pleasure arcing through her. She could feel a haze of heat enveloping her, emanating from the center of her being that resonated with his name. "Where did you learn to do this?" she asked, grunting in satisfaction as he loosened a tight muscle in her thigh.

"Actually, I bought the candles and this aromatherapy oil from the boutique," he answered. "But the idea is all mine."

"I love your ideas. Maybe I should hire you as an event coordinator. You sure know how to make a girl feel beautiful."

He rolled her over, leaving her long enough to remove his sweatpants. "And you make me feel like the most blessed man alive." His eyes glowed with the truth of his words.

She watched languidly as his hands then his mouth glided over her breasts, teasing the dark nipples to wakefulness. His lips felt absolutely heavenly as they drew upon her, and she moaned in appreciation.

Ever so slowly his hands slid down her ribcage, questing for her warm, moist center. Instant heat pooled between her thighs, spilling like honey over his fingers. He thumbed the delicate bud in the center of her folds and her body hummed in response, drawn to him as it was to no other.

So intent was she on the pleasure that she didn't notice his movement until his fingers left her. She murmured a protest that quickly became a gasp of delight as he fit his mouth to her. Her hands clamped to his head, but she didn't know if she wanted to push him away or keep him there forever.

He solved the problem by grabbing her wrists, pinning her arms to her sides as he plundered her with his tongue. Waves of pleasure engulfed her senses, reducing the universe to Michael's lips and the area he suckled. "You're killing me!"

"No, I'm loving you."

He laughed, and the sound rumbled up his throat and vibrated across the sensitive tissue he laved. With a short, sharp cry, she combusted, arching against his mouth. Even as her spasms shook her, he surged into her, meeting her fire with heat of his own.

She locked her legs around his waist, calling his name as another larger current of pleasure shook her to the bone. He answered her with a hoarse shout, spilling into her in an unending rush of ecstatic energy.

It was a long time before their senses returned. He rolled, taking her with him, stopping when she was perched above him. She opened her eyes to find him staring at her, his expression so intense it stole her breath. Alarmed, she framed his face with her hands. "What is it?"

"Do you realize just how happy you make me?" he whispered, his voice thick with emotion.

She leaned forward, trailing feather-light kisses across his face. "If it's as happy as you've made me, I think I understand."

Her smile became a sensual sigh as he flexed deep inside her. "Don't you ever get enough?" she asked, her eyes twinkling as she rocked against him.

"Of you, my love?" His hands circled her waist. "Never."

Sometime later he staggered to his feet, but Yvonne was too satiated to offer more than a token protest. She was deliciously lethargic, so thoroughly loved that her bones felt like water. If only every day of her life could end like this!

He returned, wearing the robe she had created for him and carrying a Desire gift box. "Dinner will be ready in a few minutes," he informed her as he sat cross-legged beside her. "In the meantime, this is for you."

Curious, she sat up. Though she designed everything under Desire's line, there were some items that she wouldn't dream of making for herself, much less buy. She wondered what Michael would pick out for her.

"It's not my birthday," she protested even as she reached for the box. "The bath, the massage, and the-the other thing were enough."

"I wanted to get you something special. Go on, open it."

She did, pulling back the tissue paper to reveal his gift. It was a gown of sensuous gold silk, with a bodice and three inch wide panel running down the center made of black velvet lace. It was demure, yet decadent. And it matched his robe perfectly.

She looked at him obliquely. "It's beautiful," she admitted. "But it's not mine."

He laughed. "Don't get your hackles up. Lawrence made it for me, after I told him what I wanted."

Her mouth dropped open. "You and Law made this-together?" She scrambled to her feet and shimmied into the gown in a series of movements that set Michael's blood to boil. It clung to her curves with reverence, making a mystery of her femininity, proving her a goddess made flesh.

She spun in a circle, clapping her hands as a laugh bubbled out of her. "Law has a lot of questions to answer in the morning. He's definitely wasting his talent being my personal assistant. And you!"

She leveled a finger at him. "'Fess up. My birthday was in March. So what are we celebrating? Or do you want something from me?"

Sheepish, he spread his hands. "You got me. I never could keep secrets from you." He got to his feet. "But I think I'll keep you in suspense a while longer."

Taking her hand, he led her to the bistro set in the corner, already set for a romantic dinner for two with candlelight and a single red rose for the centerpiece. He seated her and handed her a flute of champagne. "I'll be right back with dinner. Relax."

Watching his retreating back, Yvonne was anything but relaxed. She was enjoying every minute of this blissful respite, and every cell in her body was screaming in thanks. He was going way out of his way with this gesture, yet she failed to see any reason for it. Sure, Your Heart's Desire's premier fashion show was three weeks away, and the catalog was...

The catalog. Of course. They had received the galley of the catalog today, and there had only been need for one correction. Mass printing would start on Tuesday, with the first mailings to start the week before the show. Also, in a marketing blitz devised by BBC, one customer from each store would win tickets to the fashion show, with a grand prize winner receiving tickets for two, dinner at Marco's, and a limousine for the evening. Response was better than they had forecast, and it was going to get better.

When Michael returned, bearing steaming plates, she gave him an amazed smile. "I'm amazed that you found time to do this," she admitted as she sliced into the tenderloin. "Thom can't appreciate how I've all but stolen you from him."

He pushed food around on his plate, anticipation stealing his hunger. "Almost all my other projects have been funneled to assistants," he informed her. "And that's per Thom. He realizes that Your Heart's Desire is top priority."

Yvonne stared at him through lowered lashes. "And where am I in your list of priorities?" she asked, half-jokingly.

He reached across the small table and captured her hand in his. "You're the only thing on my priority list."

She laughed and gently extracted her hand. "I think we'd better make the fashion show the only thing on our lists for the next month," she said, returning her attention to her dinner.

He watched as she attacked her meal. She reminded him of a hummingbird, brightly colored and seemingly fragile, yet always in constant motion. His mouth quirked in a smile. Of course, he didn't know if hummingbirds ate like lumberjacks.

She looked up at him then. Apparently disconcerted to find him studying her, she stuck her tongue out and crossed her eyes. Michael broke into startled laughter. "Didn't your mother ever tell you your face could get stuck like that?" he asked, and instantly regretted it.

But her eyes didn't cloud with pain. "Actually, she did," she admitted, a bittersweet smile on her lips. She reached across the table and took his hand. "I think my family would have liked you."

Michael swallowed. "Really?"

Yvonne's eyes were soft. "Yes," she replied. "Even though you're not what they would have expected, they would have realized what I finally do."

"What's that?"

She glanced down at their intertwined hands, then back to him. "That you are a good man, and you're good to me and for me."

Michael's heart flip-flopped as he saw the glowing sincerity in her eyes. "I hope you still feel that way when you're ninety."

"What?"

With trembling insides, he plucked the rose from the centerpiece, left his chair, and knelt beside hers. "I had a whole romantic scheme planned out, but I can't wait anymore." He handed her the rose.

Perplexed, she accepted it. "You want me to change Desire's logo from pink dogwoods to roses?"

"Nope. That's not what I want."

Yvonne brought the half-opened bud to her nose, inhaling the delicate scent. Something gleamed at her from inside. "What in the world … ?"

She peeled back a petal, and a sparkling band fell into her palm. It was a marquise-cut diamond solitaire, at least two carats' worth, with baguette rubies and aquamarines channel-set into the gold band on either side: their birthstones.

"Oh my God. Michael?"

With a gentle smile, Michael took the ring and slid it onto her finger. It fit perfectly. "There's only one thing I want, Yvonne: you. As my lover, my friend, my wife. Will you marry me?"

CHAPTER NINETEEN

Yvonne stared down at her hand. In the candlelight, the ring gleamed as brightly as true love. Scant inches from it, the bangle shone dully. "You-you want to marry me?"

"I've never wanted anything else this much," he confessed. "The first time I saw you, a brilliant flash of red on a spring day, I knew you were going to change my life. And you have. I can't imagine being with anyone else but you. You make my heart smile."

"Oh, Michael." She was finding it hard to breathe, so frantically was her heart thudding. "I never thought—I never dreamed ... "

"Me neither. I never dreamed I could feel this happy, this whole. I didn't dare. But I think it's time we start."

Start daring. God, how she wanted to. How she needed to. But she knew she couldn't go forward, couldn't claim the future, until she'd shared her past with him.

She clasped his hand between hers. "Every moment of every day makes me care for you and want you more. You have become everything to me. And because you have, I have to be honest with you, even if it costs me everything."

Without preamble, she began. "The accident happened around eleven at night. It had been snowing, but the roadways were still clear. Our station wagon was second in line at a traffic light. When the light turned green, the car in front of us made it through the intersection, but a tractor-trailer came out of nowhere, ran the red light, and struck the driver's side. Our station wagon crumpled like a tin can as it came to rest against a pole on the front passenger side.

"It took nearly three hours for help to come and pry the top off. I remember screaming, for help, for my Mom and Dad, for Yvette. I remember the smell of blood, and the acridly sweet smell of death.

"I was unconscious when they pulled me from the wreckage. I lay in the coma for a week. They didn't tell me I had lost my family until the start of the second week. Then they said I would probably never walk again, much less skate."

She sighed shakily. "Just like that, my life had been annihilated. The only two things that mattered to me, my family and skating, were ripped from me. It broke my heart and my mind. I had no other reason to live and I knew it. The nightmares started after that. I would wake up screaming whenever I fell asleep before the hour the accident occurred. Even when they sedated me the nightmare would start, driving me to stay awake, to fight the sedatives until three in the morning, the time they pulled me from the wreckage.

"It got to the point where I was afraid of darkness. Night became my enemy. I didn't dare to sleep any more, because I knew darkness, that voracious, frigid night, would unleash the nightmares. Between the nightmares and the devastation of my life, I was being sucked down a dark whirlpool. Darkness had infected my head and my heart, pushing me further down the spiral. I knew what I was going through was because I was supposed to be dead. I wasn't a survivor; I was a fluke, an aberration. In my mind, the only way to keep the nightmares from persecuting me was to-to eradicate the problem."

She stared past him, unwilling to see the horror on his face as she described her bungled attempts at suicide. "They finally strapped me to the bed and moved me to a mental hospital for children. The next three months passed in a clouded stupor; nothing seemed real to me but the darkness. Then one day, as I was begging to die, I heard my Uncle ask me why."

A harsh breath sawed into her lungs. "I told him it was a mistake that I made it when my family hadn't. Uncle Reg asked me one simple question: What if it wasn't a mistake? That possibility had never entered my convoluted mind, but I latched onto it like the life preserver it was. Uncle Reg then told me there was a possibility that I could walk again, if I was strong enough.

"That marked the turning point for me. Poppy and Auntie Grace visited me every day, becoming the guiding force in my life. I clawed my way out of the darkness of my grief. When I was declared mentally fit, I was supposed to be released to my uncle's care, but my aunt and cousins didn't want a suicidal teen living with them, so I went to live with Poppy and Auntie Grace instead.

"Poppy and Grace loved me and took care of me, but I never felt like I belonged—not with them, not with Uncle Reg. I knew I was a burden, even though they opened their hearts and their home to me. But it was so damned hard to be there, to see Melissa with Grace, to see Jimmy ask Poppy a question and realize that I would never share even the simplest things with my parents again.

"So I became determined to skate again. I wanted to thank everyone who took care of me, wanted to honor my family, and Poppy and Grace, and Uncle Reg whom I loved more than anything else. Uncle Reg had always been close to my sister and me, and we became even closer. I was all he had left of his twin, and he was so like my father, and he understood the emptiness I felt with the loss of my twin.

"He saw to my future by suing the trucking company that destroyed my life. Once it was discovered that the driver was twice the legal limit for alcohol, the company gave me two million dollars. That kind of money could buy a lot of things, including specialists to get me back on my feet. Somehow stories passed that I recuperated in a special sports medicine facility in Canada, and we never saw any reason to tell anyone differently. I knew that if Dinah and my cousins treated me the way they did because of my illness, other people would be worse.

"So I kept my story to myself, and poured my energy into surviving. Every day after hours of physical therapy, Grace would work with me, teaching me yoga and simple ballet movements. When I was able to stand up more than I fell down, I went back to the ice."

She breathed deeply, remembering that day. "It was the closest thing to a homecoming I've experienced. It didn't matter that at first I couldn't even execute a simple jump; I was on the ice, and I was home. When I was eighteen, I made it to the Nationals, and then the World. I didn't medal, but I was so happy to be there, to achieve what my sister and I had dreamed about. But that dream came with a price."

God, she didn't want to continue, didn't want to go through it all again. But there was no turning back. "Uncle

Reg had cancer. He didn't tell me because he wanted me to concentrate on skating. I-I was devastated. I knew it was my fault. I had been so caught up in my selfish pursuit of skating that I didn't notice him getting sick. I just knew there was something I could have done, spent more time with him, made him go to the doctor. Something, anything.

"But it was too late. There was nothing I could do. I was powerless, and somebody else I loved was being taken from me. Uncle Reg knew I was taking it hard. H-He made me swear to keep on going and make my life a living monument to my family. He made me swear on my family's memory that I-that I would live.

"It was the hardest thing I have ever had to do. Not even learning to walk again was that difficult. But Uncle Reg knew that if I swore it, I would have to keep that promise. So I swore it. He died two days later."

A broken laugh-sob escaped her. "My aunt, of course, blamed me. I had poisoned him. He died because he loved me. I killed him because I loved him. And she was right. I knew I had to leave Detroit then. Leave everyone and everything I loved, so that I wouldn't doom them by loving them.

"Jeff and I had become good friends through our letters by then, and when he suggested moving to Atlanta, I grabbed it like the lifeline it was.

"You know the rest. I've spent the last decade trying to build a successful business like my father did, to do good community service like my mother did. But I've never been able to be outgoing and carefree like Yvette was. Because the darkness and the coldness are still here, even all these years later. Most days are good days, but some days ... some days I become that terrified little girl again, and the darkness wins.

"The only way I know to protect myself is to relinquish the right to love. I can care, like I care about my girls, and my company, and my friends. But I can't ever love. I loved Poppy, and now's he's dead. I can't do that to anyone else. Even if it means being alone for the rest of my life."

Silence, save for her labored breathing as her blood rushed through her veins.

She had finally done it. She had finally told someone her story. Even if she never got another chance, even if it earned her a broken heart, she was glad to expunge it from her soul.

Her soul lighter but her heart heavy, she rose to her feet. "I'm sorry, Michael," she said, turning away from him. "I never intended for anyone to get this involved in my life— especially you. But the more I tried to push you away, the more I needed you. I still do."

The ring pressed into her skin as she clasped her hand to her chest. "I don't expect you to understand. How could you, or anyone for that matter? So it's all right if you want to change your mind."

"I'm not going to change my mind."

Arms came around her, engulfing her. He turned her around, brushing her cheek with the back of his free hand, and only then did she realize she was crying silently.

"But what about my past?"

His golden eyes stared back at her earnestly. "No one should endure what you did, especially a child. No one blames you for wanting to escape the pain and terror you were going through. Your past matters to me because it matters to you, because it's a part of you. Your future also matters to me, and so does the present. Especially if you can set aside the fears of the past, say yes in the present, and make our future happy and bright."

He slipped her bracelet from her wrist. "You have hurt and been hurt long enough," he said softly, running his fingers over the scar. "Let me give you what you've given me. Let's put aside the fear and guilt and anger that keep us from enjoying life. Fear is not going to keep me from loving you. It shouldn't keep you from loving me either."

He lifted her palm to his cheek. "I don't need to hear the words now, but one day I will. Can you do that for me? Step beyond the fear? Can you do it for yourself?"

The light touch of his lips on the scar was like a brand, burning away her doubts and fears. When she spoke, her voice was a broken sigh. "Yes."

Golden eyes flared with more joy than she believed possible. "Are you going to answer yes to my other question?"

Yvonne found herself believing. Daring. "Do you really mean it? We can be a family? With a big, rambling house with a magnolia tree out front?"

Michael laughed. "You, me, and as many little Benjamins as your heart desires."

"My own family," she whispered, choking on tears. "My very own family."

Michael gently brushed an errant tear from her chin. "Does that mean yes?"

Yvonne threw her arms around his neck. "You caring, considerate man! You warm-hearted, wonderful—"

He cut her off with a kiss. "Okay, Roget! I'll settle for a yes."

Laughter bubbled out of her, loving and free. "Yes, yes—a thousand times yes!"

CHAPTER TWENTY

"Hey Mike, you got a minute?" Michael put down the sheaf of proofs he held, watching as Jeff made his way through the throng of scantily clad women. "Sure thing. What's up?"

Jeff looked around the crowded rehearsal area. "Is there somewhere else we can talk? Privately?"

Curious, he led Jeff through equipment and clothing racks to a tiny office. He gestured Jeff inside then followed, shutting the door behind him. "Is something wrong?"

Jeff got right to the point. "What the hell are you up to?"

"Excuse me?"

"Come on, Mike, drop the bull. You know damn well what I'm talking about!"

Michael straightened. Did Yvonne finally tell Jeff the truth? They had planned to announce their engagement at the celebration party after the fashion show. She still wore her mother's rings, keeping his ring on a chain around her neck for now.

He wanted nothing more than to get things out in the open. He felt like a love-struck teen sneaking out behind his parents' back. But Yvonne wanted to wait, and he discovered that he couldn't refuse her if he tried.

Yet Jeff's behavior didn't lead him to believe that he knew about the engagement. Maybe something else was bothering him. "Why don't you spell it out for me?"

Jeff's hands clenched. "You and Yvonne. I don't know what kind of game you're playing, but I want it to stop! She's on an emotional roller coaster right now, and if you're taking advantage of her..."

"Wait just a friggin' minute!" he interrupted. "I am not taking advantage of Yvonne!"

Jeff continued as if he hadn't heard. "You've insinuated yourself into her life professionally and personally. Every time I go to visit her, you're there. And tagging along while she went back home, that was a little convenient, don't you think?"

"I think you're being paranoid, that's what I think."

"Oh really?"

"Yeah, really." Michael leaned forward. "Vonne needed a friend more than anything when her coach died. And I am her friend, despite what you might think."

Jeff stared at him for a silent, tense moment before he spoke. "I am not going to let you hurt her," he said, his voice low with intensity.

"I have no intention of hurting Yvonne," Michael retorted. "If you think I could do something like that, why did you ask me to take care of her in Detroit?"

"Yvonne didn't need to be alone. You were the lesser of two evils. But I warned her about you, just in case."

He was surprised at the venom in Jeff's voice. Surprised and angry. "I would never, ever, attempt to take advantage of anyone's grief, and I resent the hell out of you thinking that I would. And I can't believe that Yvonne even listened to you."

Jeff's eyes were hard. "She didn't. She told me you were the perfect gentleman, which only makes me suspect you more. Now I'm telling you for your own good: whatever scheme you're running, stop it. When this fashion show is over and the catalog's off the ground, I want you out of Yvonne's life. For good." He yanked open the door and stalked away.

It took every ounce of willpower Michael possessed not to pursue his best friend and punch him on the spot. Only the image of Yvonne's horrified expression when she found out restrained him. He understood Jeff's desire to look out for her, but good grief! The man was acting more like a jealous lover than a friend …

My God, was Jeff in love with Yvonne? The thought floored him. What else would make him behave so irrationally? She and Jeff had been friends for years, just over a decade. Yet if Jeff was in love with her, why had he never done anything about it?

If Yvonne's actions were any indication, she had no knowledge that Jeff felt as deeply as he did about her. Although she loved Jeff, Michael knew she wasn't in love with him. She couldn't be. She called him her "big brother".

A chill crept spider-like up his spine. Would her feelings change if she knew how Jeff felt? Her loyalty to Jeff was based upon more than ten years of serious history. His letters had kept her grounded. She had moved to Atlanta because of him. She had put off every attempt Michael made to inform Jeff of their relationship.

She had agreed to marry him, but she had never told him that she loved him.

The chill settled in his gut like a fist of ice. Was Yvonne unknowingly in love with Jeff?

What would he do if she were?

Yvonne couldn't stop grinning. Tonight was the culmination of months of planning and years of dreams. The show was less than ten minutes from beginning. The backstage area was the epitome of organized chaos. Makeup artists and seamstresses flitted about, making last-minute repairs under her watchful eye.

It reminded her a little of competition, and her smile grew bittersweet as she was reminded of Poppy. Grace and the remainder of the Calhouns were out in the audience, and she was sure Poppy and her family were somewhere above her, watching in approval.

She lifted her left hand, letting the beautiful engagement ring catch the light. Her mother's rings were now on a chain about her neck, to be kept safe until her son needed them.

Her son. Just the thought of having a child with Michael caused her heart to leap. Tonight, the world would discover where her latest inspiration came from. And later, she and Michael could actually practice creating a family.

"Why in the hell are you grinning like that guy from *The Shining*?"

Yvonne turned around. Angela walked up to her, absolutely stunning in an iridescent robe of stylized peacock feathers over a black lace gown. A Cleopatra-style hairpiece completed her diva ensemble. As part of the finale, Angela would come onstage regally reclining on a litter borne by six local bodybuilders in loincloths.

"Because once Jeff takes a look at you in that, he's not going to remember his own name, much less any other woman."

"You think so?"

Yvonne heard the longing in her partner's voice. She knew Angela was more than half in love with Jeff, and that he, man that he was, was completely blind to it. Their time together in New York had been wonderful, according to Angela, but strictly platonic.

It was time to wake Jeff Maxwell up. She intuitively knew that he and Angela would be good for each other. She had created the Queen of the Nile ensemble with the express intent to shake Jeff up. And if it didn't work on him, the rest of the male population of Atlanta was sure to camp out at their Buckhead office.

Yvonne took her friend's arms. "Angela, repeat after me: 'I am the Queen of the Nile'."

"I am the Queen of the Nile."

"Say it like you mean it."

"I am the Queen of the Nile."

"That's better. Now say 'I am the original diva'."

Angela held her head high. "I am the original diva."

"I make straight men hard and gay men sorry."

Angela started laughing, but she managed to repeat it. Law passed by, then stopped. "Oh my God, Angie! If I weren't playing for the other team ... "

"This diva stuff is working already," Angela said, grinning.

Yvonne winked. "Told you so."

The assistant coordinator approached them. "Five minutes."

Yvonne clapped her hands. "Okay, everybody, gather around!" Models, staff, and helpers converged on her. She looked at them all, employees, associates, assistants. Friends.

"This night is a dream come true, not only for me, Gwen, and Angela, but for everyone associated with Your Heart's Desire. From the bottom of my heart, I want to thank each and every one of you for your hard work and determination. We have international coverage just beyond those curtains, so let's show them what Southern hospitality is all about.

"Smiling is mandatory! Have fun, and remember: get through the next two hours and we'll party like it's New Year's Eve in Times Square! Like they say in Cajun country, laissez les bontemps rouler!"

"Let the good times roll!" her staff echoed their meeting-ending cheer, and dispersed.

The fashion show was a rousing success. Yvonne featured two lines: Desire Classique, traditional styles and colors set to orchestral music; and Desire Spice, lingerie so sexy it made men steam, set to a pulsing, erotic techno-beat.

The showstopper was the introduction of the Venus line: lingerie inspired by female deities and famous queens, culminating with Angela's appearance. Afterwards, all three partners fielded questions and congratulations from the media and well-wishers.

Yvonne was so excited she nearly forgot about Michael. She knew he and Thom had entertained some of their out-of- town guests, and that Michael had sat with his parents and her foster-family during the show. But she didn't really miss him until the society reporter for the local newspaper noticed the engagement ring on her hand.

She gushingly informed her of their upcoming nuptials, and the official announcement that was to be made at the after-party. No, they hadn't set a date yet, but it would be some time in the fall.

Michael caught up with her just before she joined Angela in a limousine ride to Creole, courtesy of Better Business Concepts. He handed her a single red rose that perfectly matched the ruby-red color of her silk sheath. She smiled her love at him, and someone snapped a picture of that private moment that was to run in the paper the following day.

"Have I told you how incredibly gorgeous you are?"

She laughed huskily. "When I saw the way your eyes lit up, I had a clue. But it's still nice to hear."

"There ought to be a law against that dress. Red suits you."

She smiled. "I have Law to thank for it. It's his design. I think the dress goes well with the ring, don't you?"

"It goes perfectly, but not as great as that smile," Michael answered. He linked hands with her. "Sweetheart, I've been thinking."

"About what?"

"Maybe we should wait to make our announcement."

She stared at him, surprised. He was the one who had been pushing for getting their relationship out in the open, and she told him so.

"I know, but tonight is a special night for you and Your Heart's Desire," he explained, his fingers grazing her cheek. "Everyone should be focused on you and the show. We wouldn't want to upstage the fantastic coverage you received, would we?"

He had a point. But she'd already spilled the beans to that reporter. She was about to tell him when Jeff came rushing up.

"Vonne, you look good enough to eat!" he kissed her soundly on the lips before pressing a bouquet of roses into her arms.

She accepted them, puzzled by Jeff's effusive greeting, and Michael's reaction to it. He immediately tensed, his gaze sharpening as it swept them. She gave him a minute shrug before turning her attention back to Jeff. "Thanks, I think. What did you think of Angela's performance?"

Jeff got a faraway look in his eyes. All he could say was "Whoa."

Yvonne grinned. Plan A was a huge success. On to Plan B. "Hey, why don't you ride over with her in the limo? I'm going to ride over with Auntie Grace and the family."

He gave Michael a long stare, one that Michael matched in intensity. Finally Jeff acquiesced. "All right, I'll see you there."

"What was that about?" she asked after he departed.

Michael stared down at her, his eyes stormy. She touched his arm, her nerves sending an alarm through her. "Michael?"

He blinked. "If you want to go straight home after the party, I don't mind."

"Well, I do. Grace, Melissa, and Jimmy are staying at my place, remember? Besides, aren't we going to celebrate after the celebration?"

He smiled at her then, and her nerves settled. "Two A.M., my place?"

She smiled at him. "I'll be there with bells on. Only bells."

Michael did his level best to have a good time, he really did. But every time he saw Yvonne dancing with Jeff, every time he saw Jeff's arm lay possessively about her waist, he was seized with a fit of jealousy.

Yet even he had to admit, they made a good pair. They were striking together. People naturally gravitated toward them, making them the center of attention. They were seamless together, often finishing each other's thoughts. Why had he never noticed it before?

Jeff had so much to offer her. He was good-looking, he was successful, he was black. He knew enough of her past to help her through bouts of melancholy. He'd done it before. In fact, he had done it several times over the course of their history.

And there was history. Michael couldn't deny that. There would always be parts of Yvonne that belonged to Jeff alone.

Knowing he would ruin the festivities if he remained, Michael said his good-byes and left. Yvonne followed him less than two hours later.

She breezed into his home, all sweetness and light, giving Cutter a kiss before collapsing beside him on the couch. "I missed you," she said, kissing him as well.

He pulled the combs from her hair. "Did you?"

She stared at him, her dark eyes wide. "Of course I did. I mean, it was exciting and heady and wonderful, but you were the one who made it all happen. I wanted to acknowledge that, and us."

She looked so sincere. He wanted to believe her. But all he could see was Jeff taking her in his arms and kissing her.

And how right she looked there.

"Michael?"

She was standing beside him, her eyes concerned. "You look worn out. Let's get out of these clothes and get to bed, okay?" She held out her hand.

The ring he had given her sparkled merrily at him. He took her hand and let himself be led upstairs. He pulled her into the shower with him, wanting, needing to hold her and touch her. Her soft sighs filled the steamy shower stall as she opened for him, her back snug against his chest. Afterwards, they raided the fridge and adjourned to bed.

Damn, but he couldn't stop looking at her. She was so beautiful, and for now, she was his. But Jeff's ultimatum reverberated in his mind, warning him that time was running out.

"What's wrong?"

Quiet as it was, her voice startled him. "What?"

Her eyes, dark and mysterious, stared into him, as if attempting to divine the secrets of his soul. "I know you well enough to know you seem curiously let down," she finally said. "Would you mind telling me why?"

He slid on the bed, wrapping his arms about her waist and resting his head on her belly. She stroked his hair, a move that always helped settle him. "I do feel a little let down," he admitted. "BBC's work with your company is over. You don't need us anymore."

"But I do need you."

"No, you don't."

Her hand froze. "Wh-what?"

He couldn't look at her. If he did, if he saw hurt and confusion on her face, his resolve would be weakened. "Vonne, why did you agree to marry me?"

She gave a small laugh, but he felt her stomach muscles clench. "Because I want to be with you, that's why."

He closed his eyes, her simple statement knifing through him. Even now, she couldn't say the "L" word. Yet he had to know.

"Do you love me, Vonne?"

Her hand jerked in his hair, and in that telling moment he almost hated her. "Why are you grilling me like this?"

"Because I need to know!" Needing distance, he rolled away from her, taking a deep breath to cool his anger, and his hurt.

When he looked at her again, he discovered that she had drawn the sheet over her breasts and was staring at him with fear in her eyes.

"Vonne." He reached for her hand. It trembled in his grip. "You've never been in love before."

"So what, that invalidates what I feel?" she asked shakily. "Are my feelings any less real because I've never experienced love before?"

"No." The word was a ragged sigh. "But I want you to be sure."

"I'm sure I want to marry you." She tried to smile, but it fell flat. She wasn't sure, and they both knew it.

"How can you be sure?" he asked hoarsely. "How can I be sure? What if you meet someone else, someone who can be more, offer you more? What if there's someone else out there better for you than me?"

"You're scaring me."

He looked at her then, and was lost. Her eyes were huge, bright with tears and fear. He couldn't do it. He couldn't walk away. Not now, not like this.

"I'm sorry, love," he whispered, joining her on her side of the bed. "I don't mean to hurt you. I guess I'm just mentally exhausted."

The excuse sounded lame, even to him. She nodded once, jerky, and drew a deep, steadying breath. He diverted her attention by pulling the sheet away from her. She was curled into a defensive ball, arms and legs guarding her scarred skin, and he hated himself for doing that to her.

Gently, he laid her down, his hand trembling as it stroked across the faded network of scars that were just as dear to him as the woman they were a part of.

He pressed gentle kisses along her abdomen, his hand sliding down to the dark nest of curls between her thighs. Her responding sigh triggered a wildness in him. She was his! No matter what happened, regardless of whom she gave her heart to, he would ensure that her body belonged to him always.

He made love to her slowly and relentlessly, claiming her as his own. He branded her with his mouth and his hands as she writhed beneath him, calling his name. Fitting against her back like a living spoon, he brought her to shuddering, violent fulfillment.

Not giving her chance to recover, he turned her and cradled her against his thighs and seared her once more, each time denying himself. Finally, when she was senseless to everything but the passion, everything but him, he pinned her to the bed and slowly sank into her.

He pulled out in one long, agonizing stroke. "Do you love me, Yvonne?" he asked, his voice cracking.

"Michael…"

She moaned as he barely brushed against her sensitive flesh, teasing her. "Do you love me?" he asked savagely.

"Yes."

He sank into her, ruthless. "Then say it."

She cried out as he filled her. "I love you, Michael."

"Again."

"I love you."

"Again!"

With each stroke, she renewed her pledge until it became a frenzied mantra as she sobbed her release. One final, frantic thrust and Michael joined her, his soul reaching out to intertwine with hers. Only then did he allow her to rest, holding her close as she slipped into an exhausted slumber.

Her tears fell even in her sleep, burning like acid as they dropped onto his chest. He blinked several times, then yielded to the moisture singeing his eyes. Even as he allowed sleep to claim him, Michael held her tightly. But it wasn't tight enough.

In the morning he would let her go.

CHAPTER TWENTY-ONE

The next morning, Yvonne was too excited to remain in bed. She had dreamed about her wedding gown, and wanted to capture the image on paper before it faded.

She slipped out of bed, careful not to disturb Michael. He had worn himself out taking her company to the next level so successfully. That had to be why he was so stressed out last night. What else could explain the strange mood he had been in? As if she could even consider being with someone else. She hoped she had proven to him beyond a shadow of a doubt that she belonged to him, and always would.

With quiet movements she dressed then padded downstairs. She had been spending more and more time in Michael's house, and she had come to love it almost as much as she loved him. Cutter greeted her in the kitchen, and she roughhoused with him before letting him into the backyard. She put on a pot of coffee, then paused, struck by the domesticity of it all. What would it be like, she wondered, rushing about with Michael to get ready for work, preparing breakfast for their children before sending them off to school?

She almost laughed aloud. Prepare breakfast? She couldn't even make toast.

She carried her coffee to the large office just off the living room. She had tried not to encroach on too much of Michael's space, but he was the one taking things from her townhouse and bringing them here. Her easel and drafting table were by the window, and space had been cleared for her files and computer. Her strider was in the basement next to his weights, and one side of his huge walk-in closet was now hers. That, more than anything, showed her how serious this was. Michael was as much a clotheshorse as she was.

Setting her mug on the desk, she positioned her easel to catch the morning sun. The day was rapidly clouding over; thunderstorms would be pelting Atlanta by lunchtime. She was too happy to care.

Using a thin charcoal pencil she sketched the outline of a long-sleeved sheath with a scooped neckline and a fitted waist. With deft strokes she quickly created a detachable train that was almost an overskirt. It would be crafted of Georgian lace and sheer panels, and both would be covered with seed pearls. Instead of pure white, she opted for a shade not quite the blush of champagne or ivory, but a shade of white that reminded her of candlelight, and the night Michael had proposed.

She stepped back to survey her work. She had managed to capture most of the essence of her dream, but she wasn't a wedding gown designer. She wondered if she could convince Vera Wang to craft the gown for her. That would mean flying to New York for fittings and the cost of the gown would be expensive. Since she was only planning to do this once, she intended to pull out all the stops.

Wrapping her arms about herself, Yvonne recalled her dream: it was a beautiful cool evening, and a spectacular sunset provided a glorious backdrop. Birds and crickets harmonized to Eric Satie's Gymnopedie No. 1. She and Michael exchanged personal vows in the glow of a hundred candles then danced the night away under the canopy of a thousand stars.

For a moment the image was so powerful that she could almost smell the flowers and candles. She hugged herself tightly, her heart thumping with happiness.

She held her left hand aloft, making the jewel twinkle in the morning sun. She was getting married. Soon, she and Michael would start a family of their own. She ran her hands down her flat stomach, imagining it rounded with life, proof of their love for each other. Her deepest, most precious dream was about to come true: she would belong to a family again.

She sighed happily. She was living again. Last night had proven that happiness could be hers, that her hopes and prayers had been heard and answered.

Pounding on the front door interrupted her reverie. Her partners and assistant knew she would be staying at Michael's. She had given Lawrence the day off. Maybe it was Gwen and Angela, wanting to relive the excitement of the night before.

Looking out the window, she saw Jeff's car at the curb. She hurried to the door and threw it open. "Jeff! I'm so excited—"

He stormed into the foyer. "What the hell do you think you're doing?"

"What are you talking about?"

Jeff slapped a rolled-up newspaper against his palm. "This— this bullshit!"

She took the paper. It was the society page. Full color photos showed the boudoir setting of the fashion show. A picture of her in Michael's arms took up a third of the page. The caption read, "A Match Made in Merchandising".

"Former Olympic skater and entrepreneur Yvonne Mitchelson, 28, owner of Your Heart's Desire boutiques, surprised reporters attending her debut fashion show at the Fox Theatre with the announcement of her engagement to marketing whiz Michael Benjamin, 33, of Better Business Concepts.

"The lavish production, meant to launch the new catalog and private label, had a sizzling 'Queen of the Nile' finale featuring Desire's VP of Operations, Angela Davenport. Though the show was well received, the true finale came when Ms. Mitchelson appeared at the post-production press conference confirming her engagement. Although details have yet to be finalized, the wedding is reportedly planned for early fall."

The article went on, favorably reviewing her collection. She touched the photo, a soft smile lighting her face. "I need to remember to ask for a copy of this photo," she murmured. "I'm glad they liked the show."

"Is that all you can say, 'I'm glad they liked the show'?" he demanded, incredulous.

"Well, I didn't make it to the Olympics, and I wish they hadn't put my age in there, but it was a favorable review," she answered. "What else should I say?"

"How about, 'Oh, Jeff, how could I be so stupid?'"

"Jeff, what in the world are you talking about?"

He grabbed her by the shoulders. "Tell me that this is a joke," he pleaded. "Tell me that this supposed engagement is nothing more than a publicity stunt you and Mike cooked up."

"This isn't a stunt, Jeff," she informed him. "We were going to announce it at the party, but didn't want to detract from the show. But it's very real." She held out her hand.

Jeff stared at the ring on her finger. It was definitely real. Real expensive. "Vonne, listen to me. I know you've been under tremendous stress the last few months. I haven't been here for you lately, especially when your coach died. It's natural for you to need to turn to someone for comfort. You might even believe Mike is that someone. I know he can be very smooth when he wants to be.

"But this engagement, this is a bit extreme, even for him. No matter what he says, Mike's not the one for you."

She wrenched away from him, shocked. "I can't believe this!" she exclaimed. "Do you really think I went to bed with Michael because I was under stress? And you think he proposed to me because I slept with him?"

She sat on the couch. "Jeff, I don't know how to tell you this, but Michael and I have been sleeping together for months."

He made a strangled sound, his cheeks reddening as if she'd slapped him. "Son of a bitch!" he burst out. "I don't believe this! How the hell could you not tell me?"

She folded her arms across her chest. "We never discussed our partners before, Jeff," she reminded him coolly. "But if you must know, we didn't tell anyone earlier because there was nothing to tell. And we certainly didn't want the kind of reaction you're having right now. Besides, this really wasn't supposed to be more than a casual relationship. But things changed. It was a natural progression."

"It is not natural!" Jeff shouted. "In less than six months you go from being absolute strangers to business partners to walking down the aisle? What kind of crap is that?"

Cutter bounded into the room and inserted himself between them. He swung his head to Jeff, a low growl emanating from his throat. His loyalty was clear.

Yvonne put her hand on his back. "Easy boy," she said soothingly, using the opportune distraction to marshal her thoughts. She stood. "What Michael and I have is not crap. We make each other happy. We belong together."

He snorted but kept his distance. "Yeah, sure you do. Like oil and water. You know, maybe you believe you two belong together. I'm sure Mike promised you the moon and stars wrapped with a bow. And maybe Mike thinks you belong together, too. But he won't for long."

"You're wrong," she replied angrily.

"You think so?" he asked sarcastically. "I'm his best friend, Vonne. I've known him a helluva lot longer than you have."

"That doesn't mean you know him better."

"I think I do. Mike's not the kind of guy you want."

Yvonne's hands went to her hips. "How the hell do you know what I want?"

"I know you want someone who'll be there for you, someone to love you and care for you…"

"Michael's all that and more!"

"The man's a player!" Jeff bellowed. "He can't stay with anyone for more than a couple of months. He's been through more women than you had in your fashion show!"

"And I suppose you've been a saint all the time I've known you!" she retorted, sarcasm evident. "That won't wash, Jeff."

He tried another tack. "Did he tell you about Beth?"

"He told me everything."

That obviously surprised him. "You know he's still hung up on a dead woman and you still want to be with him?"

Yvonne forced herself to take a deep calming breath. This was not how she had planned to spend her morning! Besides, Michael was still asleep upstairs; she definitely didn't want him to overhear.

"I wish I could make you understand," she said sadly, shaking her head. "Michael and I both have ghosts we're trying to deal with. We're working through our histories by helping each other. He loves me and I..."

"Mike doesn't love you, Vonne," Jeff interrupted. His voice was low, throbbing with intensity. "He's intrigued by you, turned on by you. Hell, you may even infatuate him. But he doesn't love you. You are nothing but a game to him. He likes to make women fall in love with him, and then he tosses them away. Even that ring, as expensive as it is, is just part of the game. Money doesn't mean anything to Mike, not when there's something he wants."

She was too stunned to speak. She could only stare at him, this man she considered her best friend and the brother she never had. Something inside her began to crack, shattered by each sentence Jeff spoke.

"Vonne, think about this logically. Why would he marry you? You've given him everything he wants. He's in your bed and your company. What else could you possibly give him that he'd have to marry you for? Children? Mike doesn't seem the fatherly type to me."

Is that why he wanted to delay the engagement announcement? an insidious voice inside her head whispered. She couldn't believe it. "Jeff ... "

"Let's just say, for the sake of argument, that you do get married," he continued relentlessly. "I hope you realize you're not going to have some happy-ever-after life. You're going to be stared at, ridiculed, cursed, perhaps worse. Your life will be a freakshow, and your children will catch all kinds of hell. Do you really think Mike will stick with you through all of that? He'll come to his senses as soon as he realizes what he's getting into—which won't be long, I can promise you. You should come to yours first."

Yvonne closed her eyes in an effort to staunch threatening tears. Her earlier euphoria had vanished, replaced by bewilderment.

"How can you talk about Michael like that?" she wondered, pained. "I thought he was your friend. I thought I was your friend. How can you stand there and assassinate the character of your best friend so easily? How can you hurt me like this?"

"Vonne, I am your friend. That's why I'm telling you this. It's for your own good."

She stared at him as if he were a stranger. Her anger leached out of her, replaced by a crushing sadness. "I don't understand you, Jeff. Michael's been your friend for more than half your life. If he's as bad as you claim, how could you have been his friend all this time?"

He spread his hands. "Like you said, I haven't been a saint. But I do love you, and I want the best for you."

"You want the best for me? How do you expect me to believe that after what you just said? Can't you understand that Michael's the best thing that's happened to me? Since I've met him, my designs are practically leaping off the page, they're so vibrant. My company has grown, and sales are up."

She splayed one hand across her chest. "But more than anything else, I've learned to feel again. I'm more alive than I've been in a long time. I'm actually happy. And I have Michael to thank for that."

Jeff's expression was implacable. "Don't delude yourself. You haven't had any serious relationships in all the time I've known you. You aren't capable of defending yourself against someone like him. You're allowing yourself to be swept away by a modern-day Casanova. He will take your heart, trample it into the ground, and walk away without a backwards glance."

Balling her hands into fists, she turned away from him, afraid that if she looked at him, she would forget their friendship and attempt to wound him as mortally as he was wounding her. "You are so wrong, Jeff," she said, spacing each word carefully. "Michael illuminates me. He takes all my anger and grief and guilt and makes it disappear. I belong to him."

"Then you're a heartbreak waiting to happen. You need to walk away from him before he walks away from you."

"I won't throw this away. I can't."

"Then our relationship means nothing."

She swung around to stare at him. His arms were crossed, his face set into stark, stubborn lines. "What are you saying?"

His mouth twisted, as if he had to force the words out. "I'm saying you need to choose who you really want in your life."

Her heart slammed against her ribcage. "No."

"Who matters more to you, Vonne? A man whose rep is so tarnished he should be in politics, or the man who's loved you and been there for you for more than a decade? I need to know, and I need to know now. You need to choose between Mike and me. You can't have both of us in your life."

His words were like physical blows, pummeling her hopes and dreams. "Please, Jeff," she whispered, shaking her head in denial. "I care for you both. I need you both. Don't make me choose. It isn't fair."

"It's not fair that you settle for less, either. You deserve much more."

"Get the hell away from her."

Michael's voice cut through the charged air like a whip. Yvonne turned and saw him in the doorway, a tower of fury. She wanted to run to him, but the expression on his face as he regarded his best friend kept her rooted.

Then he opened his arms and she hurtled into them, the strength of his embrace shielding her from Jeff's betrayal.

Jeff stood his ground. "I'm not leaving. Not until I talk some sense into her. You're the one who needs to get the hell out."

Michael's hand, stroking Yvonne's back, jerked to a halt. "First you rip me apart behind my back and now you're trying to kick me out of my own house?" His voice was dangerously soft. Cutter caught his master's mood and began to growl. "Just what kind of friend are you?"

"I'm the honest kind," Jeff seethed, fisting his hands. "We all know you're not really going to marry her. Why don't you quit playing her and leave her alone?!"

"What makes you think I'm playing her?"

"Oh, please." Jeff rolled his eyes. "You are Mike Benjamin, aren't you? The man who single-handedly elevated love-em-and-leave-em to an art form! With your track record, what else could you be doing?"

"Maybe I've changed," Michael answered. "Maybe I've found something, someone, worth changing for. Maybe, just maybe, I've found the one person I could lose my heart to."

"Do you really expect me to believe that?"

"After what I just heard you say about me?" Michael shook his head. "No, I guess I can't. So much for friendship."

"You have the balls to stand there and talk to me about friendship after I just discovered that you've been sleeping with Yvonne for months?" Jeff demanded. "What kind of friend stabs his best friend in the back like that?"

"I could ask you the same question, but I won't waste my breath."

Yvonne turned in Michael's arms. "Jeff, please—"

"Mike doesn't love you, Vonne. Not like I do."

Her heart leapt into her throat, then settled in her stomach. "What?"

Jeff moved toward her, his expression heavy. "I love you, Vonne. And I'm not talking about brotherly love."

Yvonne stared at him in shock. Jeff was in love with her? Staring into his eyes, she saw the truth plainly. "Oh my God."

Jeff's expression was pained. "I know. I never said anything. But I've been in love with you for years, since I first met you."

Michael pushed in front of her. "Now who's playing games? Verbally beating me up isn't working, so now you resort to this? Give me a break!"

"You have no idea how much I want to right now."

Both men took a step forward. Yvonne looked at them, these men she loved so dearly yet so differently. Intent was clearly stamped on their features.

"Stop it! For the love of God, please stop this!"

She pushed between them. "You two have been friends for nearly twenty years! Have you forgotten that? I haven't. And now you're at each other's throats as if everything you've been through together doesn't mean anything? I can't take that. I just can't!"

She sank onto the couch, burying her face in her hands.

Silence, so loud they could hear their hearts pounding, sifted through the room. Then Jeff made a sound that was almost a groan of pain. "Mike, look at what's happening here," he urged. "You know you're wrong for her. It isn't fair to pretend otherwise. If you had any decency, you'd realize she deserves better and leave her alone."

Michael knelt in front of her. His hand shook as it threaded through her hair, a poignant counterpoint to the trembling breath he took. "You're right."

Yvonne lifted her head in alarm. She felt as if he'd just kicked her in the stomach. "Wh-what?"

He gave her arms one final squeeze and then rose. She was instantly, irrevocably cold. "I think you should listen to Jeff."

She took a deep breath, trying to find the solid ground she'd stood on minutes before. "Why?"

"Because he's right." He spoke as if the words were difficult to form. "Vonne, you deserve much better than me, reformed bastard that I am. You know my history and all my sins. I'm not the right one for you. You need someone as kind and loving as you are, not some selfish son of a bitch like me."

She felt her heart drop to the ground. "You're not like that," she insisted. "I know your heart, Michael Benjamin. I know your soul. That's not you."

His hands clenched at his sides. Those beautiful, golden eyes she loved so much were tarnished black with some inner conflict she couldn't identify. His voice was bleak as he said, "Jeff knows what he's talking about. I'm a liar and a player, and I've been called everything but a saint by more women than I can remember. Things like that are hard to change."

"I know you're not perfect," she said, voice trembling, "but you're perfect for me."

Sadly he shook his head. "I don't think so. Neither does Jeff."

"Well, I think so!"

Dashing hot tears from her eyes, she jumped to her feet and grabbed his T-shirt in her fists, her anger actually budging him. "The past is past. You said it yourself! All that matters is the here and now, and the future."

He stared down at her. His face was immobile, as impassive as if he were carved from rock. Even his voice was like granite when he spoke. "The future doesn't exist, and the here and now can change."

Stunned, she stumbled back from him as if she'd been singed. The world seemed to tilt and sway crazily. "Wh-what are you saying?" she asked, hating the desperate sound of her voice.

Jeff moved between them. "He's telling you what I've been trying to tell you. He's not going to marry you."

Her heart settled into her stomach as she stared at Michael. He hadn't moved, and he didn't return her gaze. "It's not true. Tell him it isn't true!"

"He can't," Jeff cut in. "He's been playing you all this time. Now that he's got what he wants, he doesn't need you anymore."

She moved around Jeff to stand in front of Michael, forcing him to look at her. "Is it true?" she asked, her voice cracking. "Am I really just one in a long line of women you use and discard?"

He was silent, his expression stony. He became a stranger before her eyes, and it shredded her heart.

Desperate, feeling all her dreams shriveling, she clung to him. "The last couple of months—our time in Detroit, meeting your parents, the night you proposed—was that all a lie? Was it all just an elaborate game to you? Are you saying I meant nothing, nothing at all?"

His silence was deafening. Frightened, Yvonne slapped him once, hard. "Answer me!" she cried. "Damn you, tell him it isn't true!"

Michael groaned, placing his hands on her shoulders. For a heart-stopping moment, she felt a flicker of hope. It quickly died as he pushed her away and looked down at her with eyes devoid of emotion.

"I'm letting you go, Yvonne," he said quietly. "I'm sorry." He turned away.

She stepped away from him, unable to believe the agony that roared through her. She had given him the most precious thing she could—her love—and he had spurned it.

She looked down at her hand, at the glittering solitaire that had seemed to hold such promise in its glittery facets. Now it mocked her.

With trembling fingers, she pulled off the ring. "Here. You might need this for the next fool that comes along." When he made no move to take it, she let it fall to the floor. "I'm sure you won't have to wait long."

Jeff reached for her. "Vonne…"

"I don't think I want to talk to you right now, Jeff," she said faintly. "Probably not for a long time."

Forcing her feet to move just like she had during those months of physical therapy, she moved to the front door. Grabbing her purse and keys, she willed the tears away for a few minutes longer. Difficult to do, when she felt as if family had just betrayed her.

Just as she'd predicted, rain was falling, one of those demoralizing showers Atlanta summers are famous for. It matched her mood perfectly.

She took a shuddering breath. "You know, this morning when I woke up I felt like the luckiest woman in the world. For a while there I knew pure, simple happiness. I should have known it wasn't meant to be. The curse strikes again."

With every ounce of dignity and will she could command from her fraying soul, she walked out the door without looking back.

CHAPTER TWENTY-TWO

"What do you mean, you 'broke them up'?" Angela stared at Jeff in shock, unmindful of the water bottle that had slipped from her hand and was now gushing its contents on the carpet. "Please tell me you're kidding."

He slumped on the couch. "I wish I could."

Quickly she retrieved a towel and sopped up the water as best she could. Her mind spun. The engagement announcement in the paper three days ago had surprised and pleased everyone at Desire. No one had heard from the couple since, but Angela and everyone else assumed they had gotten away for much-needed rest and relaxation. Now here Jeff was, more than a little intoxicated, shocking her with his declaration.

She retreated to her kitchen, returning with two steaming mugs of coffee. She pressed one into his hand. "Tell me."

He told her about the confrontation at Michael's house, leaving nothing out. "At first I was so sure that Mike was stringing Yvonne along like he had every other woman since Beth died. I didn't want her to get hurt. But I saw the look on his face when he picked up that ring. He looked as if he'd just watched someone die."

"I ought to dump this coffee on your head, you idiot! How could you be so stupid?"

He held his head in his hands. "You don't understand, Angie. I've always watched out for Vonne. Always. I know her, and I know Michael. I didn't want her to get hurt by him. But I was too late."

She watched him take a healthy swallow, feeling a curious mixture of pain and delight when he scalded his tongue. She knew Jeff was in love with Yvonne, just as she knew Yvonne couldn't love him the way he wanted. She wanted to help him. After all, she had firsthand knowledge of unrequited love. It hurt like hell.

Taking a deep breath, she gathered his free hand in hers. "Jeff, Yvonne loves him. It may not be what you want to hear, but it's true. And Michael loves her."

He glanced at her, his eyes burning starkly. "How can you be so sure of that?"

Wistfulness tugged at her heart as she found a smile. "Every woman wishes a man would look at her the way Michael looks at Yvonne. Believe me, he loves her."

Jeff snorted. "He sure as hell has a strange way of showing it."

She swallowed a sip of coffee then set it down. "I'm sure it wasn't easy for him to do what he did. But I believe he thought he was doing the right thing: loving Yvonne enough to let her go."

"Why? Why would he do that?"

She held his gaze for a heartbeat. "Because you couldn't."

For a long, stricken moment, he just stared at her. Then he buried his face in his hands, a low moan issuing from his throat. "Oh my God, what have I done?"

Angela put her arms around him, her heart pulsing with his pain. "Nothing that can't be fixed, God willing."

He lifted his head, his eyes burning with purpose. "I'm going to fix it, Angie," he vowed. "Whatever it takes, I'm going to do it."

"And I'll help you." And not for my own selfish reasons, she swore. Not completely.

"I've got to find Yvonne. I don't know where she went. What if she won't talk to me? What if neither one of them forgive me? They're my best friends, Angie. What if I've ruined their lives?"

He turned to her, seeking comfort. And fool that she was, she gave it to him.

"Give me one good reason why I shouldn't punch your damned lights out!"

Michael's huge fists were bunched on the collar of Jeff's jacket, and his eyes hinted that one reason probably wasn't enough.

Jeff didn't try to break free. "Go ahead. I know I sure as hell deserve it. What I don't deserve is your forgiveness, but I'll ask anyway."

Wordlessly, Michael released him, turned, and walked through the house to the deck, collapsing into a chair. It was a typical late summer day in Atlanta, oppressively humid and threatening thunderstorms. Cutter saw them and dashed across the backyard. He sniffed at Jeff's leg, then barked a question to his master.

Michael sighed heavily. "No, she's not coming today, either."

The huge shepherd yelped in dismay and laid his muzzle on his owner's knee in an obvious gesture of comfort. Michael reached and half-heartedly scratched Cutter's ears, his jaw working furiously as he fought for control.

"Do you really think it's going to be easy for me to forgive you?" he finally asked, eyes on the yard. "Do you even remember half the things you said to her?"

Jeff's sigh was ragged. "I remember everything that happened that day," he said softly. "It's been keeping me awake."

"Good."

"Come on, Mike, this isn't easy for me. It wasn't easy discovering that the woman you've been in love with for nearly a decade is in love with someone else."

Michael's voice was wintry. "So that gave you the right to hurt her like that?"

Leaning forward, Jeff dangled his hands morosely over his knees. His caramel face was stony, but his eyes were unnaturally bright. "I swear to God, I never wanted to hurt either of you like that! If I could take that day back, I would. But I thought you were playing her, Mike! I thought—"

"Thought what?" Michael cut in. "That making me out to be some kind of morally decrepit monster would make Yvonne leave me? That forcing her to choose between us was the way to go? All you were doing was tearing her apart!"

He shot to his feet, his steps ringing angrily on the wooden boards. "Didn't you see what you were doing to her? Every word you said was driving the knife deeper into her heart. For Vonne, it was like her brother was betraying her. I couldn't let you go on hurting her like that."

"So you let her go."

"Yeah. I let her go." His smile was twisted as he leaned against the rail, staring at the leaden sky. "At the time, I thought it was the right thing to do. I thought it was better if I, with my dubious credentials and tarnished history, hurt her instead of you. I even thought that if I pushed her away she would turn to you. So I did the one noble gesture I was capable of. I made the choice for her. But you know what? Being noble hurts. It hurts like hell."

He pushed off the rail, his pacing restless, anguished. "But that's not even the worst pain. Pain is when someone gives you all their love and dreams and trust to safeguard because you promised that you would never abuse them, and as soon as you have their love in your hand you willingly crush it like an empty soda can. Pain is watching hope burn out in someone's eyes and knowing you're the cause of it.

"I died inside that day. Died and went straight to hell. I lie in bed every night, wide-awake because my body and soul ache with memory. I take the long way home in hopes of catching just a glimpse of her. Every day I see a car like hers, a smile like hers. Jesus, I nearly chased a woman down Peachtree Street because she wore a suit like hers! Hurt is knowing you want to die, and she wishes you would too."

Jeff stared at his miserable friend. In all the years that he had known him, Jeff had never seen Michael this bent out of shape. He had been in love once before, yet Jeff couldn't recall seeing his friend so distraught back then.

At that moment, Jeff realized how deeply Michael loved Yvonne. His own feelings paled in comparison. He got up and moved to his friend, who was now leaning dejectedly against the rail. "Mike, I'm sure Vonne still loves you," he said, the words coming with difficulty.

Michael's laugh was humorless. "Nice try, Jeff. There's no 'still' about it. She never loved me."

"What?"

"In all the time that we've been together, even after I proposed and she accepted, Yvonne never said she loved me."

"You've got to be kidding! Never?"

Michael thought back to their last night of passion. "Not of her own free will."

"But…" Jeff's expression was one of confusion. "If she didn't love you, why did she agree to marry you?"

That question had been hounding him for weeks. "I don't know. With everything she's been through, I knew it would take some time for her to say she loved me. But I could feel it, Jeff. I could see it in her eyes, feel it when she touched me. At least I thought I did."

His shoulders raised and lowered in a poor imitation of a laugh. "I can't believe I'm this stupid, falling in love with a woman who doesn't love me. Again. Talk about your curses."

Jeff tapped him on the shoulder. "Mike, listen to me. Yvonne loves you. Just because she didn't say the words doesn't make it less true. Angie knows it. I knew it that day, when she was defending you, but I was too angry to see it. It's there, Mike. I know it is. Once you find her, you'll see it yourself. And you'll hear it too."

God, how he wanted to believe that. Needed to believe that. "Yvonne's disappeared," he said softly. "I went to the townhouse the next morning and threatened Lawrence to within an inch of his life. He hadn't heard from her. I took the first flight out to Detroit, but her house was still locked tight. So I went to Grace and had to tell her just how stupid I was, how I broke Yvonne's heart to protect yours. It took her a long time to forgive me, but she promised to let me know if Yvonne contacts her.

"It's been nearly a week. I've left messages coast to coast with no luck. The only word from her was a message on her answering machine two days ago that said she was all right. That's it. I may be a fool, but I'm not an idiot. She doesn't want anything to do with me."

Jeff looked at his despondent friend, knowing he'd give anything to set things right. "What are you going to do now?"

"I'm going up to the lake for a few days. See if I can sleep without dreaming or live without needing. After that, I don't know."

CHAPTER TWENTY-THREE

The thunderous pounding on the door jerked Yvonne from a fatigue-induced sleep. Her heart in her throat, she tugged on her robe and stumbled down the stairs to her front door, and pulled aside the curtain.

It wasn't the man of her dreams. It was Jeff Maxwell.

"Go away."

Jeff pounded on the door again. "No way. Not until you hear what I have to say."

"You already said what you wanted to say, Jeff." She leaned tiredly against the cool wood. "There's nothing you can say now, and I have nothing to say to you. Please just go away."

"The only way I'm leaving is if you call the police on me," he answered. "You know your neighbors wouldn't like that. Come on, open the door!"

With a defeated sigh, she unlocked the door. Jeff fell in. "You don't look so good."

Shivering despite the sticky heat, she pushed the door shut with her foot. She had spent the last few days dividing her time between Atlanta, New York, and the west coast, making the rounds and sitting for interviews with fashion magazines and television shows. Telling no one of her breakup with Michael, she had to endure the congratulations and questions of well-wishers with the quiet suffering of a martyr. She had returned her mother's ring to its original place. Everyone assumed it was the one Michael gave her, and she couldn't bear to tell them differently.

"How did you know I was here?"

Jeff shoved his hands into the pockets of his jeans, a sheepish expression on his face. "I was with Angie when you called her."

She ignored the import of his words. "Look, Jeff, you can't hurt me any worse than I'm hurting right now. So if you came to add insult to injury, you can leave."

"I'm sorry, Vonne," he said morosely. "I really am sorry. That's why I had to come over."

She turned away, heading for her kitchen and the coffee maker. "What do you have to apologize for?" she asked acidly. "Isn't this what you wanted?"

Conscious of Jeff's gaze on her, she went through the motions of coffee preparation. She knew she'd undergone a dramatic change since he had last seen her. Like living in a vacuum, she hadn't slept in days and she couldn't remember the last time she had eaten. While she managed to conceal most of her sorrow with skillful makeup application, she knew it would be obvious to someone who knew her.

Someone like Jeff. With a perverse pleasure, she wanted him to know just how wounded she was, even if nothing could be done about it.

"Yeah, I thought I wanted this," he said honestly, "but I was wrong."

"Discovered that a little too late, don't you think?" She got cups out of her cabinet and filled them. "Why is it that the happiest days of my life are also the worst? The day of the show, I felt like the queen of the world. It was the happiest I had been in years. And the one person I thought would understand rejected me.

"You betrayed me!" she shouted. "Do you know what that feels like? I trusted you, I needed you, and you ripped my dreams to shreds! Why?"

"Damn it, Yvonna, I'm sorry! I was wrong, and I knew then that I was."

"Then why?" she cried. "Just tell me why."

"Because I was jealous!"

Her head jerked up sharply, but Jeff's eyes were turned inward. "You see, I knew. I knew you and Mike were going to hook up. I felt it. Maybe because of what you both went through. I don't know. That's why you never met before. I wanted to keep you away from him as long as I could. I just had a feeling that if you and Mike got together I would lose you."

She stared at him in surprise. "Lose me? How could you lose me to him? I will always be your friend, your sister—"

Jeff shook his head, his jaw clenched tight. "I'm trying to come to terms with that now. But for the longest time, I didn't love you as a friend, or as a sister. I love you more than that. I always have."

Shock coursed through her again, as it had the first time she heard him make this declaration. "Oh God, you're serious," she whispered. "I thought you were just saying that to drive me and Michael apart."

"It was the wrong time to tell you. About ten years too wrong. But that doesn't change how I feel."

Suddenly feeling the need to catch her breath, she pulled out a chair from the breakfast table and sat down. She thought the need to cry had left her; she was obviously wrong. But the tears she felt were more of frustration and anger than anything else.

"Why, in the thirteen years that we've known each other, did you never say anything?" she wondered. "Why did you have to use it like a trump card in a poker game?"

"I should have told you, a long time ago," he said bitterly, turning away from her. "When I first met you at that wedding, your aloneness just slammed into me and held me. Each of your letters, each time you opened up to me, just made me want you even more. I wanted to hold you, protect you, make you happy. I still do."

She was flabbergasted. "Jeff…"

He continued, speaking over her. "You were still grieving over your family when I met you. Then came the championships, and after that, your uncle died … I didn't want to burden you with my feelings, and young as I was, I wasn't sure of them myself. Besides, you had come to Atlanta by then, and I could be with you every day. And yes, I was seeing other people, but if I'd thought your feeling were deeper at any time I would have left them in a heartbeat."

He swallowed. "Of course, your feelings never got deeper. And once I saw you with Mike, I knew they never would be."

"Jeff." Yvonne paused, trying to find words, the right words. Here was a man, a man she had known and loved thirteen years, declaring his love for her. He was handsome, financially well off, caring. Any woman would be flattered. Yet all she could think of, all she could see, was Michael.

Reaching out, she captured his hand in hers. "Jeff, I have to make you understand," she said, carefully enunciating each word. "Even if you had told me all this a long time ago, even a year ago, my answer would be the same. I will always love you, but I love you like a brother. That's all."

"And what about Mike?" he asked his voice scraping bottom. "Are you in love with him?"

"Of course I love him," she said softly. "I never saw the person you said he was, the person he believes he is. He never used me; he vivified me. He isn't superficial—he wasn't even repulsed by my scars. That alone was enough to make me love him. But when he went to Detroit with me, when he didn't leave even after he found out all the horrible things about me, when he took the darkness away, I knew I couldn't love anyone else."

Jeff looked perplexed. "What horrible things?"

Silently she gestured for him to sit at the kitchen table. She set her mug down carefully and stood in front of him. Pushing the sleeve of her robe back, she lifted her wrist, palm up.

For a long silent moment, Jeff held her hand. Then he raised his head, tears streaming down his face. "Oh God, Vonne. You tried to—you tried…"

"Yes."

"How? When?"

She withdrew her arm and pushed her sleeve into place. "Shortly after the accident. The grief and nightmares were constant, and I wanted to be free of the pain, to be with the only people who loved me. Some part of me knew it was wrong, but I desperately wanted to escape the despair I was caged in. They put me on suicide watch, they restrained me, and finally, they locked me away for a year."

Her heart heavy, she watched him struggle with her words, trying to equate what she had told him with what he knew, or thought he knew, of her. It was a difficult thing to ask of anyone—to believe, to understand, to withhold the platitudes and pity. She would not ask it of him.

"Why didn't you tell me?"

"I was afraid. My aunt and cousins had already ostracized me, because they knew it all from the beginning. I didn't want to risk our friendship. I wasn't going to tell anyone. Ever."

"But you told Mike."

She nodded. "He told me how he lost his wife and unborn child, and why. He shared his pain with me because I asked him to, despite what it cost him. When he asked me to marry him, I knew I needed to be just as honest and forthcoming, despite what it could cost me."

She retrieved her mug, her hands shaking so badly she couldn't take a sip. "Of course, it cost me everything."

Jeff got to his feet. "You're wrong. Mike loves you."

"He doesn't love me!" She spun away from him, slamming her mug against the counter, causing it to crack and send hot liquid and ceramic shards everywhere.

She quickly grabbed a towel to sop up the mess, and her tears. "You were there, Jeff. You saw how easy it was for him to break my heart. Is that love?"

"You're right, Vonne, I was there. One thing I know for sure, it wasn't easy for Mike to do what he did."

She raised pain-filled eyes to his. "Then why? Why did he do it? Did I love him too much? Did I scare him away because of my past?"

"No, you didn't," Jeff said thickly, hugging her close. "He did it because of me. Because of our history, yours and mine."

When she only stared at him, confused, he continued, "Mike thinks that you don't love him."

"Don't love him?" She had to find a chair again. "How can he think that? How could he possibly think that?"

"Mike says he's never heard you say the words of your own free will," he said. "He thought it was because there was something unacknowledged between us. He heard every word of our argument, saw the way I was forcing you to choose, saw how it was tearing you up inside. He made the choice for you, but I think he believes he doesn't deserve you. He thought you would be better off without him."

"Better off?" she echoed. "I haven't had a full night's sleep since I left. I can't eat. I can't even sketch a damn apple. How is this supposed to be better?"

"It's not," he admitted. "I was wrong. We were both wrong. Believe me, Mike regrets what he did to you. He's taking it hard."

"How do you know?"

"I saw him."

Yvonne's hand went to the lapel of her robe. "You did? When? Is he-how is he?"

Jeff's expression was drawn. "He looked as if his life had ended." He related their conversation. "He's been trying to contact you for days, and when he couldn't, he went to the lakehouse."

He cupped her cheeks. "Vonne, you've got to believe me. Mike loves you. If you recall, he never once said he didn't. He's been my best friend for nearly twenty years, remember? He hasn't loved anyone like he loves you. But he's convinced that you don't love him. That's why he went to the lake."

She was stunned. Michael thought, actually believed, that she didn't love him because she had never said the words.

But she had said the words. Their last night together, after the triumph of the show. He had taken her to such heights of pleasure that she had screamed her love for him until her throat was raw.

Then he left her, like everyone else.

"You've got to talk to him, Vonne," Jeff urged. "Call him or wait for him to call you. Better yet, go see him. Talk this out. And if you mean it, tell him you love him."

"I don't think I can chance it," she whispered, shaking her head. "If he doesn't think he deserves my love, what's to prevent him from sending me away again? I don't think my heart can withstand another rejection."

Jeff drew her to her feet. "You've got to take a chance. Where's the woman who dropped everything to move to a town she's never visited before? Where's the woman who started a multi-million dollar company from scratch? Where's the woman who was determined to walk again when everyone told her she couldn't? Would that woman let a foolish best friend and an obstinate fiancé stand in her way?"

Taking a deep breath, Yvonne squared her shoulders. "You're right, Jeff. I'm used to fighting for what I want."

"And do you want this?"

"More than anything."

He pushed her towards the kitchen door. "Then go get it."

CHAPTER TWENTY-FOUR

Jeff had already pulled her Volvo out of the garage when she came downstairs, dressed and refreshed. Dark clouds crowded out blue late afternoon sky, and thunder rumbled in the distance. "A storm's coming, Vonne," he said unnecessarily. "Maybe you should wait."

She performed her pre-driving ritual, checking the car's tires and body for signs of damage. "I can't. The phone's still out at the cabin, and we keep getting the voice mail on his cell phone. I have to go. Besides, the past few days have felt like an eternity. I need to have this settled, one way or another."

She gripped his hand. "If you would do me a favor and wait until Law gets here, I'd appreciate it."

He nodded, swallowing hard. "Okay. You've got the map, right?"

She held it up. "Right here."

"And your phone?"

"Charging as we speak." She hugged him. "Thank you, Jeff. For everything."

He opened the door and she slipped in, strapping herself in and adjusting the seat and mirrors to her liking. "Wish me luck."

"You know I do," he whispered thickly. "Just be careful."

It took every ounce of courage she possessed to make the drive from Atlanta to the North Georgia mountains, but that wasn't the reason her heart was pounding against her ribcage. The hope Jeff had given her was gradually dissolving, replaced by nagging doubt. Michael had left messages with Lawrence, Angela and Auntie Grace for five days, but she'd been too heartsick to care. When she'd finally gotten the courage to call him back, he was gone.

Now, every fiber of her being was urging her to turn around, to save herself from further pain and embarrassment. If he could push her away once, he would do it again.

She gripped the steering wheel tightly, her hands slick with sweat. Her wipers were going full tilt, but were proving ineffectual against the sheets of rain drenching the highway. She drove slowly. The afternoon had become as dark as twilight, and she knew neither she nor her car was designed for muddy mountain roads. Yet she continued. She had to get to Michael.

A bolt of lightning rammed into a large tree beside the two-lane road, toppling it onto the pavement ahead. Without thinking, Yvonne slammed on her brakes, sending her car careening off the path and into the ditch alongside. There was a crash, the sound of glass shattered, a blinding flash of white, then nothing.

Michael drove down I-85, his wipers going furiously. It was pouring rain mercilessly, and he was driving at a near crawl in the blinding storm. Yet the storm was hardly a match for his tumultuous emotions.

Three days sulking was three days too long. He was determined to find Yvonne and set things right between them. He would court her and woo her, even if he had to camp out on her front step. If she could agree to marry him once, she could do it again.

And this time, he would hear the words.

The cell phone rang on the seat beside him. "Hello."

"Mike? It's Jeff. Is Yvonne with you?"

Michael nearly dropped the phone. "What did you say?"

"I'm at her place. We, uhm, had a long talk and we settled some things between us. I told her you might be at the lake, and she insisted on going there. She's not with you?"

"Jeff, you know Yvonne hates to drive, and she never, ever gets behind the wheel in conditions like this. Are you positive?"

"Oh, man," Jeff's voice was taut with concern. "After our talk, she just took off. I told her I didn't think it would be a good idea to drive out, but she did anyway. She should have been there at least fifteen minutes ago."

Dread clenched like an icy fist in his stomach. "I'm on the way home," Michael explained. "I got on the highway a few minutes ago."

"Damn! I knew I shouldn't have let her go. I should have gone with her."

"Let me try and call her," Michael suggested. "Hopefully, she's just lost." But even as he said the words, he knew he was wrong.

It took several attempts before his fingers dialed the correct sequence, and several rings before the phone was answered. "H-hello."

He sighed with relief. "Vonne? Sweetheart, it's me, Michael."

"M-Michael?" A huge sob tore through her. "Oh, God, help me!"

Panic grabbed his heart in a frozen fist. "What's wrong, what happened?"

"L-lightning hit the tree, and it was falling and I k-knew it w-was going to hit me, but I couldn't stop... "

Michael pulled into the emergency lane. "Oh my God! Are you hurt?"

Her whimper tore at his soul. "I ran into a ditch and the airbag exploded. The windshield is busted, and my head hurts."

His heart almost stopped. "Where are you?"

"I-I don't know," she answered, her voice trembling. "Jeff told me you were at the lake, so I was coming to find you." She told him the last road marker she remembered.

She was less than fifteen minutes away. "Hold on, Sweetheart. I'm going to call for help."

"No! Please, don't hang up!"

Her terror was palpable. "Okay, I'm going to find you, and I'll stay on the line the entire time, I promise."

"Okay."

He quickly exited the highway and turned around, desperately trying to remember basic emergency skills he'd learned during college and fighting to keep the fear at bay. Guilt tore into him with the claws of a frenzied beast. Because of him, Yvonne was trapped in a car on a deserted road on a stormy night. If he was recalling the accident she was in years ago, he knew she would as well. She had every right to be petrified with fear.

He had to take her mind off the situation. "Vonne, I want you to listen to me. Make sure the engine's turned off, okay? Good. Now turn on your blinkers and the headlights if they still work."

"Okay." She was silent, presumably following his instructions, but Michael knew her calm was fragile at best. "Vonne, can you hear me?"

"I had a long talk with Jeff ... " her voice stopped with a hiss.

"Vonne?"

"Oh my God, I'm bleeding."

It was all Michael could do not to floor the accelerator. "Vonne, talk to me!"

"I don't feel so good." Her breathing was louder, labored.

"Vonne!"

"I gotta get out. I gotta get out!"

"I know, but you need to stay put."

He could hear frantic scrambling noises, as if she was having difficulty opening the door. "I can't stay in here—I can't! Please don't make me."

"You have to." Michael forced brusqueness into his voice, knowing it would have the effect of a verbal slap on her. "It's safer for you to stay in the car. You could wander off and we wouldn't be able to find you. Do you understand?"

"Y-yes."

He made a difficult decision. "Vonne, I need to get help for you. I'm going to have to hang up, but I'll call you right back, I promise."

"No!" Her voice rose hysterically. "Please don't go!"

"Vonne, sweetheart, I have to get help. If we wait…" He couldn't finish.

"Okay."

Disconnecting her was difficult, but he had to call for help. Precious minutes passed before they would let him hang up and call her again. Two rings, three rings, four.

"The mobile customer you are trying to reach …"

"Dammit!"

Michael hurled the phone down and turned up the winding road, adrenaline surging through him. Another five minutes, he guessed, before he would find her. "Oh God, please. Let her be all right. Just let her be all right."

Half a mile farther on he saw a pulsating amber glow illuminating a massive oak split in two and blocking the road. His heart in his throat, he haphazardly parked and jumped out of the car. He slipped and skidded ten yards down a sharp incline to the white Volvo, its nose buried into a tree on the opposite rise. Not daring to breathe, not daring to halt his prayer, he ripped the driver's door open.

The front seat was empty, covered with glass. But in the back, curled against the far door, was Yvonne, her hands clamped around the cell phone. "Vonne?"

She turned to him slowly, and in the dim light of the overhead, he could see the nasty gash on her forehead and the blood soaking her blouse. "Michael, is that really you?" She clumsily slid across the seat and into his arms.

He held her as close as he dared, fearful of hurting her. "I'm here, love. I'm here."

"You came for me, you really came for me."

He pulled off his shirt, wrapping it around her. She felt insubstantial in his arms, as if she would float away if he didn't hold her. "Help is on the way, darling. Just hold on."

She shivered. "J-Jeff told me everything. Why-why you made me leave like that."

Michael groaned. "It was the hardest thing I've ever done. I didn't think I deserved you. I didn't want you to regret that you didn't get the chance to search for someone better."

"Who could be better for me than you?" she asked, her voice catching. "There was no one before you, and there won't be anyone after you."

"I love you, Yvonne," Michael said, throwing his whole heart and soul into the pledge. "I never stopped loving you. You're my whole life. My whole life! Do you believe me?"

"Yes."

"Can you forgive me, for messing up your life?"

She sighed, closing her eyes. "You didn't mess up my life, Michael. You jump-started it."

"You did the same to mine," he whispered, rocking her gently. Where was the ambulance? At least a state trooper should have been here by now. Remembering what the emergency operator told him, he knew he had to keep Yvonne warm and awake.

"Do you remember, when I asked you to marry me, you said you wanted a large house with a big magnolia tree out front?"

It seemed like forever before she answered. "Yeah."

"My parents' house has a big magnolia tree in the front, just like you want. Standing under it with all the branches hanging down is like stepping into another world. They want to give us the house for a wedding present. I can't wait to show it to you."

"I'm tired, Michael. So very tired ... "

He could hear the wail of sirens in the distance. "Vonne, Vonne please—hang on, just hang on for me."

"Want ... rest."

"You can't. You have to fight."

"Tired of fighting. No more f-fighting."

"I'll fight for you, dearheart," Michael vowed, unmindful of the tears streaming down his cheeks. "I'll be your strength. Do you hear me, Vonne? Vonne?"

"It's okay, Michael," she breathed. I-I'm not afraid of the dark anymore..."

Michael gripped her hand, willing his strength into her. "Don't you leave me!" he told her fiercely. "Don't you dare leave me!"

Her fingertips brushed against his cheeks, his lips. Michael caught her hand in his, kissing her palm. He heard tires skidding to a stop, doors slamming, people running. The paramedics had arrived. But Yvonne had lost so much blood.

"I love you, Vonne," he whispered. "I need you. Stay with me. Just stay with me."

Beams of light flashed over them as the rescuers scrambled down the incline. Yvonne opened her eyes. For a moment the pain and shock receded, and she smiled gently at him. "I love you."

She closed her eyes and slipped into darkness.

CHAPTER TWENTY-FIVE

The first sound Yvonne's consciousness registered was the tinny beep of a heart monitor. Her first coherent thought was that the last sixteen years had been a dream and she was still an orphaned thirteen year-old. The idea made her want to wail in anguish.

"Oh God, no…"

"Vonne?"

Her heart tripped a beat as the familiar voice washed over her. "Open your eyes, sweetheart."

Making every effort, she blinked her eyes open. Michael's face loomed over hers. His eyes were tarnished, he hadn't shaved, and his clothes were slept in.

He looked beautiful.

"Are you real?"

Warm hands enveloped hers, gathering them to his heart. "Yeah, I'm real." He gruffly cleared his throat. "How are you feeling?"

It hurt to smile, but she didn't care. "Probably as bad as I look. Did I hurt anyone?

"No. The police say you probably hydroplaned, causing you to careen into the embankment." His voice grew ragged. "The seatbelt and airbags saved your life."

"Am I broken?"

A less-than-steady hand stroked her cheek. "Just bruised. That Volvo was built like a tank."

"Was?"

"You slid down an embankment into a seventy-year old oak tree. Some of the branches smashed through the windshield, gashing your forehead. There was blood, so much blood…" His voice faded in remembered horror.

"Michael, don't."

"If you hadn't ducked…" He swallowed heavily. The look he gave her nearly broke her heart. "I almost lost you. I pushed you away because I thought you didn't love me. And then you tried to come back to me, and when I held you in my arms, you told me you loved me then you slipped away."

Holding Yvonne's unconscious body in his arms that rainy night had made him understand exactly what she had endured as a child, why she had made the choice she had. The desolation he had felt in those heart-stopping moments was unendurable.

He closed his eyes with a shudder. "I never want to have an experience like that again," he whispered.

"Don't do this to yourself," she begged, cradling his face in her hands. "It doesn't heal, only hurts. Believe me, I know."

"I thought I'd die."

"But you didn't, and I didn't. Guess that means we're stuck with each other."

"Really?" He stared down at her, at the pale bandage against her bronze skin. He would have nightmares for days to come, he knew. But her smile was going a long way to ease some of the terror in his heart.

"Really." She caressed his cheek. "I love you."

"I never thought I'd hear you say it."

"I told you. I know I did. The night after the show."

"Because I forced you."

Her smile became a laugh—a slight one quickly extinguished by her protesting ribs. "That night just reaffirmed it. I loved you before then, before you proposed. I might have even loved you the first time I saw you. I know I definitely felt a connection. But the day I actually realized that I was falling in love with you was the day you told me about Beth. I loved you so much that the words just didn't seem adequate enough, so I was trying to show you instead."

"And fool that I am, I thought you didn't tell me because you didn't feel it."

He gathered her hands in his again. "Yvonne, about the things I said…"

"I know, and I forgive you."

"But…"

She grabbed his shirt and tugged his face within inches of yours. "I've waited half my life for you, Michael Benjamin. I'm not about to give you up."

"But…"

She shut him up the only way she knew how. When she finally broke the kiss his eyes were glazed. "Hey, are you all right? I could press my buzzer for a doctor."

His answering grin was beatific. "Who needs a doctor? You're the only medicine I need."

She laughed away the pain. "Flattery will get you everywhere."

He gave her a lecherous wink. "I'm hoping it will get me laid."

"Michael!" Grace Calhoun's shocked exclamation startled them both.

"Married! I meant to say married."

"Good." Grace hurried into the room, followed by Michael's parents. "It's about time you make an honest woman out of her."

Edward Benjamin deposited a huge bouquet of balloons in a chair by the window. "Absolutely. Besides, it will be nice to have season tickets in the family."

"Edward!" Amelia failed miserably to keep the laughter from her voice.

Edward reached over his son's shoulder to clasp Yvonne's hand. "What I meant to say is, my son couldn't have made a better choice, and you are a welcome addition to our family."

Michael's smile was for her alone. "I couldn't agree more, Dad."

"Speaking of family," Grace interrupted, "there's a whole bunch of yours waiting outside."

"Mine?" Yvonne asked, confused.

"The waiting room's packed," Grace answered. "There're several women, two men, and two girls all claiming that you're their sister."

"Is no one running my company?" she cracked, but couldn't quite keep the emotion out of her voice. Spiritually, they were her family.

Grace sat beside her, across from Michael. "There's someone else here. Your aunt."

"Dinah?"

Michael answered her. "I called her, after I talked to Grace. I thought she should know."

"We took the same flight down," Grace added. "We had a long and interesting discussion. She wants to see you."

"See me?"

"Are you up for it?" Michael asked, squeezing her hand.

Yvonne closed her eyes, silently thanking God for giving her another chance.

"Vonne?"

"I'm not seeing anybody until I see Lawrence," she said. "If I know my assistant, he's packed the perfect lingerie and accessories for receiving hospital visitors. And he'd never forgive me if I let anyone else see me with my hair standing all over my head."

She was right.

EPILOGUE

Michael stood frozen, staring at the arrangement of roses. Behind him, a string quartet played Pachelbel's Canon. It was Yvonne's favorite piece. He closed his eyes and let the familiar tune wash over him, thinking of her.

A hand closed on his shoulder. It was Jeff. "Are you going to make it?"

Michael took a fortifying breath. "Yes."

Jeff looked closely at him. "Are you sure? You look like you're about to pass out."

"Pass out at my own wedding?" He shook his head. "Vonne would kill me."

"Not before you say 'I do'," Jeff quipped. "Don't worry, though; I got your back. We'll prop you up if we have to."

Despite his lightheartedness, Michael knew Jeff still had a long way to go before he was completely over Yvonne. Angela was definitely influencing his recovery. If Jeff didn't realize what was right in front of him, Michael was going to spell it out in no uncertain terms. After the honeymoon.

Behind them, the harpist struck a muted chord. Everyone turned to watch Kiki and Shanté scatter rose petals down the aisle. On the bride's side sat nearly all her employees as well as friends and her Mentor Atlanta protégés. Sitting in the front row, beside Grace and her family, were Dinah and her children, Yvonne's cousins.

He still found it hard to believe that minor miracle. In the two months since the accident, Dinah had reached out, giving Yvonne what she so desperately desired: connection to family. They still had distance to travel before they were completely reconciled, but that distance was growing smaller daily.

A hush fell over the assembled guests. Michael turned and paused, his breath caught in his throat.

Yvonne strolled sedately down the flower-strewn aisle, the ivory silk of her gown warming to gold in the glow of hundreds of candles. She was unescorted, save for a tiny gilded photo of her family that hung from her bouquet. He couldn't see her expression through the veil, but he could feel her smile.

Only a few of the assembled guests knew the obstacles Michael and Yvonne had overcome to be together. To many, it was a fairy tale come true. The ceremony was poignantly simple as Yvonne and Michael shared their vows. Few eyes were dry as the minister pronounced them man and wife.

He lifted her veil. She smiled brilliantly up at him, her eyes bright with tears. "I love you, Mrs. Benjamin," he told her, his voice thick. "Forever, and always."

She reached up to wipe a stray tear from his cheek. "I love you, Mr. Benjamin," she told him, her voice clear and steady. "Always, and forever."

Michael swept Yvonne into his arms and let out a whoop of joy. As if on cue, the string quartet broke into the "Hallelujah Chorus." The botanical garden rang with applause and laughter as the couple recessed down the aisle in the glow of hundreds of candles. For them, commitment wasn't required, but definitely desired.

ABOUT THE AUTHOR

Seressia Y. Glass lives in Georgia where she works as a Human Resource Trainer. Her writing career began early and by the time she finished elementary school, many of her short stories had been made into plays. She was the winner of the first "Living the Dream" essay contest for the inaugural Martin Luther King, Jr., holiday in Atlanta.

2007 Publication Schedule

January

Rooms of the Heart
Donna Hill
ISBN-13: 978-1-58571-219-9
ISBN-10: 1-58571-219-1
$6.99

A Dangerous Love
J. M. Jeffries
ISBN-13: 978-1-58571-217-5
ISBN-10: 1-58571-217-5
$6.99

February

Bound By Love
Beverly Clark
ISBN-13: 978-1-58571-232-8
ISBN-10: 1-58571-232-9
$6.99

A Love to Cherish
Beverly Clark
ISBN-13: 978-1-58571-233-5
ISBN-10: 1-58571-233-7
$6.99

March

Best of Friends
Natalie Dunbar
ISBN-13: 978-1-58571-220-5
ISBN-10: 1-58571-220-5
$6.99

Midnight Magic
Gwynne Forster
ISBN-13: 978-1-58571-225-0
ISBN-10: 1-58571-225-6
$6.99

April

Cherish the Flame
Beverly Clark
ISBN-13: 978-1-58571-221-2
ISBN-10: 1-58571-221-3
$6.99

Quiet Storm
Donna Hill
ISBN-13: 978-1-58571-226-7
ISBN-10: 1-58571-226-4
$6.99

May

Sweet Tomorrows
Kimberley White
ISBN-13: 978-1-58571-234-2
ISBN-10: 1-58571-234-5
$6.99

No Commitment Required
Seressia Glass
ISBN-13: 978-1-58571-222-9
ISBN-10: 1-58571-222-1
$6.99

June

A Dangerous Deception
J. M. Jeffries
ISBN-13: 978-1-58571-228-1
ISBN-10: 1-58571-228-0
$6.99

Illusions
Pamela Leigh Starr
ISBN-13: 978-1-58571-229-8
ISBN-10: 1-58571-229-9
$6.99

2007 Publication Schedule (continued)

July

Indiscretions
Donna Hill
ISBN-13: 978-1-58571-230-4
ISBN-10: 1-58571-230-2
$6.99

Whispers in the Night
Dorothy Elizabeth Love
ISBN-13: 978-1-58571-231-1
ISBN-10: 1-58571-231-1
$6.99

August

Bodyguard
Andrea Jackson
ISBN-13: 978-1-58571-235-9
ISBN-10: 1-58571-235-3
$6.99

Crossing Paths, Tempting Memories
Dorothy Elizabeth Love
ISBN-13: 978-1-58571-236-6
ISBN-10: 1-58571-236-1
$6.99

September

Fate
Pamela Leigh Starr
ISBN-13: 978-1-58571-258-8
ISBN-10: 1-58571-258-2
$6.99

Mae's Promise
Melody Walcott
ISBN-13: 978-1-58571-259-5
ISBN-10: 1-58571-259-0
$6.99

October

Magnolia Sunset
Giselle Carmichael
ISBN-13: 978-1-58571-260-1
ISBN-10: 1-58571-260-4
$6.99

Broken
Dar Tomlinson
ISBN-13: 978-1-58571-261-8
ISBN-10: 1-58571-261-2
$6.99

November

Truly Inseparable
Wanda Y. Thomas
ISBN-13: 978-1-58571-262-5
ISBN-10: 1-58571-262-0
$6.99

The Color Line
Lizzette G. Carter
ISBN-13: 978-1-58571-263-2
ISBN-10: 1-58571-263-9
$6.99

December

Love Always
Mildred Riley
ISBN-13: 978-1-58571-264-9
ISBN-10: 1-58571-264-7
$6.99

Pride and Joi
Gay Gunn
ISBN-13: 978-1-58571-265-6
ISBN-10: 1-58571-265-5
$6.99

Other Genesis Press, Inc. Titles

Other Genesis Press, Inc. Titles (continued)

Bodyguard	Andrea Jackson	$9.95
Boss of Me	Diana Nyad	$8.95
Bound by Love	Beverly Clark	$8.95
Breeze	Robin Hampton Allen	$10.95
Broken	Dar Tomlinson	$24.95
By Design	Barbara Keaton	$8.95
Cajun Heat	Charlene Berry	$8.95
Careless Whispers	Rochelle Alers	$8.95
Cats & Other Tales	Marilyn Wagner	$8.95
Caught in a Trap	Andre Michelle	$8.95
Caught Up In the Rapture	Lisa G. Riley	$9.95
Cautious Heart	Cheris F Hodges	$8.95
Chances	Pamela Leigh Starr	$8.95
Cherish the Flame	Beverly Clark	$8.95
Class Reunion	Irma Jenkins/	
	John Brown	$12.95
Code Name: Diva	J.M. Jeffries	$9.95
Conquering Dr. Wexler's Heart	Kimberley White	$9.95
Crossing Paths, Tempting Memories	Dorothy Elizabeth Love	$9.95
Cypress Whisperings	Phyllis Hamilton	$8.95
Dark Embrace	Crystal Wilson Harris	$8.95
Dark Storm Rising	Chinelu Moore	$10.95
Daughter of the Wind	Joan Xian	$8.95
Deadly Sacrifice	Jack Kean	$22.95
Designer Passion	Dar Tomlinson	$8.95
Dreamtective	Liz Swados	$5.95
Ebony Butterfly II	Delilah Dawson	$14.95
Echoes of Yesterday	Beverly Clark	$9.95

Other Genesis Press, Inc. Titles (continued)

Other Genesis Press, Inc. Titles (continued)

Other Genesis Press, Inc. Titles (continued)

Magnolia Sunset	Giselle Carmichael	$8.95
Matters of Life and Death	Lesego Malepe, Ph.D.	$15.95
Meant to Be	Jeanne Sumerix	$8.95
Midnight Clear	Leslie Esdaile	$10.95
(Anthology)	Gwynne Forster	
	Carmen Green	
	Monica Jackson	
Midnight Magic	Gwynne Forster	$8.95
Midnight Peril	Vicki Andrews	$10.95
Misconceptions	Pamela Leigh Starr	$9.95
Montgomery's Children	Richard Perry	$14.95
My Buffalo Soldier	Barbara B. K. Reeves	$8.95
Naked Soul	Gwynne Forster	$8.95
Next to Last Chance	Louisa Dixon	$24.95
No Apologies	Seressia Glass	$8.95
No Commitment Required	Seressia Glass	$8.95
No Regrets	Mildred E. Riley	$8.95
Nowhere to Run	Gay G. Gunn	$10.95
O Bed! O Breakfast!	Rob Kuehnle	$14.95
Object of His Desire	A. C. Arthur	$8.95
Office Policy	A. C. Arthur	$9.95
Once in a Blue Moon	Dorianne Cole	$9.95
One Day at a Time	Bella McFarland	$8.95
Outside Chance	Louisa Dixon	$24.95
Passion	T.T. Henderson	$10.95
Passion's Blood	Cherif Fortin	$22.95
Passion's Journey	Wanda Y. Thomas	$8.95
Past Promises	Jahmel West	$8.95
Path of Fire	T.T. Henderson	$8.95

Other Genesis Press, Inc. Titles (continued)

Other Genesis Press, Inc. Titles (continued)

Order Form

Mail to: Genesis Press, Inc.
P.O. Box 101
Columbus, MS 39703

Name _____
Address _____
City/State _____ Zip _____
Telephone _____

Ship to (if different from above)
Name _____
Address _____
City/State _____ Zip _____
Telephone _____

Credit Card Information
Credit Card # _____ ☐ Visa   ☐ Mastercard
Expiration Date (mm/yy) _____ ☐ AmEx ☐ Discover

Qty.	Author	Title	Price	Total

Use this order form, or call 1-888-INDIGO-1	**Total for books** _____ **Shipping and handling:** $5 first two books, $1 each additional book _____ **Total S & H** _____ **Total amount enclosed** _____

Mississippi residents add 7% sales tax